RAID

AND THE KID

HARRI NYKANEN

Translated by
Peter Ylitalo Leppa

Ice Cold Crime LLC

Originally published in Finnish as *Raid ja Poika* by WSOY, Helsinki, Finland. 2003.

Translated by Peter Ylitalo Leppa

Published by
Ice Cold Crime LLC
5780 Providence Curve
Independence, MN 55359

Printed in the United States of America

Cover by Ella Tontti

Library of Congress Control Number: 2012938091

ISBN-13: 978-0-9824449-4-8
ISBN-10: 0-9824449-4-X

RAID

AND THE KID

Cast of Characters

Raid..Hit man

Jansson.....................Helsinki PD detective lieutenant

Huusko......................................Jansson's colleague

Susisaari....................................Jansson's colleague

Kempas.................Head of Helsinki PD undercover unit

Captain Tuomela..................................Jansson's boss

Matti Porola (the Kid)..........................Grocer's son

Nina Liljeblad.......................Greedy flight attendant

Erika Liljeblad...........................Nina's younger sister

José Hernando.......Bolivian produce warehouse worker

Eila Tuuri.............................José's former girlfriend

Henri Aho.......................................Former cop, PI

Diego......................................Bolivian drug boss

Simon...................Bolivian gangster living in Finland

Lopez brothers.............................Bolivian gangsters

Hietama..Finnair CFO

Kallio..............................Finnair security officer

Day-o, day-ay-ay-o

Daylight come and me wan' go home

Day-o, day-ay-ay-o

Daylight come and me wan' go home

(Banana Boat Song)

Prologue

The man's name was Armano Zetov.

Zetov was at the fortune teller. An old woman in black garb was reading his tarot cards, but the cards didn't tell her that only a thin, translucent sliver remained of Zetov's forty-two-year life. As a measure of time, that amounted to precisely three minutes. Nor did the cards tell her that a man was seated on the fourth floor of the building opposite them, a rifle equipped with a silencer and a telescopic sight resting on a table beside him. The window was cracked open.

The man watched as a black 700 Series BMW with dark, tinted windows rolled to a stop in front of the fortune teller's building. The driver, dressed in a leather coat, with a clean-shaven head, stepped out of the car to have a cigarette. The man at the window picked up the rifle, raised it to his shoulder, and aimed it at the driver's forehead. Through the scope, the crosshairs quartered the driver's head. The man set the weapon back down in his lap. The driver took a cell phone out of a holster on his belt and exchanged a few words with someone. Then he put it back in the holster.

Again, the gunman raised the weapon to his shoulder, but this time, he brought the front door into the crosshairs. When Zetov stepped outside, the gunman took aim, steadied his breathing, and smoothly squeezed the trigger. The weapon bucked, the bullet struck Zetov in the center of the forehead, and he crumpled to the sidewalk.

The driver dove behind the car, and the man at the window watched Zetov's motionless body through the scope. The rear door of the car flew open, and the man panned his rifle to the right. A boy of about eight, dressed like a miniature adult, sprang from the car. He dashed over to Zetov, and pressed himself against the man's limp body, smearing his face with Zetov's blood.

The man at the window looked at the weeping boy for a moment. Then he broke down his rifle, packed it into a gym bag, and left the apartment.

1.

He was running as fast as he could, but his legs felt dead, like wooden pegs, almost as if he were dragging them along behind him. His breath came in gasps, and drool was dripping from his chin. Style points were of little concern when he was running for his life.

Toward evening, the fog had thickened, but he could still make out the spruce forest across the field. That meant his stalkers could see him, too. A dirt road on the left led through a field of low bushes. The nearest hiding place lay in the forest across the field, but the last thing he wanted was to get stuck in the mud and become human target practice.

He cut left onto the curving dirt road, and a wet branch struck him sharply across the face, but he plodded on.

They had killed Sepi—shot him dead, right in front of his eyes—and they'd kill him too, if they caught him. A little pain was nothing. It would take a lot more than that to get him to stop and wait for death.

He tried not to think about Sepi, tried to concentrate on running. One foot in front of the other, as quickly as possible, yet with a loose stride: left, right, left, right…

Shit, shit, shit!

He had always detested sports, especially running, and he vowed that if he ever made it out of this alive he'd change his ways. In a couple of years, he'd run a marathon to the roar of a crowd.

Him running a marathon? A laughable idea, though he didn't feel much like laughing—he felt like crying.

He had always detested sports because sports had detested him. Though his congenital hip defect had been surgically repaired, he had always been the klutz whose gait brought even the gym teacher to laughter.

"Pick it up, Daffy! Quit waddling like a duck," his classmates had jeered.

Running the mile had been nightmarish torture for him. He didn't recall—or want to recall—how long it had taken him, sometimes walking, at other times reeling.

Swimming had been more of his thing, and diving—three minutes under water without a breath. But this was no swim meet, nor a breath-holding competition.

His right foot slipped into a wet hole in the trail and he lost control, nearly plowing into a thick pine branch before regaining his footing. It took a while to get his rhythm back.

He had run almost a mile already, but wouldn't last much longer. He had to think of something soon. What the hell was he going to do?

The lake! he thought, fanning a paltry cinder of hope. It renewed his strength.

The trail would lead to Nygren's house, and from there to the lakeshore, where he'd find the boat.

Or would he? The house had been deserted for years, and its peculiar owner had passed away the previous fall. He had seen Nygren every so often in his father's store, a tall, wiry man with a long trench coat, boots, sunglasses, and a murky reputation. Some claimed Nygren to be a hard-core criminal, a fugitive from justice. A couple of weeks earlier, he had seen a sun-bleached fiberglass boat on Nygren's property. If it was still there, and he could launch it quickly enough, he might be saved. If the oars were gone, he could paddle with his hands, as long as he could get out of shooting range.

"Please let it be there, please let it be there," he blubbered, not really knowing to whom he was addressing this heartfelt plea.

A shot came from behind, and a bullet plowed a long, fruitless furrow into the path in front of him. He guessed the bullet to have flown a good hundred and fifty feet.

"Mommyyyyyy!"

The outburst came involuntarily, without any thought of his mother. She would have been little help now, and had played no part in his life since he was two years old. He didn't even remember her, and didn't want to. His father had hidden all the photos, which he hadn't seen until he was thirteen. He had found them in a folder crammed into an old cabinet in the attic, yellowed photographs of a sober-faced woman. In one photo, the woman held an infant in front of her, not clutched to her breast, but dangling from the end of her arm like some repulsive creature. That creature was him. Seeing the photos hadn't sparked any emotion in him whatsoever.

Shouting for mommy wouldn't help. He'd need a miracle at the very least, and those were rare.

Another shot rang out from behind. The bullet went by so wide that he couldn't tell where it had landed. All he knew was his fear, which was so great that it burned and froze at the same time. His stomach, too, ached and churned. The thought of calling a time-out for a nature call in the bushes crossed his mind. The idea nearly made him laugh: him squatting down behind a tree while the killers waited, then up with the trousers and on with the chase. Like something out of a cartoon.

Another shot went off, way wide again. That's when he realized they didn't *want* to hit him, they just wanted to stop him. He wouldn't die until he'd told them what

5

they wanted to know. If Sepi hadn't been packing his grandfather's laughable rattletrap pistol, an old 6.35 Baby Browning, the men would've quickly found what they wanted, and both boys would be dead. Sepi had managed to shoot one of them—even if only in the foot—before taking a bullet to the forehead and another to the chest.

In the confusion, the kid had made a break for it and gotten a small head start, which was dwindling by the second.

The one with the bullet in his foot had stayed back by Sepi's car with another man, while the other two gave chase.

The kid let out a bitter howl, like that of a wounded hound.

Soon he would die, and there was nothing he could do about it. And somehow he had always been positive that he was destined for greatness. He had never known where this now fading certainty had stemmed from, but it had been an inseparable part of him. It was like a promise that couldn't be broken, granted to him by a supreme power in the presence of witnesses. Perhaps he imagined that if there was any justice in the world, he'd be paid for all his suffering with an equal proportion of manna and bliss.

He had been created for a grander purpose—at least that's what he had told his father on numerous occasions. His father had always responded with a sad look, his eyes full of pity…

Fuck that! Pity was a plague. That had been his mantra for years. Nobody had pitied him when he was beaten at the school's spring party, his new pants torn to shreds. Nor had they pitied him when he was locked in a broom closet for three hours after school, with no choice but to soil his pants…

Why should he feel pity for anyone else? Except for Chocolate Ear and Sven Dufva, his pet rabbits, the latter named for the heroic soldier in Runeberg's poem. True pity was what he felt every time he realized that one day he would bury Chocolate Ear in a little shoebox beneath an apple tree, his sprightly legs forever limp.

And with tears in his eyes, he had likewise pitied the dying Sven Dufva as Colonel Johan Sandels looked on kindly with the words, "The bullet found its mark, chose not the empty head, but the noble heart..." Or something in that vein.

The trail emerged from the forest into the field. A leap over a shallow ditch, and Nygren's house was still a good hundred yards off. From somewhere behind, he heard the sounds of his stalkers as they came thrashing through the scrubby birches.

Only fifty more feet. The gate to Nygren's property hung open. He slipped through, and pressed on toward the yard. The main house stood on the right, with an old barn and sauna to the left, near the lake. He glanced toward the water where he could make out the boat moored to a spindly dock...

Suddenly his foot caught on something, probably the edge of a rock jutting from the ground, and he came crashing down face first.

The impact briefly paralyzed him, and before he could get up, he felt their hands close around his arms and haul him roughly to his feet.

The men were obviously brothers, both with the same laughable whiskers. Aside from that, there was nothing laughable about them. The fat one had shot Sepi.

They wrenched his hands behind his back, both of their chests heaving from the long chase. Beads of sweat glistened on their faces. The thin one held his arms, while the fat one knelt down, took a deep breath, and

7

spat on the ground. Then he rose, cursed in Spanish, and slammed the butt of his gun into their captive's forehead. Blood began to run from the wound. Then the fat one pressed the gun barrel against his temple.

The thin man joined in the fun and shook him about like a ragdoll.

His muscles began to tremble. The fat one slapped him hard on the cheek.

"Let him go."

The boy heard the voice, but it took a moment to realize that it wasn't his imagination. They all turned at the same time.

The fog had thickened, and the surface of the lake had begun to melt into the mist. It seemed as though the man had simply materialized out of the fog. He was dressed in a faded sweater and worn-out jeans. His hair was tousled, as if he had just rolled out of a pile of hay in the barn.

He stood in a carefree manner, one hand behind his back, seemingly oblivious to the idea that he might have walked into the wrong place at the wrong time. The expression on his face was almost cordial.

The fat man looked at his partner, who nodded. Then he raised his gun.

The man from the fog stood in the same position, save for his hand, which moved fluidly, as though rehearsed a thousand times before. The gun came up, fired, and the fat man found himself with a gaping hole in his shoulder. Then his gun hand dropped, and the pistol tumbled to the ground.

The thin man glanced at the shooter, made his decision, and thrust his hand beneath his coat. His gun rose, but far too late. The man from the fog sent a bullet through the thin man's shoulder as well. Through the mist, the man's face was blank, as if he were taking potshots at cardboard cutouts on the shooting range.

The thin man looked down at his shoulder and began to scream and curse.

The boy felt his legs starting to melt. He collapsed on his back in the grass, which felt now like the finest down comforter in the world. So sweet, soft, and secure. Like his very own bed with a fresh change of sheets.

The man's face loomed over him and he tried to focus. He glimpsed into the man's eyes...blue, like two holes in a gray cloud before they faded into the ashy fog all around.

Then he heard himself utter a peculiar sound.

Had he not quit crying when he was eleven, he might have mistaken that sound for sobbing.

2.

Even dead, she was beautiful, though the man was not. He'd been stabbed to death, his face and neck mottled with lacerations and puncture wounds, his chest the same. He lay in the hallway near the bedroom, mouth gaping open, his tongue nestled between two rows of white teeth, a kitchen knife protruding from his chest. The lower half of his face and neck were smudged with blood, which had soaked into the rug and formed a grim, foreboding stain. Blood splatters sprinkled the salmon-colored wallpaper.

In addition to a large brass bed, there was a tall armoire, a mirrored table laden with cosmetics, a couple of erotic prints on the walls, and a nightstand beside the bed.

In comparison with its surroundings, the contents of the nightstand seemed oddly unbecoming: an overflowing ashtray, a half-empty whiskey bottle, and a crinkled sheet of aluminum foil with traces of white powder.

The woman had died in a more becoming manner. She lay on her back on the living room floor. No wounds were visible, but blood stained her hands and shirt sleeves.

She was blond and about thirty years old, a Swedish-Finn who clearly tended to her appearance. Her hair was neatly brushed, and her nails carefully manicured. She had on a dark blue skirt, a pair of mid-high pumps, and a blue naval jacket with gold buttons.

A strip of white shirt showed from beneath her jacket. One could easily imagine her at the meat counter of Stockmann's, buying the best cuts of meat. And then to the liquor store for a few bottles of French wine with a nice bouquet.

Her appearance didn't disappoint. The victim's name was Nina Liljeblad, a Finnair flight attendant. Her passport and driver's license had been found in a handbag on a table in the foyer.

Jansson stood next to her.

"Still wearing her coat."

Tykkylä, the coroner, came in from the bedroom with his ratty leather briefcase. Camera flashes flickered on the walls. One of the investigators was brushing for fingerprints in the foyer.

"Won't get much outta this, least not on the first go-around. The man was stabbed multiple times, but the cause of death was a stab wound to the heart. No evident wounds on the woman. Some minor abrasions on the face, with some swelling. Both deaths occurred in the last seventy-two hours, but we'll have a more exact time when we find out where she's been over the past few days. You probably noticed that she was still wearing her coat."

"Think it's what it looks like?" asked Jansson.

"It's usually just what it looks like. A kitchen knife's the murder weapon, and there's blood on her hands and clothing. The guy was probably high on coke. It's possible she suffered a heart attack as a result of a cocaine overdose. We won't know till the autopsy and the results from Forensics come in, if we ever know. But it doesn't look much like a sudden bout of illness. A young, healthy woman doesn't die just like that."

Jansson, a Helsinki PD detective lieutenant, put the pieces together in his head.

"So it looks like she came home from the airport to find him snorting coke. Somehow, they started fighting before she even got her jacket off. She grabs a knife from the kitchen, stabs him in the bedroom, and then ODs on coke."

"Looks that way. The stab wounds are more like sloppy jabs, which would be consistent with an upset woman."

"Seems odd she'd go into a frenzy the second she gets home. No foreplay whatever, just sticks him in the ribs right off," said Huusko.

"Drugs can make you do odd things. She was probably doing coke on the way home, too. Maybe she got upset once she realized he was dead, took some more, and the combination was fatal."

Jansson glanced at Huusko and nodded.

"Any more questions?" said Tykkylä, as he snapped his briefcase shut.

"What do you recommend for a bad case of jock itch?" said Huusko.

"Amputation."

Tykkylä left, snickering at his own joke. In the foyer, the tech who was lifting prints chuckled as well.

"Good advice for many an ailment," said Jansson.

"That's what happens to people who spend all their time around corpses."

"But I hope the jock itch was a joke," said Jansson seriously.

Huusko was in a blossoming relationship with a florist from Vantaa, and Jansson was genuinely concerned. The woman was the ex-wife of a murdered criminal, and Huusko had gotten to know her while investigating his death. Jansson felt she had had a positive influence on Huusko, who seemed more balanced now. He had even told Jansson about his future plans a few times, and that he got along with the woman's daughter, who was in grade school.

Jansson often felt somehow responsible for Huusko. After Huusko almost died from a gunshot wound, he had been adrift for years. Jansson had always tried to help when it felt right, and had loaned Huusko some money during hard times. After Jansson bought a flat in Herttoniemi the past spring, he had rented it to Huusko at well below market rates. But of course, he didn't want Huusko to feel indebted. And now he was fretting over Huusko's relationship as if she were a potential daughter-in-law.

As far as Jansson was concerned, all Huusko needed was a good woman to get him back on his feet. This florist, Lea Vuorio, was just that woman.

"It was a joke. Just a joke."

Huusko squatted down and peered into an expensive-looking suitcase that had fallen over in the foyer.

"She probably just got off her shift on a flight."

Huusko began removing the contents of the suitcase and piling them on the floor.

"Expensive tax-free aftershave for her man, two sets of headphones, brand-new Boss sunglasses, and an unopened bottle of perfume. So she comes bearing gifts, but whacks him at the first hello. What kinda game is she playing?"

"A lousy homecoming game, at any rate," said Jansson.

"Lousy, and the last… But what if there was a third person?"

"Third wheel, you mean?"

"Yeah. Say the guy's got another lady here, the girlfriend walks in and asserts her feminist rights by grabbing a kitchen knife and skewering him to her heart's content."

"A fine theory...very fine indeed," said Jansson.

Adjacent to the bedroom was another room with a closed door. A dog's fading, yet still furious bark sounded from behind the door. Jansson glanced at Huusko.

"It's theirs. It was already in there when I arrived. Some kind of utility room."

"Has it been fed?"

"I snuck a little water through the door. Grumpy little devil. Hardly bigger than a hedgehog."

Jansson went into the kitchen and looked in the refrigerator. A row of dog food cans were lined up on the lower shelf. He opened one of them and dumped the contents into a bowl from the cupboard.

Huusko was right: the dog was more than a little ornery, but its fire was starting to fade. It greeted Jansson with a snarl at first, then seemed to tire, and sat down.

The dog could have come off the shelf of any toy store. It stood about a foot tall and was only slightly longer. Its white fur was longish and fluffy. Jansson didn't recognize the breed, but its appearance was consistent with some kind of terrier. The dog was clearly young, hardly more than a puppy.

Jansson knelt down in front of the dog and slid the bowl toward its snout. It growled and stared Jansson in the eyes.

"Quit your complaining and eat up. You'll feel better. Probably haven't had two crumbs in as many days."

The dog couldn't resist the tempting smell and licked at the food with its little pink tongue. Then it sat up, took a small bite, and, with some difficulty, swallowed.

"I'll get you some fresh water to wash that down."

Jansson brought the dog some water in a kitchen bowl. After greedily gulping it down, the dog took another mouthful of food.

"Not so bad, huh? Eat your fill. I'll just go see if I can find out who hurt your momma."

Jansson returned to the foyer. Huusko was on all fours, studying a blue notebook.

"Here's her work schedule and a few scribbled notes. For Sunday it says 'Jose' with an exclamation point. Is the victim's name José?"

Huusko handed the notepad to Jansson, then pulled the woman's wallet out of the suitcase and started to rifle through it. Jansson paged through the notebook. In addition to her work schedule, there were a few names and times. Probably reminders of engagements she had made.

"Here's her car keys—she drove from the airport. Would've been easier for us if she took a taxi."

"Too easy," Jansson mumbled.

"Why can't we have it easy just once? The gods have something against us? If so, the union must've negotiated terribly on our behalf."

"The man looks southern European, maybe even South American. Definitely not Finnish," said Jansson.

Huusko nodded.

"Nor does he live at this address. The only things we found were hers," Huusko said, glancing around the room. "I guess that's pretty obvious. No man could stomach this much sweetness."

Jansson had noticed the same thing. In the living room, two antique china cabinets displayed a collection of elaborate cups and saucers. The chest of drawers, table and shelves were likewise laden with little trimmings of glass and silver, powder boxes, crystal

15

animals, and candlesticks. A lumpy, wine-red sofa echoed the fabric wallpaper of the same tone. Several large, ornately-framed oil paintings of traditional subjects hung from the walls: fruit baskets, couples in fancy 19th-century outfits basking in the bosom of nature, a row boat on a glassy lake. A huge crystal chandelier hung from the middle of the ceiling.

Huusko ran his fingers through the crystals and they tinkled against one another.

"Must have had a thing for bling."

"Looks to me like an older person's home. Maybe her folks live abroad and gave her the house keys."

"Same thing crossed my mind."

Jansson went to the living room window, which looked out onto the front yard. Cypresses and Chinese pines were growing in the lawn on either side of the front walk, which was flanked by perennials.

Directly across the street was a single-family home of the same 1950s vintage, with similar stucco siding. Despite a couple of apple trees in the yard and a hawthorn hedge bordering the street, Jansson could see directly into the front window of the house. That meant that the reverse was true as well.

Jansson glanced at his watch: 1:36 P.M. "Soon as Sanna gets here you can go interview the neighbors."

"Right. I imagine our blonde here would attract plenty of attention, especially men's, so we got a decent chance of finding an eyewitness."

A forensic investigator came into the living room.

"The male is all yours now."

"Could you process those prints as soon as possible?" said Jansson. "We need a name."

"We'll do our best."

Huusko shifted the body around a bit and began searching the victim's pockets. Nothing there. The man's jacket had been in the foyer, but those pockets had been empty as well.

"Mystery number two. Where's his stuff? No wallet, no cell phone, no keys. Not even a bus ticket. Doesn't really fit the picture. I'm guessing he didn't walk here or drive a moped."

"Search the house a little more closely," Jansson said. "Maybe she took his things first and then killed him."

"Why?"

"No telling what a coke head might do. Maybe she was jealous or wanted to keep him from leaving. Check the trash, too."

"Awright."

Huusko examined the man's abraded hands and cracked fingernails.

"He sure wasn't a desk jockey."

"But he did have work. In other words, he's probably lived in Finland for many years. Shouldn't be difficult to get an ID."

"If he's Latino, cocaine and the Colombian drug cartels come to mind," said Huusko. "Latino, a beautiful stewardess, an opulent home, everything seems to fit."

"That's painting with a pretty broad brush if you ask me," said Jansson.

"Well, a good theory could get us off with a bang."

Jansson glanced at the blood splatters on the wall, then went back to the woman's body. He examined her bloodied hand and sleeve. In the bedroom, the forensics tech was picking through the ashtray, putting the contents into a series of small plastic bags. After extracting DNA from the cigarettes and comparing it to the victims, Forensics would determine if anybody else besides the victims had been in the room.

"Anything on the handle to the bedroom door?" Jansson asked.

"Yep. Fingerprints."

"No blood?"

"Nope."

"Strange."

Huusko heard Jansson's remark.

"Why's that strange?"

Jansson thought for a moment, then pointed to the wall between the bedroom and living room.

"There's blood on the bedroom wall and door, but none on the door handle. What does that tell you?"

Huusko looked at the door before answering.

"That the door was almost shut. If it were open, it would've been between the victim and the wall, and there wouldn't be any blood on the wall. And the splatters would be on the other side of the door."

"Exactly, but why is there no blood on the handle?"

"Why should there be?"

"The woman's hand is bloody. How could she open the door without leaving blood on the handle."

"Maybe she's a lefty."

"We know the knife was in her right hand because the blood is on her right. In her state of mind, she'd have left plenty of blood on the knob."

Huusko looked at the forensics tech.

"Whaddya think?"

The man nodded. "Jansson's right."

"So it was staged?" Huusko asked. "Someone else stabbed the guy and smeared blood on her hand and clothes. The killer made sure not to touch the door handle so as not to leave any prints. That what you mean?"

"Precisely. For her part, the woman was so high, she was completely oblivious."

"There goes my feminist theory."

Huusko approached the floor-to-ceiling armoire, and opened the left-hand door. A dense row of designer clothing hung from the rod.

"Expensive taste."

He opened the right-hand door.

"Hel-lo!"

Jansson went to see for himself.

The armoire was crammed with merchandise of every stripe, each in its original packaging. Stereo headphones, MP3 players, silk scarves, ties, sunglasses, and wristwatches. In the lower half of the cabinet were at least twenty bottles of cognac and whiskey. Jansson knelt down to have a look, though he knew immediately where they had come from.

"Pilfered outta the plane's tax-free cart. Ms. Liljeblad appears to have been quite the sticky-fingered klepto," said Huusko.

Susisaari's red compact pulled up in front of the house and joined the police cruiser and Huusko's white Ford loaner. Susisaari got out of the car briskly. Jansson had heard that she had enrolled in the station's fitness classes, and he could see that she had lost weight. She approached the entrance with a nimble stride, and gave a quick wave when she spotted Jansson and Huusko in the window.

"I feel old suddenly," said Jansson.

"Come on now. Aged to perfection."

Huusko went to open the door, and Susisaari breezed inside with a fresh gust of autumn air.

"What'd you find out?" Jansson asked.

She took a notepad out of her pocket. "I haven't gotten hold of the mother yet, but I spoke to her younger sister. The sister had no idea what this might be about, and didn't know anything about the guy. She was pretty frank about the fact that her older sister had plenty of male friends, both here and abroad, but she didn't know them. Apparently, they aren't all that close. The father's dead and the mom lives in Florida. Last time she was here was three months ago."

Susisaari flipped to a new page in her notepad.

"I found one entry on her record from a couple years back...resisting arrest. She got into a fight with another woman on the terrace bar of the Kulosaari Casino. Police were called when Liljeblad pulled a Swiss Army knife out of her purse. She gave the officers some trouble before wising up. Later we got word that the fight had started over her friend snorting too much coke in the restaurant bathroom. Nothing more."

"Pulling a knife fits the picture—seems like the hot-tempered type," Huusko noted.

"No thefts on her rap sheet?" asked Jansson.

"No."

"What about the flight she was on?"

"Regular flight from Madrid. I got hold of the two other stewardesses from the flight. According to them, nothing out of the ordinary happened on the plane."

"What did they think of Liljeblad?" Jansson asked.

"Fun-loving...a party girl, basically. Hung out with a posh crowd, spent lots of money on herself, lots of boyfriends. Supposedly a favorite among the pilots, but she did good work. A couple of complaints were filed against her. According to some customers, she had acted rude and arrogant."

"Any recent boyfriends?" asked Huusko.

"The stewardess I talked to told me she was dating a South American man who was living in Finland. She didn't know anything about him except that his name was José. She had tried to find out more, but Liljeblad was tight-lipped about him. Normally she was pretty open about her boyfriends and actually bragged about

20

them. That's all I got… Except I put in a request for the phone records."

"Good."

Huusko snapped his fingers. "I knew something was missing. No cell phone. These types always have a phone."

Jansson nodded. "I'll head over to the station to write up the report. Why don't you two knock on some doors with a photo of our man. If nobody IDs him, one of you can ask around the Latino circles in Helsinki. Shouldn't take long. If that doesn't turn up anything, we'll send the photo over to the press. We need a name for this guy, pronto. Malmberg and Lehto can help out if needed, and if we're really in a jam, I can get more help."

"How's Tuomela?" asked Susisaari.

Jansson paused at the door.

"Lucky it was mild… Three weeks of sick leave under close observation."

Captain Tuomela, their boss, had suffered a heart attack the previous week. He had been rushed directly to the same hospital where, one year earlier, he had undergone a bypass operation. He had recovered well from the surgery and returned to work after six months of sick leave. Jansson had headed up the Violent Crimes Unit during his absence, and didn't miss the role in the slightest.

"Well, still feels nice to be in the field again," said Susisaari, struggling to conceal her happiness.

After having attended a lieutenant-level training course, Susisaari was now back at the Violent Crimes Unit for a couple of months. In total, her classes would last another year.

Jansson knew that the next vacancy for a VCU lieutenant wouldn't open up until Captain Tuomela's retirement set off a chain reaction. Only then would

Susisaari get her post. The next to go after Tuomela would be Jansson.

"Well, we got you back at the right time," said Jansson. "Isn't that right, Huusko?"

"That's right. Me and her go together like Laurel and Hardy... Or mustard on a brat."

"Yeah, just like that," Susisaari mumbled.

"Be nice now," said Jansson as he turned to lead them in. He stopped in the entryway, thought for a moment, then slipped the dog's leash off its hook. Susisaari watched him curiously.

"The victim left an orphaned puppy," said Huusko.

Susisaari was immediately interested. When she spotted the little white dog on the rug, with its head nuzzled between its paws and its ears pricked, she couldn't help but blubber, "Ohhh...now who is this? Are you mommy's little cutie? Wonder what breed it is?"

She bent down in front of the dog and reached out her hand. The dog didn't budge, just watched her curiously with its brown button eyes.

Jansson bent down as well. The dog got up, hesitated briefly, then came to Jansson's side. He clipped the leash onto its collar.

"You must have meant to say daddy's little cutie."

* * *

Jansson had spent better than half an hour typing out the short press release, but was still unhappy with it. The language seemed stiff and clumsy.

Jansson looked at the dog lying under his desk.

"Even you could do better. Much better."

The dog stared at Jansson from behind its furry bangs.

22

"Just as I thought," said Jansson, and he adjusted himself into a position that tested the very limits of the chair's weight capacity.

Jansson had once decided to put all of the most interesting cases of his career down on paper. One night in bed, just before falling asleep, he had roughed out the first story, written it in his head, complete with a title. He had felt good about his unique prose; it seemed both humorous and profound. But after settling down at the computer the next day, he found he had begotten a tired yarn, a parade of words with no trace of originality or rousing emotion. At that moment, in one fell swoop, he had lost all faith in his literary aspirations.

Jansson got up and looked at the dog.

"You be a good dog and wait here. I have to do something."

Jansson brought the report to the service desk, where it would be faxed to the Finnish News Service. After that, there would be no going back to his office. As the news spread to every media outlet in the country, his phone would begin to ring, and he had no intention of revealing anything more than what he had written in the report.

Deputy Chief Hakala called, and Jansson, confident that the incident would interest Hakala, gave him the latest. Afterwards, Jansson called his wife to tell her that he'd be working late. She wanted to know when he'd be home so she could shoo off her latest French lover before he arrived. Jansson promised to call and warn her.

Just before four o'clock, Jansson called Huusko, who sounded busy.

"I was just about to call you. They found some coke under the lining of her handbag."

"How much?"

"Two ounces. Too much for her own use. I'd say she's been moonlighting as a mule. Probably how she's funding her habit. All of which means that the case for the murder being connected to narcotics is getting stronger."

"Let's keep that in mind. What about the neighbors?"

"That angle's getting interesting too. A guy who lives in the opposite building saw some yuppie SUV parked out in front of the apartment on Sunday evening. Two foreign-looking men came out of the building and got into the SUV. This neighbor was pretty sure it was a dark green Land Rover Freelander, since his co-worker has the same car. But he didn't see when the car got there, nor has anyone else up to this point. According to Liljeblad's co-workers, she left work in the same red Mazda that was in front of the building. What do you think?"

"Ask around some more and put out an APB on the Land Rover. Forensics can examine the Mazda."

"The APB's already out. It doesn't look like this is as clear cut as we thought."

"Has anyone identified the man?"

"No."

"If the guys who got into the SUV were foreigners, maybe it was a rental."

"Let Lehto and Malmberg work that out. We've got plenty to do already. Some of the neighbors should be coming home from work about now."

"Very well. I'll be here late if something comes up."

"I'll call right away," Huusko promised. "What'd you do with the little mutt, by the way?"

"He's right here."

"I see."

"What do you mean, I see?"

"Don't you think Liljeblad's mom or sister might want it?"

"Maybe."

Jansson called Lehto and directed him to contact the Department of Motor Vehicles for information on all Land Rover Freelanders, as well as to start calling rental agencies. That left Malmberg with the responsibility for identifying the murdered man.

"Take the photo and ask around Latino neighborhoods, restaurants, friendship societies, whatever you can think of."

Jansson ended his embargo, and returned to his office. The dog followed him in, its head cocked to the side, its stubby tail wagging. The phone rang, but Jansson ignored it. He opened a window and breathed in the autumn air, which had been rainy and foggy all week, but now seemed to be clearing. Jansson decided to hang his hammock between the apple trees when he got home. Then, later in the evening, as one by one the lights of the city went out, he'd gaze at the starry sky from beneath a warm blanket. Just lie there and take in the rich scent of the apples, the mud, the grass, and leaves. But not until evening, and only if he got home at a reasonable hour.

The phone rang again, and after hesitating for a moment, he answered, "Jansson."

"I called asking for the investigator of that double murder and they connected me with you."

"We didn't say anything about a double murder, just two deaths. Anyhow, I'm the lead investigator."

"Is there a difference? Well...I just happened to be listening to the news when they gave a description of the male victim...er...the male... I think he might've been my co-worker."

"What is your co-worker's name?"

"José Hernando. Hasn't been to work in two days, and we haven't heard anything from him. He mentioned he was going to his girlfriend's in Oulunkylä for the weekend... Isn't that where the murder happened?"

"You mentioned the two of you were co-workers... What did this José do?"

"Same thing as me. I work for a produce wholesaler, so everything you'd expect to do there...drive truck, wash produce, pack, sort... Odd jobs."

"And what would your name be?"

"Seppo Ollila."

"Why don't you give me your phone number and I'll have an investigator call you shortly to set up an interview. We'd like to meet with you this evening. Would that work?"

"I guess so."

Jansson called Malmberg and gave him Ollila's number. Then he booted up his computer and signed into the police database. According to records, José Hernando lived in Roihuvuori, on Vuorenpeikon Street. His occupation was listed as warehouse worker. Though he had lived in Finland for seven years and had a common-law wife and one child, he was not a Finnish citizen. Hernando was from La Paz, Bolivia. How ironic that the man had to come from La Paz all the way to Finland to die.

Jansson felt something brush against his leg. The dog was standing at his feet, peering up at him. Jansson bent down and offered his hand, which the dog licked.

"What in the world are we gonna do with you?"

The dog licked Jansson's index finger.

"You think for the time being you'd like to live in an old wooden house under a big poplar?"

The dog woofed softly.

"I suppose you would… But remember, no promises. And just for the time being. Is that clear? My wife is very kind, but I think she's more of a cat person."

Jansson clipped the leash onto the dog's collar, closed the door behind them, and padded off toward another door, which was dimly visible at the end of the hallway. The dog stumbled along beside him for a bit, but then caught on to the cadence of Jansson's gait. Jansson beamed down at the little creature, now trotting along happily at his feet.

"Now there's a born police dog if I've ever seen one. Keep that up and you'll be promoted to deputy chief in three years flat. Then again…you might be too gifted for management."

3.

It smelled like smoke in the house. Not raw and acrid, but soft and mild, like a tough man's aftershave. The fumes were the result of an insufficient draft and a flue that had been out of use for years—the stove no longer vented properly.

Raid wasn't bothered by the smell. It only brought to mind a certain nostalgia, something real. The smell of smoke belonged to a lifestyle that demanded less of itself: it was enough if one had warm clothes, dry firewood in the shed, wool in the storehouse, bread in the rafters, and potatoes in the cellar.

Neither the lake nor the forest beyond the field were visible through the lingering fog. The forest's yellowing canopy, which signaled the arrival of the first frosty nights, lay in the distance. Everything beyond the furthest apple trees had simply faded to gray. The normally sharp contours of the barn and sauna were a haze through the fog, like watercolor on damp paper.

The cream-white tiled stove and wood oven were last used in the spring, and Raid had started with only a small fire so that the stove and flue could dry out and get acclimated to the heat. A natural gas heater was also running at full tilt. In three hours, the temperature downstairs had risen to sixty degrees Fahrenheit. Outside, it was ten degrees colder.

Raid had a good sleeping bag. He would stay plenty warm. As soon as the stove was hot he had made some coffee, the aroma of which mingled with the smell of smoke, damp furniture, old wallpaper, and bed linens.

What was left of the sandwich toppings still lay on the table next to the coffee: bread, sausage, cheese, butter, and a jar of sliced pickles.

The kid sat at the table and glanced nervously about. He wore a US Army jacket, baggy cargo pants, and black running shoes. His face was pale and he ran his hands through his short hair.

"Who are you?" he asked.

"The owner of this house."

"Did you buy it? Or are you a relative of Nygren's?"

"Nygren was my uncle."

The boy's restless eyes fell on Raid.

"Uncle? Then you must be…"

"And you?"

"Me? Porola, Matti Porola… I remember you now. You came here last fall with Nygren."

"That's right."

"Did the cancer get him?"

"Yes. He's dead."

"Some cops were here asking about him after you guys left."

"That so?"

"Yup. Didn't say why. Was he a… Don't take this wrong, but was he a criminal?"

"Yes, and you?"

"You mean what do I do? I work at my dad's store here in town. I help with sales…drive the truck…that sort of thing…" The boy realized how ordinary his résumé sounded, and added, "I studied for over a year at the community college in Kuopio. I'll be outta here as soon as I can. I got lots of plans, and staying here to rot isn't one of them."

"Must be a dangerous line of work nowadays, being a shopkeeper's helper."

The young man tried to muster a laugh. "I must've passed out... Got to drinking yesterday... Still have a hangover, and then the running..."

"Why did you run here?"

"Sorta by chance, at least at first. Then I remembered Nygren had a boat here. I was heading for the boat... What happened to the guys who were after me? Are they dead?"

"What do *you* think?"

"I saw both of them get hit. Awright... That's your business... At any rate, I'm damn thankful. If there's anything I can do to help..."

"Who were those men?" Raid shaved off a slice of cheese with his knife.

"Must have been some misunderstanding, I can't think of any other explanation... Not that I'm not thankful for your help."

"Seemed like a rather serious misunderstanding."

"These foreigners always get shit wrong... Easily offended. They got their vendettas and what not... I dunno. They spoke Finnish with a heavy accent...and a little English, too."

"Make yourself a sandwich," said Raid.

"Not right now, but thanks."

The boy rose with some difficulty, and Raid noticed that one of his legs looked stiff. The boy shook out his leg.

"Damn, they had me running like hell. Must have been almost two miles."

"You planning on doing some more?"

"I have to go."

"Suit yourself."

"My dad's probably waiting."

"Send him my best."

He stopped at the door, peeked out the window, and turned back toward Raid.

"I wonder if you could help a little with one more thing. See...my car broke down. You think maybe you could give me a ride to town?"

"Call your dad. Or a taxi."

"I don't have a cell phone with me."

Raid nodded toward a cell phone lying on the table. "You can use that one."

The boy took the phone and put his finger on the keypad as if to dial. Then he stopped and set it back on the table.

"Maybe I'll just walk. Just remembered he's got some kinda Lions Club meeting all evening... Can't be much more than a couple miles."

"That's not too bad," said Raid. "But it'll be dark soon."

The young man was still stalling.

"You must be in pretty serious trouble," said Raid quietly.

The boy couldn't look him in the eyes.

"And you got me involved when you stumbled onto my property."

The kid considered his options for a moment before making his decision. "Can I interest you in some serious money?" he said.

"What, should I start playing the lottery?"

"I got something going that might net a few million, but I need some help... I figure you must have some good contacts."

"Bad ones, too. From every walk of life."

"Okay, I'll tell you what it's about, but this stays between you and me. Promise?"

"Let's hear it."

"Cause I'm in deep shit if someone finds out, and maybe you, too."

"Sit down," said Raid.

The boy glanced outside one more time and came back to the table.

"Thirty pounds of snow…you know, cocaine. That's what this is about. A couple weeks back I was unpacking a big shipment of bananas… Buried under the bananas I found a big package wrapped in layers of plastic. I opened it up and found some white powder inside. First thing I thought was it's flour or something, but it didn't take long to figure it out, no matter how hard it was to believe. There was thirty pounds of coke in there, I'm not shitting you. Obviously meant for someone else, but someone screwed up and sent it to us… Coke goes for about seventy-five grand a pound, so the whole thing works out to more than two million euros. Think about it…that's *more* than winning the lottery."

"So what happened?"

"Well, I didn't hear from anybody, so I told my best friend Sepi about it. We've done all kinds of shit together, so I trusted him a hundred percent. He was pretty stoked about it and wanted in right away. We figured we'd connect up with a guy that Sepi knew and sell it off in Helsinki. Even at half price, we'd make a million. With that kinda money you could buy a nice pad in downtown Helsinki, or even move out of the country."

The boy sank his hands deep into his pockets.

"Well, this dude that Sepi knew was supposed to have connections, but fuck if that was true. Bunch of clowns, every one of 'em. Pooling all their money, they bought all of *one* ounce. And that was at a discount. We got a couple grand, and almost all of that's gone 'cause Sepi wanted to stay in a five-star hotel and drink all the booze from the mini-bar. That shit probably costs more than our coke."

"So how did those men find you?"

"Sepi couldn't keep his trap shut. Kept acting like some big shot drug lord, bragging that he's got pounds of coke. I guess word got out…I don't see how else they found out."

"So he gave out his address?"

"Even he isn't that stupid…least I don't think so. But he gave his cell number to at least a couple guys. Maybe that's it. Or maybe they figured out from the produce vendor where the bananas went. First time I saw them was yesterday, and I knew right away what was up. Four foreign toughs lurking around a one-horse town like this. Pretty easy to guess that shit was gonna hit the fan."

"Did you say four?"

"Yeah.

"Then what?"

"When I left the store last night they followed me, so I called up Sepi and picked him up. We were headed toward Korpela when they cut us off, and we wound up in the ditch. They came up to the car, and one of 'em had a gun. Luckily, Sepi had a little 6.35 Baby Browning strapped to his ankle, so he pulled it out and shot the guy. Hit him in the leg, right here." He pointed to his right calf.

"But then they…they shot Sepi… In cold blood… Horrible to see him die."

He turned away for a moment in an attempt to calm himself.

"Thanks to Sepi, I managed to get away with about a hundred-yard head start, but two of them came after me. I got this bum hip, you know. Even with the surgery, I've never been the best runner. Anyways, they were catching up, not that they were big track stars either…

One of them was kinda fat… They'd have killed me on the spot if you hadn't been there."

"How far behind were the other two?"

"Maybe a mile."

"So they heard the shots."

"Where are the two that were chasing me?"

"Out in the grain shed."

The boy raised his hand to silence Raid.

"I don't wanna know what happened. That's your business."

"Your friend didn't happen to tell them where the cocaine is?"

"He died instantly. The bullet hit him in the head… Fucking sons of bitches. Sepi was my only friend."

The boy briefly turned away again to collect himself.

"So where is it?"

He glanced at Raid and wondered if he was being conned. Then he realized that with his life in peril, it didn't matter. Besides, the man seemed trustworthy, he reasoned to himself. A trustworthy outlaw, even if an outlaw first. Dad had said that Nygren had been a criminal, and that Nygren had left his estate to a nephew, who was an even worse criminal. Dad's police friend had said so. On the other hand, he should be grateful for it. Only an even worse criminal could have stood up to those thugs. Had he stumbled onto an honest, ordinary citizen's property, he and the ordinary citizen would now be dead.

"I hid it in the woods," said the boy. "In a crack in the rocks."

"And nobody else knows about it?"

"I'm sure of it."

The boy glanced restlessly out the window. It was nearly dark outside.

"What should we do? They could be here any minute. How long was I out?" the boy asked.

"Ten minutes."

"Any second, then."

"You should go to the police. They'll be taking you in anyways, as soon as your friend's body is discovered."

"So two million just falls down from heaven, and I'm supposed to give it away?"

"Heaven? Or hell?"

"Same difference to me. You help me sell it and I'll pay you well. With your contacts, we can get a good price for it. Afterwards, we'll just go our separate ways."

Raid got up and pitched an armful of wood into the stove. He put his hand against the rounded flank of the stove, which was slowly beginning to warm.

"First off, I'm on vacation. Second, I'm not a drug dealer."

The boy looked confused.

"Does it really matter to a criminal what he does, as long as it pays?"

"To some, no. To others, yes."

"So which type are you?"

"The worst."

"So you're not interested?"

"No."

The boy looked disappointed.

"I gotta go… Dad's probably worried."

"If you're gonna be a drug lord, you'll have to get used to your mommy and daddy worrying."

"But you didn't give a shit what your parents thought."

"They didn't think much of it. They were already dead by that time."

"Both of 'em?"

"Yep."

The boy thought for a moment.

"So why'd you get involved?"

"I didn't. You involved me."

"Well, thanks."

Raid stood up. "Why don't you do me a little favor before you go."

"What?"

"I'm going for a little evening drive. I'll bring you home afterwards so your dad doesn't worry. Here."

Raid gave him one of the guns he'd taken from the thugs.

"I don't even know how to use this."

"Pretty poor credentials for an aspiring drug lord."

"I intend to use my head, not guns."

"A fine idea…in theory. Lock the door. And don't shoot me when I come back."

"What if you don't come back?"

"Then you'd best make yourself scarce."

* * *

Diego Estefani was seething with anger. From the word go, everything had gone wrong, bad luck dogging him at every step in this cursed frozen land.

He had laid the groundwork with care, mapped out the route, and entrusted the important details to the most trustworthy men. The initial trial shipment had gone like clockwork, and the bosses had lavished him with praise and promises of large shares of the profits. But praise and promises didn't cost them anything.

The second shipment had also gone without a hitch, but that's where the smooth sailing ended. José had yielded to his more carnal interests and started consorting with that loony stewardess. The woman

36

inhaled cocaine like a vacuum, and her behavior became erratic when she got high. Now her habits appeared to be rubbing off on José. The previous spring, they had sent a couple of men to have a chat with him, but to no particular end.

When the third shipment had arrived, José had been so high on the job that the coke, which had safely arrived from halfway across the world, went to the wrong address on the last leg of its journey. Had José done his job, the coke would have continued over the border in the banana crate to a Russian grocery store. There, it would have been distributed to the middlemen, and finally, rushed up the nose of some newly-rich Russian in a gleaming St. Petersburg commode.

Diego was accountable for the success of the operation, and for salvaging what was left to salvage, including his own life. The bosses took responsibility very seriously, and the fact that one of them was Diego's uncle, Joseph Espocio, didn't help Diego at all.

Once José had finally realized what had happened, he had gotten scared and promised to help find the coke. Initially, second cousin or not, Diego had meant to off him without further ado. But then it dawned on him that José still had some use, at least for a little while longer.

With José's keys, they had gotten into the produce warehouse, but had to break down the office door. The entire office was in shambles before they found the distribution records in a file cabinet, and even with those, it had all been in vain.

The bananas had been split into twenty shipments, and they couldn't ransack twenty grocery stores.

Uncharacteristically, Diego had gotten good and drunk, and called a Russian whore up to his hotel bedroom.

In the early morning hours he had knelt down and prayed that Jesus and Mary would have mercy on his miserable soul, him having drifted into perilous waters in this godforsaken corner of the world.

And the Virgin Mary heard his heartfelt plea. A Russian middleman that Simon knew called to tell him that two country boys were brazenly hawking thirty pounds of coke all over Helsinki. It was pretty clear whose cocaine the boys were peddling as if it were their own. Simon asked the vendor to score a hit and get the boys' cellphone numbers with the promise of much larger deals. One of the boys had fallen for it, and using the number they had found out where he lived.

They had come into town yesterday and checked into a local hostel. Simon, who had lived in Finland for six years and spoke the language well, had gone to find out about the boys. That evening, it became clear that the kid with the gimpy leg was the son of a local grocer. And with that, the whole picture came into focus: the grocer's son had found the coke in the banana crate and realized that it wasn't flour. Afterwards, he had pulled in his friend, and together, the starry-eyed pair had traipsed off to Helsinki with dreams of millions to peddle their stolen wares. Diego had been almost humored by their naïveté.

Now he wasn't humored at all. This wretched day had been merely an extension of an equally wretched night spent on a hard hostel bunk, followed by a cheerless breakfast and a tasteless lunch at the service station restaurant. French fries and a noodle of meat. The coffee was no better, though it claimed to be Colombian.

And now the idiot brothers who had gone after the boys, Juan and Rafael Lopez, were missing, and not answering their phones. The whereabouts of the cocaine shipment, too, was still a mystery, and it was no small inconvenience that he now had a bullet hole through the meaty part of his right calf.

And Simon. How long does it take to ditch one fucking body? He didn't have to bury it at the center of the earth. And why did he always get stuck with the dumbest guys from LaPaz, when there were plenty of qualified men to choose from.

Diego dialed Simon's number.

"Get over here. What's taking you?"

"I'll get there. Hard digging…the ground's so full of roots and rocks. My new shoes are all messed up already…"

"Didn't you hear the shots?"

"What about them?"

"Well, if you heard them, someone else did, too. Or maybe you think you can shoot off guns in Finland without turning any heads?"

"Well, there's nothing but woods here."

"Just hurry up."

Diego was mostly irritated that the little brat had managed to catch him off guard, the bullet hole in his leg a pounding and persistent reminder of that gaffe. But who would have imagined the scamp would have a gun in an ankle holster?

Diego felt the blood trickling into his shoe, his foot sliding around in the slime. He tightened the tourniquet, an old scarf he had wrapped around his calf, and wiped the excess blood away with a handkerchief.

The windshield of the car began to fog up, and he cranked down the window. The warm air from the heater and the damp air pouring through the window mingled as it swept across his face.

The shots had Diego worried. If his amigos were too trigger happy, one of the bullets could have easily hit the boy. And then who would tell them where the thirty pounds of coke were?

Another worry occurred to Diego as well. Perhaps the men's absence was due to just that. They had killed the boy and realized what that meant. So now they were hiding in the woods for fear of what would happen if they came out. He cursed quietly. If they had killed the boy, they had good reason to fear him, and if not him, then the bosses. The bugs of the rain forest had received meals of fresh meat for far less. Diego stared at the woods, which faded into the fog about fifty yards away.

Being a city kid, he didn't go into the jungle unless he had to. But even the Bolivian jungle seemed less foreboding than this Finnish one. At least in Bolivia there was life and sound. Here, the forest was deathly silent, with only the faint sound of a few birds and the rush of wind in the canopy. Almost as though the woods were watching his every move, ready to strike at the moment he let down his guard. He was afraid of the Finnish forest, and had no desire to set foot in it. And that was saying nothing of wolves and bears.

From the trees, he heard a rustling sound and the crackling of dry twigs. Shortly, Simon emerged from the fog with a shovel. Once he reached the road, he inspected his shoes worriedly, and began to wipe the fine yellow sand off with a handkerchief.

Simon was known affectionately as Wingtip-Simon, as he wouldn't think twice about going into the fields to pick rock in fine Italian leather shoes. He always kept a small piece of chamois in his pocket for renewing the shine.

"I'm lucky you had your lights on…coulda got lost in the fog."

"What'd you do with their car?"

"Covered it with brush. How's your leg?"

"Hurts like hell."

Simon tossed the shovel into the car and glanced around.

"Where's our amigos?"

"Not back yet."

"Did you call 'em?"

"Neither one's answering."

"What the fuck are they doing?" said Simon. "Maybe they're lost in the fog."

"Phones don't get lost."

"Maybe their phones are dead."

Diego was beginning to suspect the same. It seemed strange, but every other possibility only seemed stranger.

"Or maybe they fell in a ditch or a lake, and the phones got wet. Everywhere you look here, there's a lake. But why'd they shoot?" wondered Simon. "They weren't supposed to kill him."

"There's no telling with those idiots."

"We can't leave 'em here. They'd go whining to the bosses."

Diego knew that Simon was right, but even so, he was inclined to leave them to wade through the thickets. Maybe they'd even get stuck in a swamp and wind up as wolf dinner. His foot was throbbing and he wanted to see a doctor.

"Where you think this road goes?" Simon wondered aloud.

"We got two choices, either wait here or go look for 'em. If we go look for 'em, the idiots will probably come back while we're out there and call the bosses saying we ditched them in the middle of a job."

"You're the boss. Your call. It'll be getting dark soon, though."

Diego honked the horn three times.

"We'll give 'em ten more minutes."

Ten minutes felt like an eternity, and they exchanged only a few words. After three minutes of silence, Simon brought up the fact that Diego wouldn't be able to tell a Finnish doctor that the wound was a gunshot wound, because the doctor would notify police immediately.

"What, should I say it's a bee sting?"

"Think of something believable."

"Like, for example?"

"Maybe just say you were on a farm and you hurt it in the hay loft. You didn't notice the pitchfork in the haystack and it stuck you in the leg."

"And that's your idea of believable?"

"Just an example."

At eight minutes, Diego spoke up: "You'll have to come with me to the doctor and make something up. You speak Finnish."

Simon didn't seem enthusiastic. "I know a Spanish doctor who might be willing to keep his mouth shut for the right price."

"Good."

Both men stared silently at the digital clock on the dashboard.

"Time's up," said Simon.

"You drive," snapped Diego, and he walked around to the passenger's side.

The fog was so dense that Simon could drive no faster than fifteen miles an hour on the narrow dirt road. After about five hundred yards, they spotted a light on the right-hand side of the road, and as they drew nearer, an old farm house came into view.

A moped, car, and tractor were parked in the yard. A tan dog on a tie-out was barking wildly.

"The shots came from further off, and more to the left," said Simon. Diego agreed.

"Let's keep going."

After half a mile, the road terminated in the yard of another house. As the house lights came into view, Simon stopped the car and killed the headlights.

"The shots came from somewhere around here."

Diego studied the house. The lights were on in the downstairs windows and in one of the outbuildings, but there were no cars or other means of transport in the yard.

Simon drummed his fingers on the steering wheel and fidgeted.

"Just thought of something."

"What?"

"Maybe the kid didn't come here by accident."

"How so?"

"What if he ran here 'cause he knew someone here. Someone who's in on the coke deal, and Juan and Rafael walked into a trap. Maybe the shooter was someone else, and our amigos are dead."

Diego thought for a moment. Then he felt the spot in his cheek starting to twitch, and as he studied the area, he felt suddenly afraid. The old house loomed out of the fog, and the parched apple trees creaked in the wind. It all seemed like something out of a horror movie. The Lopez brothers had vanished as though swallowed up by the earth.

"And here's another thing. Maybe the coke disappearing wasn't an accident either. What if these kids were just helpers."

"So who would've been behind it, then?" Simon asked.

"The Russians… They could be ripping us off. They knew when and how the shipment was getting here. But that would mean José was in on it, 'cause he's the one who fucked up the address."

"You're not telling me you truly trust him."

Diego thought for a moment. "No. I don't truly trust anybody. But how come these kids have the coke?"

"None of us have actually seen it yet, it's all talk at this point. Maybe these kids got suckered too, just so we'd believe the bit about the shipment mistake."

Diego watched the house, his nerves tingling under the unmistakable threat of danger. He judged it best to back the car away from the house.

* * *

It was completely dark outside now. The air had cooled, and the fog had begun to lift, though it was still thick enough to obscure the lights in the homes on the far side of the lake. The wind began to rise, and the nearly leaf-bare branches in the apple trees rattled against one another. Beneath each tree was a ring of fallen apples. Raid took one and bit into it. His palate puckered at the sweet, sour juice, and the mild scent of the earth rising from the ground mingled with the flavors in his mouth. He picked up several more and crammed them into his pockets.

Raid circled behind the barn, and continued on into the meadow flanking the road. The dew had already settled on the grass, and it quickly soaked into his pant legs, but his thick hiking boots kept his feet dry.

He could make out the road, a pale strip in the darkness, and he trod lightly along the shoulder. After walking for about a hundred yards, he stopped.

On the other side of a gentle slope, a car was parked on the side of the road. The headlights were out, but the parking lights and dome light were on. Raid could hear the purr of the engine.

A man was seated in the car, talking on a cellphone. Another, this one in a leather jacket, was standing outside the car, kicking at the sand to fight off nerves and the cold. He knocked impatiently on the window. The man inside waved him off angrily, and he withdrew a couple of steps.

Raid drew his pistol from beneath his belt, cocked it, and disengaged the safety. He veered away from the road and circled back in toward the car. Once within about twenty yards, he knelt down. The man in the car hung up the phone, opened the window, and barked at the other, who answered in an apologetic tone. There was no mistaking the pecking order here. The man waiting outside circled to the driver's side and got in.

Raid crept low round the back of the car. Once behind it, he dropped to his knees. He was certain that he wouldn't be seen in the passenger side mirror, since the side of the car was almost touching the bushes in the ditch. The driver's side mirror, on the other hand, was more dangerous, but Raid had a plan.

* * *

"Let's get the fuck outta here," Diego finally hissed, "I can't wait for those idiots anymore."

Just then, the engine died.

"What the fuck?" said Diego. "Don't tell me…"

He hauled his legs out of the car in spite of the pain in his leg, grabbed onto the door to support his weight, then righted himself. That's when he felt something cold at the nape of his neck. It took only a moment for him to realize what it was.

* * *

Raid watched as the man in front of him raised his hands slowly into the air. The guy in the driver's seat was still trying to wrestle his own gun out of his coat pocket.

"Throw the gun in front of the car," Raid barked.

The man stalled briefly, then threw the gun.

"You speak Finnish?" Raid asked.

"Yes."

Raid patted down the man in front of him and found a gun holstered beneath his arm. He took it and stepped back a few paces.

"Take five steps away from the car."

The one who knew Finnish interpreted for his boss. Raid snatched the gun off the ground and jammed it into his waistband.

"What are you doing here?" he said.

"Is this private property?"

"Yes, it is."

"I'm sorry. We didn't know… We were just waiting for a couple of friends."

"Are they lost or something?"

"I don't know. Maybe."

"Then I might know where they are."

"Where?"

"Not far. We'll go see."

"Are they alive?"

"Hopefully."

The man regarded Raid warily, but said nothing.

"Your boss can drive. You take the passenger seat, and I'll give directions from the back seat."

The man translated Raid's instructions, and his boss said something back in Spanish.

Raid spoke up, "Your friends'll be needing a doctor. You can pick them up and take them to a hospital."

The man pointed to his boss's foot.

"Him too."

"Looks like it's going around. You can ask for a volume discount."

"I'm saying I'll have to drive."

"Fine. But pull the apple out of the exhaust first."

The man did so, then sat down behind the wheel. The other squirmed into the passenger seat. Raid sat in the back with his gun drawn.

"Straight ahead."

The car crept along in first gear, as though the driver expected something to leap out onto the road. He stopped in front of the gate.

Raid directed the driver to get out and go to the barn. He nodded toward the door.

The driver got out, walked to the barn, and opened the door. He groped around in the dark and found the light switch.

Two men were sitting on the ground, their hands tied to one another, their mouths gagged with duct tape. Their clothes were stained with blood.

"Untie their legs and help them up."

The man dug a folding knife out of his pocket and cut the ropes on their legs. Then he took one of the men by the arm and began to haul them up. The men, still bound to each other by their wrists, tried to help as much as they could. Once they were on their feet, the driver tried to remove the duct tape from one of their mouths.

"Leave it. I like it better when they're quiet. You'll have plenty of time to chat in the car. Don't untie them till you're on your way."

The driver managed to get the bound men over to the car. When he opened the back door, they all but fell inside. The driver took the wheel again.

"One more thing," said Raid.

"What?"

"Don't come back."

"We'll probably have to."

"Not anymore. What you're looking for doesn't exist anymore."

"Where is it?"

"Destroyed."

"Why? It was worth over two million euros."

"Drugs are bad for you."

The driver translated for his boss, who answered with a few terse words.

"I don't believe you, and neither do they. That kid stole it from us, you know. You think they're just gonna forget the whole thing?"

"Hopefully. I'm on vacation."

The man smiled. "You don't know who my friends are."

"I know enough. I don't want you around here anymore."

"They don't give a shit what you don't want. If they don't find the stuff, heads will roll."

"And if they come here, even more heads will roll."

"Looks to me like the only people here are you and the kid. There's a lot more of them. All professionals."

"As professional as those two?" said Raid, nodding toward the bound men.

"They won't make the same mistake twice."

The boss in the passenger seat rattled off something in Spanish and nodded at Raid.

"He says you can have a share if you return the stuff."

The boss said something more and the driver translated.

"In cash, he says. Two hundred grand. Tax free."

"Adios."

The driver looked at his boss, who nodded stiffly.

Raid stood in the yard for a while and watched their departure. The door to the house opened and the boy came into the yard with the gun in his hand.

"Are they gone?"

"Yep."

"I figured I'd come help, in case something happened."

"Thanks."

He looked at Raid for a while before admitting meekly, "Still, just about shit my pants."

* * *

The kid was sitting in the rocking chair, swaying. From time to time, he took a quick sip from the beer bottle in his hand. It was clearly hard for him to believe that it was over.

"You sure they won't come back?"

"Nope."

"Sorry to nag, but you saw yourself what kinda people they are."

"You think I need your advice? Call your dad, so he doesn't worry."

"And tell him what?"

"Same as usual. A lie."

The boy picked up a phone and dialed the number. This time, someone answered.

"It's me. I tried calling, but you weren't home... At a friend's house... No... Sepi's dad? ... I don't know... The battery was dead... You don't know him... Be home soon... Bye."

The boy glanced at Raid.

"What about your mom?" Raid asked.

"She died. Long time ago."

"Tell me about it."

"Why?"

"Because I wanna know."

49

"Bullshit... And even if you did, I don't wanna talk about it."

"Why not?"

"Don't wanna talk about that either."

"What do you wanna talk about?"

"What about how we're gonna turn this coke into cash."

"You're not a good listener. I'm not a drug dealer."

"You won't have to sell a thing. Just provide the contacts and have my back. Anyhow, I've told you about me, let's hear about you."

"That's not how it works, unfortunately. I ask the questions, you answer them. Just because you happen to run away from some thugs, stumble onto my property, and I save your life doesn't mean we're partners."

"Maybe not, but you're the one who shot them. Won't be long before they come after you, too."

"Maybe I should've let them shoot you."

"With enough money, you wouldn't have a care in the world anymore. A year or two out of the country, and the whole thing will be history."

"I'm guessing you're fond of your dad?" said Raid.

"What do you mean?"

"If they don't find you, they'll sure find him."

The boy mulled this over for a while. "You think they'd...?"

"I don't think so. I know so."

* * *

A light was on in the room over the store.

"Dad's watching the ten o'clock news," said the boy.

"What're you gonna say?"

The young man was quiet for a while.

"What am I gonna do?"

50

"Take him outta town for a while."

"He won't go...stubborn old codger. Won't leave the store."

"Then there aren't many options."

"I ain't tossing the jackpot out the window. This kinda thing happens once in a lifetime. Look around. Would you wanna live the rest of your life in a cow town like this? I, for one, have other plans."

"Maybe I would, if I had the choice."

"You don't know what you're talking about. You can't possibly think small towns are fun."

"I was born in a small town. And you couldn't buy beer at the gas station then, either."

"Being born in one isn't the same as living in one. And it's easy for you to talk when you've lived all over the place. Denmark, Sweden...who knows where else."

"I've been in a lot worse spots than this town."

"I haven't. And I don't want the highlight of my life to be the Kuopio community college. Hardly even any good-looking girls here, least not single ones... And none that would give a guy like me a second glance."

"There's someone for everyone."

"Really? Maybe for everyone else...not for me. Take a look. You think there's a big demand for gimpy gofer boys among the local ladies? At least in the big cities you can get some if you got money, if not otherwise."

"I'm just giving you some free advice. Do what you like with it."

The kid got out of the car, but paused before closing the door.

"Final offer: half the profits."

Raid pulled the door shut and drove away.

4.

Jansson had scheduled a meeting in the VCU conference room for eight in the evening. In addition to himself and the dog at his feet, Huusko, Susisaari, Officer Malmberg and Lieutenant Kempas were there. The day had been long for everyone, and the prevailing mood was one of exhaustion. Even Kempas yawned. He looked at the dog and then at the others, to see if anyone had noticed.

"What's that thing doing here?" Kempas finally asked.

Huusko leveled a finger at the puppy. "It's a bona fide K-9. Sniffs out the clues."

Kempas sized up the dog with a passing glance.

"Kinda small for a police dog. I got bigger dust bunnies under my bed."

"Now don't go selling him short. Many have, and they've regretted it."

Jansson scratched the dog behind the ear. "His owner was one of the victims, so I'm taking care of him for now."

Kempas took a closer look at the dog. "Living, breathing evidence, huh?"

"You know what its name is yet?" asked Susisaari.

"Nope. I just call him 'doggy.'"

"Come on. The poor thing needs a name, doesn't he? You can't just call him doggy.'"

Susisaari couldn't resist petting the dog. It stared her down with its little brown eyes, but didn't spurn her touch.

"I wonder what breed it is," said Malmberg.

Malmberg was pushing fifty, and stout. It was difficult to believe that he had once been one of the country's best sprinters. Of course, he carried his excess weight very well. Jansson knew that Malmberg was president of the police golf team.

"Think it's a boy or a girl?" said Susisaari.

"Take a peek between its legs," said Huusko. "Last time I checked, that was the only way to find out."

"Let's talk about something other than the dog for a while. Work, for example," said Kempas. "What's the situation, and what are we doing about it?"

Jansson leafed through his notepad before glancing up at the others.

"Since we've linked the case to the drug trade, Lieutenant Kempas is here. I'm referring to the cocaine in Liljeblad's purse. When we find quantities in excess of personal use, Narcotics gets involved... Anyhow, the woman's been identified, and based on a tip from the public, we believe the male has, too. Malmberg interviewed the caller, am I right?"

"Yes. In that respect, the case is clear. One of the man's co-worker's identified him: José Mario Hernando. The man had been working at a produce vendor for a couple years. Didn't come to work for two days, and he'd always been the punctual type. Has no criminal record. He was in a common-law marriage with one child, but he did have a reputation as a ladies' man, and was bragging to his workmates about the blonde stewardess he was seeing."

"Pride goes before a fall," Kempas droned.

"I'm telling you, those blondes are dangerous. Oughta be outlawed," said Huusko.

"Huusko and Sanna, what about you guys? Anything to add? You go first, Huusko."

"Well, another neighbor saw a dark SUV in front of Liljeblad's apartment building, which tallies with the first tip we got. According to him, the SUV got there around half past seven, but didn't stay long. He didn't get a look at the driver, though, since it was already dark and there weren't any streetlights in front of the building. He also observed Liljeblad coming home in her Mazda, or more accurately the car, not Liljeblad. The Mazda got there about a half hour before the SUV."

Malmberg remembered something and cut in, "Lehto's getting the footage from the airport parking ramp, and the data from her employee ID badge to see when and where she swiped it. Staff parking is in section P-1, next to international departures. That'll tell us exactly when she left."

"Good. Go on, Huusko."

"Later on, this same witness had been out with his dog and wondered about the barking and howling coming from the building. But that's it. He didn't notice what kind of SUV it was, or remember the plate number. But we haven't gotten hold of all the neighbors yet."

Sanna tore her eyes away from the dog. The little white creature had clearly stirred some kind of nurturing instinct in her.

"I called the rest of the numbers in Liljeblad's cellphone directory. Looks like she was quite the hot-blooded type. About a month ago she raised a stink at a hotel that Finnair uses in Madrid. She broke some furniture in what must have been a drug-fueled rage. But she paid for the damage and the hotel never notified her employer."

"Did anyone know the boyfriend?"

"José Hernando seems to have been a pretty new face. None of her friends knew much about him, but they all wondered why she was dating some foreign warehouse worker when she had such high standards for men. According to one of her coworkers, she had a relationship with one of Finnair's top bosses. At least she had hinted at it and joked about not having to worry about anything. Anyhow, the co-worker believed her. Liljeblad was apparently very direct, when it came to her sexual needs. Another reason the co-worker believed her was that Liljeblad had never been fired, despite numerous infractions. Many others had been let go for much smaller mistakes, which seemed to indicate that someone at a high level was protecting her."

"We know she felt confident enough to steal inordinate amounts of tax-free goods from the plane," said Jansson.

Kempas was toying with the metal wristband of his old wind-up watch, as if it were a miniature fitness machine.

"Customs is investigating the thefts with the Vantaa PD. The company has sustained large losses, but they've written it all off on the books as normal inventory losses and non-marketable goods."

"So why are they investigating?" said Huusko.

"One of the firm's assets protection people is a former officer who didn't buy these write-offs so easily. He couldn't get permission to investigate, so out of frustration he told a cop friend of his. The cop got in touch with Customs, since they deal with the tax-free market, and they quietly opened an investigation with the help of the guy from assets protection. At the same time, luck had it that one of the airport catering guys got busted for drunk driving. They found a hundred bottles of tax-free cognac and all kinds of other airplane staples in his trunk, plus double that in his apartment. After that, they had a setback and the case went cold."

"What happened?" asked Jansson.

"The guy from assets protection got busted with ten cartons of tax-free cigarettes and he got the boot. He claims he was framed so they'd have an excuse to fire him, and that's certainly what it looks like. The timing was just too convenient."

Jansson stood up and the dog did the same, as if to follow. Jansson seemed surprised.

"Sit."

The dog sat and cocked its head, awaiting its next command.

"Based on preliminary forensic evidence, it appears that the woman killed the man first under the influence of drugs, then died of a cocaine overdose. This is all speculation until we get the autopsy reports, though. It is, however, possible that both were murdered and the woman was made to look like the murderer. At a minimum the killings didn't happen exactly like someone wants us to believe."

"Any ideas on a motive?" asked Malmberg.

"Drugs are on the top of the list. She, the boyfriend, or both of them got in over their heads, or they made a mistake that they paid for with their lives," said Huusko.

"These South American gangsters are a mean lot," said Kempas.

Huusko perked up momentarily. "Does Narcotics have any intel on cartels with connections to Finland?"

"Only what we can get from Interpol, not much more."

All eyes turned to Kempas, who had a reputation for being stiff-lipped on account of his determination to horde every last crumb of data that he deemed significant. This time, he surprised everyone with his candidness.

"One of the Bolivian drug cartels is doing business with the St. Petersburg mafia. Interpol believes that they're building a new cocaine route to Russia. A route right through Finland would be one option. There's plenty of demand in Russia, and they can also redistribute the stuff to central Europe and Scandinavia. It's even possible that the drugs go to Russia in raw form, and get refined in local labs. We've also received some intel from Sweden that backs up Interpol's findings."

"What sort of intel?" asked Jansson.

Kempas seemed to be regretting his candidness already. He squirmed in his chair for a moment.

"A couple of Bolivian gangsters operating out of Gothenburg were here in Finland. They're considered the cartel's reps for Scandinavia."

"What were they doing here? You must have tailed them, right?"

"The second time. The first time, we got the tip too late … They met up with some other Bolivians and a certain crooked lawyer by the name of Ari Saramaa."

Saramaa was among the country's most recognized business attorneys, one who had made his name as an expert on tax shelters. White collar criminals eager to shelter their ill-gotten nest eggs, and in fear of getting caught, lined up outside of Saramaa's office door. Saramaa would build a buffer between the crook and his assets such that connecting the two would demand no end of time and effort.

"Do you know why they met with Saramaa?"

"We don't exactly have a mike in his office, though we ought to. And a camera in his shitter, too. That sort of scum doesn't deserve privacy. Bastard costs us the upkeep of more than a few prisons."

"You don't have a hunch?" said Huusko.

"No, but it smells fishy, that's for sure."

The dog stood suddenly and began to growl as the sound of crisp footsteps approached from the hallway. Everyone there recognized the gait. Without bothering to knock, Deputy Chief Hakala glided into the room.

"Nice to see my staff working so diligently." Then his eyes stopped on the dog, which was staring at him intently.

"What's with the dog?"

"He's an eyewitness," said Huusko.

"From Liljeblad's apartment?"

Jansson nodded.

"What's it doing here? This isn't a dog shelter."

"It's not like we could just leave him at the house. Just imagine what the animal rights people would say. How would that look for us if it made the tabloids?"

Hakala thought for a moment.

"Not good," he said. "So what are you gonna do with it?"

"He's staying with me till we find him a new owner."

"Good. Well, not sure if it's good or not, but it'll do for now. Any new developments?"

"The male victim has been identified. He's a native Bolivian who's been working at a Helsinki produce warehouse for the past few years."

"Was it a murder and overdose or a double murder?"

"Not sure yet. There's some other possibilities."

"What do you mean?"

"Well, the investigation is barely underway."

Hakala couldn't think of any more questions.

"Well, carry on, then. Let me know what you find out."

He turned on his heels and disappeared into the hallway. The dog settled down at once and lay back down on the floor.

"Good dog... Atta boy," said Huusko. "You let us know whenever Hakala comes around."

"So who exactly was investigating these tax-free thefts?" Jansson asked Kempas.

"Inspector Keijo Alanko from Customs, and Pekka Kallio from Finnair's assets protection."

Jansson wrote down the names.

The sound of hurried footsteps came from the hallway, and Lehto breezed in with two video cassettes in his hand.

"Sorry I'm so late, but it was worth it. Okay if I show these?"

"Go ahead," said Jansson.

Lehto slid a cassette into the VCR and flicked the TV on. The picture showed a dim parking garage with a few cars sprinkled here and there. One of the cars furthest from the camera began to pull out. Lehto pointed to the time stamp at the bottom of the screen.

"Liljeblad left work at exactly 7:08 P.M."

The car drove out of view, and Lehto swapped the cassette out for the other.

"I went through all of the ramp's cameras, but the car only showed up in this one. Watch carefully now. This is from the camera at the exit of the parking ramp."

This time the car was closer to the camera, and the image was quite clear.

"Take a look at the time," said Lehto as he paused the video. The time stamp showed 7:14 P.M.

"The trip from Liljeblad's parking spot to the exit is about thirty seconds. Where was she for the other five minutes?"

"Do you know?" asked Jansson.

Lehto seemed pleased to have the room's attention. Only rarely did he get the chance to display his sharp intellect to the higher-ups.

He hit play again and stepped to the side of the television.

"The car's gonna go past the camera soon."

Lehto tapped the screen with his finger.

"Did you see it?"

"Rewind," said Jansson.

Lehto rewound the tape a bit and pressed play.

This time Jansson saw it. The camera had captured the car from the rear on the driver' side. On the opposite side of the car from the camera was a streetlight that shone through the windows of the car. The light revealed a crisp silhouette of someone sitting in the passenger seat.

"Liljeblad wasn't alone," said Lehto before anyone else could take credit for noticing. "Which explains the missing five minutes. She was waiting in the ramp for her passenger."

"Do you know who it was?" asked Kempas.

"No. I have Finnair's work schedule, so I can find out when and by what means everyone left work. On the other hand, it could be someone other than a co-worker. Anyone can just walk in there."

"The tape doesn't necessarily have anything to do with the murders," said Kempas. "She could've just been dropping a colleague off on the way home."

"Whatever the case, this is good. Well done," said Jansson.

"Columbo himself would've probably been jealous," said Huusko.

"But not you?" said Lehto.

"I'm entirely immune to human shortcomings."

Jansson jotted something down in his notepad.

"Let's figure out our assignments for tomorrow. First thing in the morning, Lehto will find out how Liljeblad's co-workers got home. We need to find out who her passenger was. Malmberg will be in contact with the DMV to look for all dark-colored Land Rover Freelanders, if we don't receive any reports on it beforehand. All patrol officers will be asked to keep an eye out for the vehicle on their regular patrols. Huusko and Sanna, I want you two in my office first thing in the morning."

"What about the dog?" said Huusko. "What's his job?"

"He'll keep the bosses at bay."

* * *

Jansson didn't make it home until around ten in the evening. The dog was curled up in the passenger seat the whole way home, as if familiar with the routine. When Jansson opened the door, the dog bounded into the yard and took in the surroundings. Then he sniffed his way over to the base of a cherry tree that stood near the garage.

"Will this do?"

Jansson shuffled about beneath the apple trees and stopped to take in the night air. The aromas were juiciest at this time of year, with an abundance of apples in the trees, and just as many on the ground. Once the kids had left home, there had been little use for all the fruit, and most wound up joining the zucchini vines on the compost pile. In years past, they had made jam, cider, and purees to be put into the children's backpacks and shared with relatives. Winter varieties had been wrapped in paper and stored in the cellar until Christmas. The zucchinis had been used to make a type of relish. Unopened jars of it up to ten years old were still lined up in the cellar. What used to be bright yellow zucchini drowned in vinegar had faded over the years to a pallid gray.

A hedgehog snuffled out from beneath the gooseberry bushes and waddled off toward the hawthorn hedge, which prompted a growl from the dog, but it stayed at Jansson's side. The local fauna also included a couple of brown hares that had once eaten an apple tree sapling that Jansson had planted.

"Good dog. Leave the little ones alone and chase the big ones away."

The dog cocked its head and stared at Jansson.

"Right here under the apple tree is where I usually relax in my hammock. Listen to that poplar rustling in the wind…nice, isn't it? How 'bout we go say hi to my wife? She's a sweetheart…even if she tries to seem a little gruff. You make a good impression, okay? Jansson dug out his keys, opened the door, and stepped into the foyer, where an old chaise lounge, coat rack, and a corner cabinet were tastefully arranged. Roll-up floral shades hung in the windows. The dog scented the air first, then the women's shoes under the coat rack.

When the children were small, the entry had been a perpetual scene of disaster. Heaps of rubber boots, ski boots, shoes, and skates littered the floor, and mittens, stockings, hats, and scarves knit by two grandmothers jockeying for position burst from the cabinet doors. Now it all seemed so sterile.

Jansson stepped inside and let the dog into the kitchen.

"Go on in."

His wife was watching television in the living room.

"Who are you talking to?" she called out.

"We have a guest."

"Who?"

She came into the kitchen and glanced around before noticing the dog.

"Where'd you get the dog?"

"He's an orphan. Mommy was murdered."

"Why'd you bring him here?"

"There was no place else. She was single."

Jansson's wife gave the dog a once over.

"What's his name?"

"We don't know."

"Has he eaten?"

Jansson loved his wife's practical sensibility. Everyone else had treated the dog like a stuffed toy.

"Yes."

She took a deep plastic bowl out of the kitchen cabinet and filled it with water.

"Thirsty?"

She set the bowl down in front of the dog, and the dog looked inquiringly at Jansson.

"Go ahead, have a drink."

The dog lapped up a few slurps out of what seemed to be courtesy.

"Good-looking dog," Jansson's wife conceded. "What breed is he?"

"Don't know. Probably some kind of terrier."

"Looks almost like a puppy. Was his owner the one in the news?"

"Yep."

"You don't think her relatives would look after him?"

"Doesn't look that way."

She looked at him knowingly.

"Would you mind telling me what your plan is here?"

"What do you mean?"

"You know what I mean."

"Well...I can't just abandon him... And besides, he trusts me."

She laughed. "Taking care of a dog is a big responsibility."

"I know."

"Do what you like... You're almost all grown up, after all."

Jansson looked at the dog and bent down to scratch behind its ears.

"What would you think about living in an old house like this, with an old, lazy, almost-grown-up like me?"

The dog didn't seem to object.

5.

In the early hours of the morning it began to rain.

First a light patter on the roof, then a steady beat as it began to pick up.

Raid was sleeping in the main room downstairs. He awoke, sat up, pulled the shades aside, and looked out into the yard. He had turned off the exterior lights, and it was dark outside; but even so, he could see the branches of the apple tree swaying in the wind outside the window. The metal frame of the oven, or perhaps the latch, popped from the heat. Raid had thrown in an armload of wood just before retiring for the night, and the old house had squeaked and creaked as the air warmed and the timbers dried. He looked at the phosphor hands of the alarm clock on the window sill: twenty minutes past three. He could almost hear the second hand tick.

Raid had awoken to a strange dream.

He had been sitting in a sun-bathed meadow, at the edge of which stood a small boy wearing a blue blazer. The boy was so distant that Raid couldn't see his eyes, but knew that the boy was looking at him. Then it had begun to rain, and the boy walked toward him. The sky had darkened with each approaching step. By the time the boy was standing in front of him, the sky was dark purple, and lightning had begun to streak across the sky. The boy just stood there and looked at him silently, with somber eyes. There was blood on his face.

Raid had recognized the boy in the dream. It was the boy whose father he had shot in Stockholm the previous spring. While sitting in the back seat of a car, surrounded by tinted glass, he had watched his own father die. Then he had burst from the car and thrown himself upon his father's body.

In the dream, Raid had felt a powerful desire to explain. To tell the boy that his father had been a criminal, and had arranged the killings of many of his own countrymen. But he was unable to speak, and the boy just stared at him with those dark, clear eyes.

Then Raid had awoken. He had lain there for a moment, tried to remember the sequence of the dream, and how he had felt, but could only recall a vague sense of shame. Not because he had killed Zetov, but because he had done it in front of the boy.

Though Raid had killed many, and assaulted many more, the incidents never visited his dreams. With the exception of his first. Then, he had been just seventeen, and still living in Gothenburg. Three Yugoslavian gangsters had attacked him, and he had stabbed one of them to death. Sometime later he had seen the thug's mother in the streets, dressed in black, and that night, he had a nightmare in which the mother condemned him for the murder of her only son.

Killing Zetov hadn't bothered him in the slightest. Zetov had been the head of the Russian mafia in Sweden. At his bidding, at least half a dozen Russians living in Sweden had been killed. Zetov treated his countrymen just as the grand dukes of old treated their serfs. He determined the course of their lives, and their deaths. If Zetov demanded it, a Russian grandmother would have no choice but to pack a suitcase full of amphetamines and smuggle it to Finland or Sweden. And if she didn't, things would go badly for her grandchildren and great-grandchildren.

Over time, Zetov had become so pompous that he wanted all others to call him czar.

Finally, his serfs had had enough, and they pulled together a collection for Raid's services. Zetov's death had been cause for celebration in more than a few Russian immigrant families.

Zetov had considered himself indispensable. But though his absence created a brief vacuum, his businesses were quickly taken over. The Yugoslavs got a slice, the Turks another, and the third went to the Russians.

Everyone had supposed the Yugoslavs to be the killers, since Zetov had been fighting turf battles with them for years over tobacco-smuggling. Toward the end of summer, Raid had received a tip that the heat was now on him. His bag was always packed, and he had taken it and left for Finland. He felt certain that the whole thing would blow over in a few months, as the Russians had enough on their hands with the Yugoslavs and the Turks. Besides, even Zetov's own had hated him.

Raid unzipped his sleeping bag and got up. He groped through the darkness to the coat rack, stepped into a pair of cut-off rubber boots, swung his jacket over his shoulders, and went outside. He sat down on the stone steps, the cold seeping through his clothing. The porch roof partially sheltered him from the rain, but the wind still drove a few stray drops into his face.

The last time he had been here was exactly one year ago, with Nygren. Only once they had reached Lapland had he realized the true reason that Nygren, suffering from cancer, had wanted him along. Not as a chauffeur, nor a bodyguard, nor a mercy killer. He was there because Nygren felt responsible for Raid's having taken the wide gate in life. Nygren was not just his uncle, but also his godfather, whose boldness and sophistication Raid had admired more than anything else as a boy. Nygren had known it, and in Lapland he had asked Raid to forgive him for not having lived up to the duties of a godfather.

In addition to the old Mercedes, Raid had also inherited Nygren's cabin. Perhaps Nygren had wanted to provide him with a refuge, a place to renew his strength and reflect on his life. Or perhaps Nygren thought that the place would remind Raid of how it would all end for everyone. That he, too, would have to settle his affairs in the end. If not with others, then at least with himself.

And now he was in almost the exact same position as Nygren had been with him. The shopkeeper's boy had stumbled into his life, and Raid had plucked him from the hands of his would-be killers. He had seen the boy's nervous adulation, though the boy had tried hard to conceal it.

Were it not for the Bolivians, he'd have no quandary. Raid would have returned to Sweden, and the boy would have stayed here to help his father with the store. Pricing products, organizing shelves, and other myriad duties of retail life would have kept the boy's mind off crime. In time, the boy would have taken over as owner, provided the shop hadn't been replaced by a big box store by that time.

But now, the situation was different—the thugs would be back, that was certain. With the stakes of the game as high as they were, they wouldn't leave without a second round. The gunshot wounds would set them back maybe a day or two. And when they returned, the boy would be a lamb for the slaughter.

Raid also knew that he himself would not escape unscathed, even if he'd left Finland the same day. He had manhandled them enough that they would take their vengeance in one way or another, sooner or later.

Even so, something about his predicament humored him: he had left Sweden to escape the Russians, and once in Finland, had run headlong into the South Americans.

If he were to stay, he would have few choices. He could kill the whole lot of them. He could have done that back at the barn, but he didn't want that many bodies on his own stomping grounds.

The second option was much more tempting. Somebody else could do the dirty work on his behalf, and he knew who could do it best. He could get in touch with Lieutenant Jansson, someone he always seemed to cross paths with in Finland.

Raid was certain that Jansson would be an easy sell. All the detective would need would be a little background information. With a few names, times, and places, nothing could hold Jansson back.

Raid rose and stepped into the rain for a moment to enjoy its soft touch. Then he went back inside, kicked off his boots, and crawled back into his warm sleeping bag.

6.

Huusko was watching her sleep. The moon was full, and its light fell into the room through the gaps in the shades. The woman had curled up on her left side, her right hand dangling over the edge of the bed. One leg, from her calf down, lay bare on the bed.

Huusko bent down and kissed her lightly on the cheek. She stirred and pursed her lips. Huusko gazed at her face with an enchanted look. She rolled onto her back and the sheets slipped aside, revealing one of her breasts. Huusko wanted to reach out and touch it, but he quashed the impulse.

He slid into bed, lay on his back, and quietly pulled up the covers. It was past one o'clock, and he was tired, but he wanted to enjoy his good spirits for a few more moments.

It had been many years since he had been this happy and satisfied with life. Beside him lay a woman he was in no hurry to get rid of. How many other mornings had he awoken in a strange bed, glanced at the strange face beside him, pulled on his clothes, and left like a thief, without a single warm feeling from the previous night.

Now he wanted to milk the shared hours of the morning as long as he could. He felt more strongly than ever that he had found a woman he wanted to hold onto.

Before drifting off, he resolved to not make any of the many mistakes that had undermined his previous relationships. He would become the perfect man for this naked, moonlit woman, whose shoulders teemed with tiny freckles.

Huusko arrived at work just before eight to find Susisaari already in Jansson's office. Jansson had a steaming mug of herbal tea in front of him, something his wife had bought from an organic market. It was supposed to improve his digestion.

"I think I know what breed Liljeblad's dog is," said Susisaari. "I was looking at some dog sites on the net last night and found an identical looking dog. It's a West Highland white terrier, a westie."

"A westie," Jansson repeated. "You hear that, Huusko? Sanna figured out what kind of dog it is. A westie."

"Sounds like a whisky brand. Might as well be a Scotch retriever. What else is new?"

"Not much. Sanna's still interviewing relatives and coworkers with Lehto and Malmberg. You can concentrate on the foreigners that were seen in front of the apartment. Check all the hotels to see if they've had any Hispanic customers. You could ask around the victim's workplace, too. It'd be a great help if we could figure out which one was the victim, and which one the unlucky bystander."

"My guess is she was the victim. I can say from experience that I know the type. Even dated a few, although lucky for me I got out in time. Real hostile…the type that drives a man crazy till he resorts to the only way he knows to shut her up, a knife or a pistol."

"An in-depth analysis from our top expert on women," Susisaari snorted.

"Every romance for that sort of woman is just another opportunity to try to squeeze something other than blood, sweat, and tears from a guy. What possible use would she have for a Bolivian warehouse worker?"

"Maybe he was well-endowed," Susisaari said.

"You can be well-endowed in other ways, too."

"Maybe she was getting cheap cocaine from him," she said.

"Could be a kind of symbiosis where they feed off each other," said Jansson. "She smuggles in coke and he finds sellers in the source country and buyers here. I imagine it'd be pretty easy for a stewardess to bring drugs into the country."

"Narcotics could track down her flight history from…say…six months back," said Susisaari.

"What about the stolen goods she had in her wardrobe?" said Huusko.

"What was the name of the customs guy Kempas mentioned?" said Jansson.

Susisaari riffled through her notes. "Alanko."

"Have a chat with him, too."

Malmberg strode into the room. "Looks like finding that SUV isn't gonna be as easy as we thought. We got several dozen Land Rover Freelanders in the country, almost all of them dark colored, and many of those dark green. The DMV promised to fax us a list of all the vehicles and their owners.

"Send it to Huusko as soon as you get it," said Jansson. "Now let's saddle up and ride. Let me know right away if something turns up."

* * *

Huusko checked a car out of the station garage and headed for the produce warehouse in east Helsinki.

He left his car in the customer parking lot and found the main entrance. A female guard was seated in a glass booth next to the door, and Huusko told her his business.

"Personnel issues usually go through the finance director, but the CEO has requested that any inquiries on this issue go through him."

"That works too."

The woman called the CEO's secretary and exchanged a few words with her.

"Looks like the management team is in an important meeting just now, but they'll be free in about a half hour. Can you come back later?"

"I'll wait."

"You can wait in the cafeteria just inside. I'll let you in."

The woman opened the door and showed him the way to the cafeteria.

"I'll come and get you once the meeting is over."

Huusko bought some coffee and a glazed donut, and brought them to a window table. Through the window, he could see the loading docks where the semis were being unloaded.

He bit into his donut and glanced around. On one wall was a glass display case with a few trophies from corporate sports leagues, a dish and a pennant. Next to the case was a large black-and-white photo of a gray-whiskered man, which Huusko supposed to be the founder of the company.

Only a few customers were in the coffee shop. A couple of tables away sat a dark-haired man reading the newspaper with his back to Huusko. The man glanced out the window, then turned to look back. Huusko got up, walked over to the man and took out Hernando's picture.

"I'm from the Helsinki police. Do you recognize this man?"

"Yes... I just heard today what happened."

"Are you two from the same country?"

"No, he's Bolivian. I'm from Chile."

Huusko sat down, and the man moved over a bit.

"Do you have any idea why he was killed?"

The man seemed to withdraw somewhat.

"Did it have anything to do with drugs?"

"Drugs are never a good thing."

"I agree. Was José mixed up in drugs?"

"He used them sometimes. I used to play badminton with him, and we'd go partying sometimes. I know he was a user."

"Who did he get them from?"

"That I don't know. I have a wife and three children. I don't want to know anything about drugs...wouldn't wanna get mixed up in that sort of thing. I have a good job here, a nice apartment, and a good family. I don't want to mess that up. I am grateful to Finland for what it has done for me."

"But you think he was killed because of drugs?"

The man stared sharply at his coffee cup.

"I didn't say that... It's possible."

"Did he sell drugs?"

"Maybe... I think so."

"Did you know his girlfriend?"

"The one that was killed?"

"Yeah."

"No."

"But you knew some other one?"

The man paused again.

"José has a child, you know. He used to live with his child's mother, but he left them after he met this other woman."

"Who is his child's mother?"

"Eila... Eila Tuuri. They lived in Roihuvuori, where she is a kindergarten teacher. A good woman—José was stupid to leave her."

"Did he tell you anything about his new girlfriend?"

"Just that she was this hot blonde…and a flight attendant."

"Where did they meet?"

"I don't know… I never even saw her. Sometimes I thought he made the whole thing up."

"Do you know any of his other friends?"

The man shook his head.

"Are there any other Bolivians working here?"

"No."

"Do you know if he knew any other Bolivians in Finland?"

"No."

"You must have José's cellphone number."

The man dug his phone out of his pocket and scrolled through the directory till he found it. Huusko jotted it down.

The guard appeared at the door of the coffee shop and gestured to Huusko, who gulped down his coffee and got up.

"If you think of anything, give me a call."

Huusko gave the man his card. *If you think of anything, give me a call.* A good closing line, and one that had often yielded results. Business cards were free. Although on one occasion a con man had pulled out one of Huusko's cards in a restaurant, pretending to be the police. Later, he complained that the card hadn't had the desired effect on the ladies.

"I forgot to ask your name?"

"Jesús Alvaro."

Huusko wiped the bits of sugar and jelly off his mouth and set off to meet the CEO.

* * *

Kirstilä, the produce company CEO, bore a family resemblance to the man on the wall of the coffee shop, though he was thinner, and much younger. His careful, pale-blue eyes gazed at Huusko from behind a pair of thin, frameless glasses.

"Are you here because of Hernando or the burglary?"

"Hernando. We need some information about him. We're trying to find a motive for the murder."

"I doubt that I'll be much help. He was with us for just over a year. A good worker. That's about all I can say."

"What did he do here?"

"Unpacked crates, packed them, loaded trucks, that sort of thing."

"Why did he come *here* for a job?"

"I don't know. Perhaps someone told him that we were looking. We first hired him as a temp, and since he was a hard worker, and conscientious, we held onto him."

"Did he do anything unusual here?"

"I'm not sure what that would be. He did his job and that sufficed."

"Do you have any guesses as to why he was murdered?"

"Certainly not."

"Did he ever miss work?"

"Just the usual, the occasional flu, nothing more... Although a week ago he did miss work and never gave a reason for it. He claimed that he was on vacation, and had forgotten to notify us."

"Do you have a third shift here?"

"When necessary."

The man looked at the clock, and Huusko got up and thanked him.

"Does that help you?" asked Kirstilä.

76

"A little."

"Could you do me a favor and ask your worthy colleagues to return our calls? We'll need a police report so we can make a claim to the insurance company."

"I'll try to remember."

* * *

Huusko had almost reached his car when Jesús Alvaro stopped him, and steered him out of sight behind a nearby van.

"I did see José meet two other men one time. They looked South American and spoke Spanish."

"When, and where?"

"Around the corner. A little over a week ago... I was at the ATM on my lunch break and saw him go into a car with them. The guys looked pretty shady to me. Later, I asked José about it, but he wouldn't say anything. Seemed to me he was afraid of something."

"Describe the men."

"Fancy clothes, one of them had a mustache... I remember the car...an SUV, dark green, brand new."

"Did you get the plates?"

"No, I only saw the car from the side."

As Alvaro hurried off, Huusko muttered to himself, "Thank you, Jesus."

* * *

José Hernando's former live-in girlfriend was at work at an east Helsinki kindergarten. The playground was filled with monkey bars, swings, and other things to keep the kids occupied. Half a dozen kids were playing in the sandbox, around which stood three women.

Huusko stopped beside a boy who was kneeling on the ground. His cheeks were flushed and he was dressed in blue overalls and a bomber hat. He was beating a plastic bucket with a tiny shovel.

"Patty-cake, patty-cake, baker's man…"

"Do you know which of your teachers is Eila Tuuri?"

The boy gaped silently at Huusko while he licked at the string of snot hanging down to his chin.

"I hope that was tasty."

Huusko went over to the sandbox, where the women were standing.

"Eila Tuuri?"

The group of women assessed Huusko carefully.

"That's me," said a thin, wary-looking woman with a two-year-old girl in her arms.

"Could I have a few words with you privately?"

The woman set the girl down in the sand and followed Huusko.

Huusko didn't stop till he reached the fence, then he turned and introduced himself.

"I suppose you know why I'm here?"

"José? I read about it in the paper and guessed it was him."

"Why didn't you contact us? We were asking for information."

The woman pursed her lips and her face hardened.

"When he left Heidi and I, and went off with that whore, I decided then and there that I was done with him."

"Who do you mean by 'whore?'"

"You know."

"Did he move in with this woman?"

"He moved into his friend's vacant apartment in Roihuvuori, a few hundred yards away from us, but even that seemed to be too far for him. Twice he didn't even

78

bother to pick up Heidi on his weekend."

"When did he move?"

"About six months ago."

"Do you know his new address?"

The woman didn't remember the building number, but she gave such precise directions that Huusko felt sure he could find it easily.

"Have you seen him since?"

"He's come to visit Heidi, but otherwise no. I didn't care to hear about his new life."

"Do you have any idea why he might have been killed?"

"It's that whore… Those kinds of coke-snorting psychos are dangerous. She knew just about every drug dealer in town. Whoever did it, they were after her; José just happened to be there."

"You don't think José could have gotten mixed up in something?"

"Maybe…but only after he met her. I knew she'd be trouble, but he made his own decision."

"Have you ever met her?"

"No, and you couldn't pay me enough…"

"How do you know about her, then?"

"I've just heard things here and there."

The woman looked suddenly guilty, and Huusko decided to wade in a little further.

"Did you hire a private investigator to follow him?"

Huusko saw immediately that he was on target.

"José got caught in a lie, but I wanted to be a hundred percent sure."

"What did the PI find out?"

"That they had a relationship. That was enough for me."

"Did you receive a report? Or any pictures?"

"I burned them."

79

"Do you remember what they consisted of?"

"Nothing having to do with any murder, but they didn't leave any room for doubt as far as their relationship went. You can ask the private investigator if you're interested."

"Do you remember his name?"

The woman told him.

"Thank you."

Eila Tuuri turned hurriedly away, but Huusko caught a glimpse of a tear welling up in her eyes. She didn't return to the sandbox, but headed off toward the building instead.

* * *

It seemed to Huusko that he was running the steeplechase. He had cleared the first few hurdles, then came the water jump, and then off to the home stretch. Private investigator Aho was the water jump, and the water was plenty deep and muddy.

Aho was a former cop, someone Huusko knew well. The man had worked at the vice squad toward the end of the seventies when they began getting tips that he had taken bribes from Helsinki prostitutes to turn a blind eye to their trade. And not just money, either. A fuck here, a fuck there. It was all part of his benefits package.

He finally got caught in the act, and on the clock, on top of a whore in a seedy Kallio flat, his pants around his ankles and his gun tucked in a shoulder holster. He tried to claim he was only pumping her to get intel on her pimp.

The story made the rounds at the station, and even at the ministry, but he was still hanging on somehow. A rumor went around that he knew of several police chiefs who had frequented the same prostitutes he had. But the story leaked to the tabloids, and in the end Aho was reluctantly let go. Huusko had joined the department just in time to meet him, but he doubted the man would remember him.

After leaving the police, Aho started a security company that attracted a clientele connected to the department. Some suspected that this was the way he was being paid to keep mum.

But Aho was no businessman. With the aid of his salacious lifestyle, he drove the business into bankruptcy. Half a dozen guarantors, among them a couple of police officers, had to shoulder the hundred grand in debt.

The most hot-blooded guarantors went after him for the money, but he took exile in Sweden for a few years. Upon his return, he set up shop as a private investigator, but his reputation dogged him from the outset.

So Aho was a rat that needed proper handling, lest he seal his lips out of sheer obstinacy.

Aho had suggested that they meet at the Ursula coffee shop. Huusko arrived at noon. The air was chilly, and Aho was sitting at a sidewalk table with a broad-brimmed hat and a thick hunting jacket on. The outdoorsy getup was a sham, as was everything else about the man. Huusko sat down opposite him, and Aho offered his hand from across the table.

"I believe we've met before?"

"Yep. I joined the department right around the time you left."

"Is Tuomela still with homicide?"

"Yes, but he's on sick leave. Heart trouble."

"Like the rest of us…at this age."

Huusko looked at Aho's watery eyes, certain that his hat concealed a saucer-sized bald spot. To some, a bald spot could be a sensitive topic, and Aho was doubtless no exception.

"I mentioned on the phone that your customer advised me to get in touch with you because you have some information on a certain José Hernando."

"Right, the Bolivian guy. What's he done?"

"Died under mysterious circumstances."

"Where? In plain Finnish, please."

"At his girlfriend's."

"The stewardess's?"

"Right."

"So in plain Finnish, he had a heart attack while fucking," Aho cackled.

"Not nearly so romantic. He got intimate with a kitchen knife."

"Oh, it was that guy. Read about it in the tabloids. So things didn't go so well for old José, then. I guess life is full of surprises, death being the biggest."

Huusko made a point of committing these astute words to memory.

"What'd you find out from trailing him?"

Aho held up his hand as if to stop him.

"Easy, now. Information is my living. I sell it, trade it, or steal it. If I give you a little, you give me a little more. Understand?"

"So, in plain Finnish, you're asking for a bribe?"

"No. In plain Finnish, I'm merely suggesting a trade, perhaps a little display of leniency."

"If it's just about leniency, I could maybe forget your cellphone number and plate number. I know a few rough characters who're still looking for you. And they're still pretty hot under the collar."

With a peevish look on his face, Aho dug a photograph from the inside pocket of his coat and slid it across the table to Huusko. Hernando was easy to recognize. He was sitting around a restaurant table with two Hispanic men, looking like a servile disciple at the hands of his two stern masters.

"Where was this taken?"

"At the Scandic Marski Hotel. I followed our José for almost a week. I figured he had a date with the lady before these two hombres piled in. They looked suspicious enough that I snapped a picture. I had a nice parking spot in front of the hotel."

"When was this?"

"Look at the time stamp."

Huusko took a look. The photograph was taken on May 13, at 6:22 P.M.

"You got anything else?"

"Nothing of any interest. Your typical hydraulic action—in and out, in and out, ad nauseum. There wasn't much our Bolivian friend could say. Once I had enough evidence there was no point in following him anymore."

"So what makes you think I should be interested in these guys?"

"Just an old cop's hunch. Those guys aren't from the Rotary Club. They sat at the table for nearly an hour, and it seemed like José was getting hauled over the coals. He was scared, anyhow. Afterwards, they got in the elevator. I waited for over an hour, but when they didn't come back, I took off. That tells me they were probably staying at the hotel. You got the hotel and the date, so that should get you somewhere."

Huusko nodded. He could trust that an old cop's hunch wasn't completely off the mark. Then he got up and slipped the photos into his pocket.

"Sure you didn't forget anything?" said Huusko, staring Aho in the eyes.

"I'm sure. You're not gonna tell those thugs anything about me, are you?" he said nervously.

"I'm not afraid of Vallenius, but that Somero's crazy. Been to therapy, even."

"In other words, a complete psychopath," said Huusko, and he took his leave, satisfied to have ended on that note.

* * *

"Nina was always like that. Her whole life, it was always me first. Everything of hers had to be nicer, better, and more special. Toys, clothes, shoes, boyfriends. Ever since she was a little girl, she was the princess. Our father died when she was six, and Mom probably wanted to make up for it… She's four years older than me."

Nina Liljeblad's younger sister, Erika, at least in appearance, was the polar opposite of her sister. She was on the shorter side, a stocky-looking brunette. Her hair was short, and her clothes stylish, but a bit dull. A thin silver bracelet clung to her wrist, and black-jeweled earrings hung from her ears.

Susisaari got the impression that the younger Liljeblad was a woman who did not wish to be seen too much, but who nevertheless had a distinct character. Her clothes and jewelry were clearly high quality, perhaps from a high-end boutique. And in no sense was she *un*attractive. With a little effort, she could have had plenty of company at any bar.

"It sounds cruel, but we were about as distant as two siblings can be. When I was younger, I sometimes felt like I was a changeling, or fathered by somebody else.

Susisaari was sitting in Erika's office at the University of Helsinki Sociology Department, where she worked as a researcher.

"How often did you see each other?"

"Whenever we had to. Which was whenever Mom came to Finland, and we had to make arrangements for her. Usually we wound up fighting over some petty detail."

"When did you last meet?"

"Three weeks ago. Mom went back to Florida at the beginning of September, and we brought her to the airport. Our mother is not in good health."

"Did your mother stay with either of you?"

"No. She owns an apartment that we rent out for the winter. She didn't get along all that well with Nina, either, though you'd think the fights would've ended at puberty. I'm usually the one to visit her and take care of her things if needed. Nina's always been more of a globetrotter... Of course, that comes with her work."

"You must have known something about your sister's life. Friends and men, for example."

"Nina's had a lot of boyfriends ever since high school. I guess it's obvious she was the most beautiful girl in the school. For her junior year, she was an exchange student in America. You'd have thought she'd become more mature, but it just made her worse. Her host family was very wealthy, and I guess the superficiality rubbed off. Normal life became nothing to her. We belonged to the dullest of the dull, the upper middle class. Nina got a job at Finnair and became a flight attendant. On a flight, she met a rich man, a businessman twenty years her senior, and they got married. The marriage lasted about a year and a half. Nina got a nice settlement, and she used it to buy a house in Oulunkylä. After the divorce, Nina lived the wild life for many years. We met only rarely."

"Did you know about her drug use?"

"I heard about it from Mom when she went to Nina's place once without calling ahead. She had keys to the apartment so she could water the flowers, and let the dog out when Nina was away. Anyhow, she found her completely wasted... Did she die of an overdose?"

"The autopsy hasn't been completed yet."

The woman studied Susisaari.

"What else could it have been?"

"Don't know, we're still investigating. Did she have any significant relationships after the divorce?"

"She went out with some pilot for almost a year, but apparently that was just a fling, or just for show. In that world, a pilot is supposed to be the cream of the crop."

"What about José Hernando?"

"She told me about him in passing the last time we met...that she had some hot Latino who'd left his family for her. I never met him and she never said anything more... I don't think it was anything more than that, though. Two weeks ago, I went to dinner with a couple of work friends at an Italian restaurant. Nina was there with some guy... He looked well over fifty, and certainly was no hot Latino. But there was no mistaking their relationship."

"Do you know who this man was?"

"No. But he wasn't Nina's type. And if she *was* dating him, he must have been somebody important. Maybe an executive at the airline."

"Do you remember the exact day?"

She took a glance at her desktop calendar.

"It's right here. Thursday, September second, Around sevenish."

"What restaurant?"

She told him.

"Do you remember which table it was?"

She searched her memory for a moment.

"Just as you get inside it's the first left, close to the corner."

"Did Nina see you?"

"No, she was sitting with her back toward me. I made up some excuse and we left. I wouldn't have stayed if you had paid me... That's the last time I saw her alive..."

Seemingly out of nowhere, a tear ran down her cheek, and she quickly wiped it away.

"That doesn't mean I wouldn't want to find the people responsible for her death... We had fun sometimes, when we were kids. She wasn't always such a pain in the ass. I'm supposed to be an expert, but I still don't understand what went wrong in her upbringing... She had few if any women friends, and what few she had were always outnumbered by her enemies. She was the type that doesn't even bother to act friendly unless somebody is useful to her."

"Did she ever mention being afraid of anybody?"

"Not to me. People like her only disclose things that make others jealous... Not that I want to portray her as a monster, but I couldn't describe her as a kind person. Unless she wanted to be, and then she was very kind. She could also be pretty violent. Sometimes she'd fly into these rages... Which is apparently what happened here. She went off on the guy about something..."

"So you think she killed Hernando?"

"Who else? I know she's been violent before. I heard it from a mutual friend."

"Are you referring to the incident at the Kulosaari Casino?"

"You know about it, then... Yes."

Susisaari stood up.

"You mentioned her dog... The dog is in police custody now. Would you like to adopt it?"

The woman laughed. "Is it under arrest? No, I'm allergic to dogs. That's one reason I never went to her place."

"Any other relatives who might?"

"Just Mom, and she's a cat-lover."

"Would you happen to know the dog's name?"

Erika shook her head.

"Sorry. She had a black poodle before, but it died about six months ago. Someone gave her a new one a couple of months ago, a little terrier, but I never heard its name. Mom would certainly know."

* * *

Back on the street, Susisaari's cell phone rang. It was Huusko.

"I've been running around town like a panic-stricken moose, but I think I'm getting somewhere. I'm off to the Scandic Marski Hotel next to ask about a couple of Hispanic-looking men that stayed there. They met with Hernando last spring. What about you?"

Susisaari told him about her meeting with Liljeblad's sister.

"Is it alright if you go ahead to Hernando's apartment on Vuorenpeikon Street and call the maintenance guy to open the door? I'll come straight there. I won't be long here," said Huusko.

"Come as quickly as you can."

"I always do."

* * *

The phone number for the property management company was on the bulletin board in the downstairs entryway, and Susisaari dialed it. She had expected the maintenance man to be somewhere on the other side of town, but he happened to be raking leaves in the neighboring yard.

"I'll be a couple minutes," he promised, and kept it. In two minutes, a forty-something man in blue overalls and a ball cap came cutting across the yard.

"Something wrong?" he asked.

"Just a few things to check out."

"I should probably ask to see your badge."

Susisaari showed him her badge.

"But where's your silver star?"

"At home next to my cowboy boots."

The apartment was on the third floor. The maintenance man sifted through a giant ring of keys attached to his belt, and Susisaari noticed that each one had a number.

"Do you know the owner of the apartment?" she asked.

The man looked at the name plate on the door.

"Rodriguez. Some foreigner. Doesn't ring a bell. I do remember seeing a darker fella around here every now and again. But who knows if he's the same guy."

"Have there been any complaints about disturbances or anything of that sort?"

"You'd have to ask the building manager. He deals with complaints. Or the association president."

He found the right key and slipped it into the lock. Susisaari watched the man take a whiff of the air as he opened the door.

"Doesn't smell like a body, anyhow. It wouldn't be the first time I've opened a door to find the owner dead on the floor. One time…"

Susisaari interrupted the man's reminiscences.

"I'll need the key."

"This is a master key. I can't just…"

"I'll take good care of it."

Susisaari plucked the key ring from his hand and slipped the key off. Then she thanked him and closed the door behind her.

A few free newspapers and some junk mail lay at the foot of the door. Susisaari stepped over them and went inside.

The apartment was a rather large studio with an alcove, and all the markings of short-term residence. A drab chipboard bunk in the alcove, a no-frills trestle table next to the window, and a rickety shelf with some magazines and a few books. Bags of clothing and moving boxes full of things were still piled against the wall. The television lay on the floor, as did a cheap stereo system. José Hernando's living conditions didn't have the slightest hint of luxury.

The doorbell rang. Susisaari peered out the peephole to see Huusko staring back.

"You just couldn't wait, could you?" he scolded. "How's it look?"

Huusko stepped inside and took a look around.

"Very cozy."

He went to the kitchen and opened the refrigerator.

"Sad."

The contents of the fridge were a half-empty package of some kind of salami, a bottle of ketchup, a couple of eggs, and half a bag of potatoes.

"Even my fridge looks gourmet next to this."

Susisaari was emptying one of the cardboard boxes onto the floor: clothes and shoes. She stuffed the things back into the box and grabbed another: sweatshirts and other winter things. She went through the pockets of all the coats and pants. Empty.

Huusko's cell phone beeped to notify him of an incoming text.

"Jansson's learned how to text. We have a meeting at three."

He glanced at the clock: One-thirty.

"We got time to grab something to eat," said Huusko as he glanced into the closet. A few shirts, a tie, a blazer, and a pair of pants hung from the rail. The jacket and pants pockets were empty. Some socks and underwear lay on the shelf.

Susisaari went into the bathroom, which was even drearier than the rest of the apartment. The ceramic tiles were yellowed and ancient. The grout was crumbling and the shower basin was cracked.

In the medicine cabinet were a couple of old, shriveled toothbrushes, an opened box of condoms, some aftershave, and deodorant. A plastic laundry hamper stood next to the shower.

As Susisaari dumped the contents of the hamper onto the floor, she heard a metallic clatter. She swept aside the stinky socks and underwear, looking for the source of the sound. Something was inside a rolled up T-shirt. She peered inside to find an expensive-looking precision scale, which she brought into the living room.

"Take a look at this."

"An electronic scale. Not hard to guess what that's for."

"Cocaine."

"Probably a good idea to get a dog in here."

* * *

When Huusko returned to the station, a report of all incoming calls to the tip line was waiting on his desk. He dropped half of the stack onto Susisaari's desk, and both began scanning the tips.

Huusko read off the sheet: "*A red Mazda driven by a blond female was observed at a traffic light on Kiitoradan Street in Vantaa. A passenger was also observed. Unknown whether passenger was male or female.* That doesn't help much."

"Then there's this: *If it was that bitch I think it was, then she got what she deserved.*"

"I guess Liljeblad had no shortage of enemies."

Huusko scanned quickly through the next few tips. Completely useless, but the fourth captured his interest.

"Listen to this: *She was a drug user. You should see if it had something to do with drugs. It must not be too hard for a stewardess to smuggle drugs, right?*"

"I don't suppose there's a name there?"

"Nope."

"And another tip on a red Mazda," said Huusko. "*I seen a red Mazda over by the Oulunkylä ball fields right around that time. There was a man and women having sex in the car. I was out walking my dog and saw everything from about fifty feet away. Shameless, you know...in that kind of place. I says to myself, don't anybody have any morals or common decency anymore? Osmo Lepistö.*"

"I guess not," said Huusko. "We'll have to give this huffy Osmo a call. There's even contact information here. Actually appears to be a proper lead."

Susisaari was staring at her paper so intensely that Huusko had to have a look.

"You find something?"

"*Think about how many euros worth of tax-free goods disappear from airplanes and warehouses every year. Millions. She knew all about it, and meant to open her mouth about it. That's why she was killed.*"

"There a name?"

"Just an alias: Pilot."

"What was the name of that customs guy who was investigating the tax-free thefts?" said Huusko.

"Alanko."

"How about we have a chat with Alanko?"

"Right now?"

"You know I'm a man of action."

7.

Väinö Porola was a third-generation shopkeeper. His grandfather, a traveling salesman, had founded the shop in the 1920s after noticing that there was no competition for miles around. The shop had flourished due to the circumstances of the times, and his grandfather had then founded two smaller shops, which also quickly became profitable.

Grandpa had died just after the war, and Väinö's father, Taisto, having just returned from the front lines, wound up taking over the shop. As his first order of business, Taisto had taken the list of all outstanding credit the shop had extended, and visited all those customers to determine their ability to pay. For those who were able, he arranged a payment plan. For those with no money, and none on the horizon, he crossed out their outstanding balances.

Väinö took over the shop in the early seventies after his father suffered a stroke and was moved to a nursing home. As his first order of business, Väinö scrapped the service counters and remodeled the store into a sort of supermarket, even though the aisles were so narrow that two shopping carts were barely able to pass one another.

Times were bad for village shops—small towns were emptying out as people followed work to Sweden. Fortunately, the building was paid for, and Väinö had also inherited some forested land and a portfolio of stocks.

During the seventies, Väinö had also met Riitta.

She had moved to the town from Kuopio to work as a teller at the local bank. They had seen each other regularly at the bank when he had business there. But Väinö wasn't much of a ladies' man, and they got acquainted slowly, in fits and starts.

The relationship grew more serious when Väinö, emboldened by her hints, asked Riitta to the dance.

They were married in 1979, and Matti was born the following year. In hindsight, it was not a good year.

The marriage had already begun to cool, and the fact that Matti was born with a congenital hip defect did not help. He was also often sick and cried a lot. Had he been cute enough, perhaps their relationship could have endured, but Matti was unusually ugly. Riitta blamed Väinö—how could someone as beautiful as her give birth to such a homely child.

She reminded him often of the unerring beauty on her side of the family. Väinö's family, on the other hand, looked like they all had been thrown together on a dreary Monday morning—clearly not examples of God's best work. And the life of a shopkeeper's wife was not nearly as rosy as Riitta had imagined.

She held on for four years, then packed her bags, emptied their bank account, and left.

For over a month, they heard nothing from her. Then she called to tell them that she was in Stockholm. She asked Väinö to begin divorce proceedings and to send the rest of her belongings to the address she provided.

After a year, they received a letter from her, informing them that she was living with a Turkish man, and was expecting. She asked Väinö to send money, as they had purchased a new apartment that required an expensive décor, as well as a washing machine, a vacuum, a color TV, and much more.

Väinö didn't respond to the letter, and after a couple of weeks she called to lambast him, claiming that half of the store, as well as the rest of his assets, were hers. Väinö was a good-natured man, but now he was livid, and dished it back. He asked her what kind of a mother could abandon her sick child, and not even remember him on his birthday.

Riitta hung up on him. From then on they heard nothing from her until five years later when Väinö received a letter from Riitta's sister. He learned that Riitta's Turkish husband had stabbed her to death for dancing too closely with his cousin.

Though the years right after Riitta's departure had been difficult, things had gradually improved. Matti spent his days at the store, doodling in the office or lounging on the stairs, reading cartoons.

City folks had been gradually buying up the vacated properties in the area for summer cottages, and the crumbling local farms had been revitalized. The new summer residents brought new life to the village. Dozens of new cottages were built on the lakeshore. Even Väinö made out well by selling off some of his land as cabin lots.

During the summer, he kept his shop open twenty-four hours a day. If someone's sauna party ran low on beer or sausage, he willingly opened the doors. He sold gasoline and propane whenever it was needed. But during the winter, the town went dead, and the store struggled.

A couple of female interests he had found in the personals section came to visit. One even stayed at the shop for a few weeks, but ultimately both attempts fell through. Väinö admitted that it wasn't solely their fault.

Väinö always felt sorry for his son. The boy was quiet and kept to himself. His dad always bought him the best sporting gear, bicycles, and skates in an attempt to compensate for something. And a black-and-white puppy, a spaniel they named Rob, short for Robin Hood.

Soon the dog vanished. After a few weeks it was found drowned, bobbing in the lake with a wire around its neck, which had apparently been fastened to a heavy rock. When the wire came loose from the rock, the dog rose to the surface.

Väinö would have bought him another dog, but the boy didn't want one. Instead, he got a pet rabbit later on.

When Matti reached the age of thirteen, he underwent hip surgery in Helsinki, and within six months was able to walk with a nearly normal gait. The operated leg tired sooner than the other, and at nighttime, it often hurt enough that Matti had to take powerful pain medications.

A couple of smooth years followed, but toward the end of his adolescence, Matti began to change. He became obsessed with role-playing games and violent movies. Väinö often thought that Matti himself didn't know who he was.

His school work began to suffer. Though Matti had been teased at school, he had done well in spite of it, managing an A- GPA. His first year in high school went equally well, but then his grades plummeted, and he dropped out the following year.

Since the shop would soon be in need of a successor, Väinö talked the boy into enrolling in business classes at the Kuopio community college. But that too proved to be a mistake. Matti attended classes for a good year before dropping out and returning home. Soon enough, the college called to inform Väinö that Matti had been arrested for using and selling pot. The case was apparently to be heard in court in the near future.

Pot!

To Väinö, this seemed incomprehensible. His son goes to study in Kuopio, a tranquil little town, and comes back a drug dealer? It was difficult to believe.

What had they done to his boy...his little boy?

Väinö had called the Kuopio police department and got hold of the officer in charge of the investigation, who had told him the whole story.

After returning home, Matti had decided to stay and work at the store. Väinö hadn't asked about the reasons for his son's return, instead pretending as though nothing had happened. Only two weeks later did he finally say, "Some policeman from Kuopio called about some drug charges. Mind telling me what's going on?"

Matti had glanced at his father's sullen face.

"I got mixed up in some things. Got caught in the wrong place at the wrong time."

"Were you using?"

"I tried it a couple times."

"Was it worth it?"

The boy shrugged his shoulders.

"What about now?"

"I quit."

But that seemed doubtful. Matti's main man Sepi had started hanging around more than seemed necessary. Sepi had lived in Helsinki for two years, and if Kuopio had a bad influence on a child, then Helsinki was many times worse. Sepi was definitely that influence.

One day, Väinö sensed that something had happened. Matti was both restless and raucous. Two days later, he went with Sepi on a trip to Helsinki. When they returned, Matti brought his father an Italian silk tie as a gift.

"How'd you pay for this?" Väinö had asked.

"It wasn't that expensive. I got it on clearance."

Then Sepi came to pick up Matti. Väinö had watched as the boys whispered in front of the store like two conspirators.

Three days later a couple of foreign-looking men came into the store, one of whom spoke Finnish well. They picked out a couple of odds and ends before loading an entire crate of bananas into a cart.

"Don't you have any more?" asked one of them.

Väinö went into the back room to check, but all the bananas were gone, even though three crates had arrived only a few days prior.

"I'm afraid we're out."

"None at all?"

"I thought there were some, but I thought wrong. That oughta be enough…"

"There's a lot more of us. And we like bananas."

"Could I interest you in some oranges? Apples?"

The man shook his head. They still bought something, and the other man asked, "Do you have any empty crates? We could use as many as you have."

"Take a look by the loading dock. Help yourselves."

The men paid, and Väinö watched as they went to the loading dock to inspect the crates.

They carried two of them to the car and drove off. Väinö had wondered as he watched them leave. With only three men in the car, where was this big crowd?

When Matti returned, Väinö told him about the foreigners who had come to clean out their stock of bananas.

"When?"

"An hour ago."

"How many guys?"

"Two. And one in the car. Why?"

Without replying, he had run back to the car.

"What's gotten into that boy?" Väinö had muttered to himself.

* * *

Raid parked the car behind the store so it wouldn't be seen from the street. The building was similar to hundreds of others in small towns across the country: a pale-yellow two-story wooden building, built after the war. A large window facing the street was cluttered with old soda signs and a few flashy ads. A set of steep concrete stairs flanked by metal railings led up to the entrance. A woman's bicycle waited alone in the bike rack next to the stairs.

The shopkeeper's Volvo station wagon was parked next to the loading dock, which was heaped with empty beer and beverage cartons. In the front yard stood a gas pump that dispensed only premium gas, and a shed for the propane tanks. To the rear of the building were a couple of apple trees and a few berry bushes.

Raid stepped into the store, which took him back thirty years to the general store of his own childhood. The same smells and easygoing atmosphere, all despite the fact that it had been converted into a supermarket. Now only meat products were served from behind the counter.

A young girl sat at the register. The shopkeeper, standing behind the meat counter, noticed Raid, wiped his hands, and came to greet him with an extended hand.

"Glad you came, I didn't want to bother you…"

"I would have come anyway. For groceries."

"I was sorry to hear about your uncle… Let's go in the back room if that's okay… I'll be right back."

He stepped over to the girl at the register, and Raid heard him say, "I'll be busy for a bit. Just come get me if someone wants to buy some meat."

He led Raid to the back room and closed the door.

"Please sit," he urged as he bustled about.

Raid sat down in an old creaky chair. The shopkeeper remained standing.

"This is difficult for me, but if it's alright I'll speak frankly."

"Sure."

"I've known for some time now that Matti's been on a dangerous path. His professor called a few months ago to tell me that he'd gotten mixed up in some drug deal in Kuopio, but since he was a first-time offender he got a suspended sentence. Yesterday he came home late and told me some unbelievable things. I didn't sleep a wink, and I can't shake this feeling... Is it true?"

"What?"

"He says some guys were after him, and that you saved his life."

"That's true."

The shopkeeper kneaded his brow.

"That's what I was afraid of. I want to thank you... I still don't understand, though... Matti didn't really tell me what's going on. Obviously something pretty serious..."

"What did he tell you?"

"That he's gotten mixed up in something, and it's not safe for him here... Do you agree with that?"

"Yes."

"He was trying to get me to close up shop and leave town for a week...at least."

"That would be smart. You're not safe here, either."

"I don't think he was telling me everything... I don't care about myself. But if my boy's in danger, I can't leave him..."

The shopkeeper leaned on the desk and lowered himself into a chair. He buried his face in his hands and spoke, almost as if to himself.

"I'm a third-generation shopkeeper. I always wanted Matti to take my place. This is good, important work…"

"Dad."

The shopkeeper stopped and turned toward the door. Matti stepped in.

"Dad, I want you to listen to him. You've got to leave. When they don't find me, they'll come after you."

"What good would I be to them?"

"They're trying to get something back…something I have."

"And what might that be?"

The boy thought for a moment.

"Remember when I said that banana shipment went bad? It didn't. I found thirty pounds of cocaine under the bananas. It was supposed to go somewhere else, but it wound up here. Now they want it back."

"So give it back."

"It's too late for that."

"Well, let's call the police. I know the chief well…"

"No! Listen to me. I stole thirty pounds of cocaine, so I'm just as guilty! I'd go to prison for sure."

"We don't have to say anything about you. We'll pack the stuff back in the crate, I'll call the police and tell him we just found it… No need to say a word about you. The chief is a friend of mine…he'll trust me."

The shopkeeper looked to Raid for support.

"Wouldn't that be the smartest thing? We'll just put it back and call the cops."

Raid didn't respond.

"Dad…there's more. These men killed Sepi…he was involved. If the cops catch those guys, they'll find out about us."

The shopkeeper fell silent and stared at the floor.

"Did you hear me? These guys are killers. They shot Sepi, and they'll shoot you too, if you don't get outta here. Close the store, and say you'll be back next week. I'll let you know when it's safe again."

The boy set his hand on his father's shoulder. "I...I don't want anything to happen to you..."

Väinö sighed deeply. Then he rose and looked first at his son, then at Raid.

"I've done nothing wrong, and I'm not going anywhere. I have to stand by my son, no matter what he's done. A father can't just leave his own flesh and blood..."

"That'll just make things more complicated," said the boy. "Let's not argue, alright? I'll clean up my own mess. You've already done enough for me."

He turned to Raid. "Talk some sense into him, will you?"

"Your son is right. You should go. We'll fix things while you're away."

"And how is that? By killing them all? Is there really any other way?"

"Yes."

"For example?"

"That depends on what happens."

"So you'll protect him?"

"Who else could?"

"But why would you do that? There's nothing to keep you from leaving."

"That's right."

"So why?"

"I'll tell you when I find out."

8.

Huusko was observing Susisaari's driving. She pulled the stick shift briskly and purposefully, although perhaps her lane changes were a bit too aggressive. Susisaari noticed him watching.

"How's my driving?"

"Better than mine."

"Which doesn't say much."

"No, it doesn't."

Susisaari glanced over with a tentative look.

"Is it just me, or has Jansson changed?"

"Changed how?"

"He seemed a bit down. It's a tough case, of course."

"Maybe it's Tuomela. They're friends, you know… And besides that, he's the one having to fill in for the guy on top of everything else."

"Could be."

"How's things with you?" Susisaari asked after a while.

"Not bad. And for once that's actually true."

"I heard you're renting Jansson's pad?"

Huusko laughed.

"When he told me he found a vacant flat, I thought it was one of his friend's. Then I found out he'd bought the place with his wife as a retirement home."

"Steep rent?"

"Practically free."

"He's not much of a businessman."

"That's for sure."

"How's it going with your girlfriend?" The word girlfriend felt strange coming from Susisaari's mouth.

"You don't have to answer that," she added.

"It's going well...least for the time being."

"I don't understand what's so wrong with me that I can't hold onto anyone. I'll be an old maid soon, at this rate."

Huusko studied Susisaari from head to toe.

"I can't find anything wrong with you. Might be a tad prickly, but that's what a lotta guys like... You gonna stay with us once you get your lieutenant's stripes?"

"Hopefully."

"Don't you think it'd be smarter to go someplace with a vacancy?"

"It would, but that's not what I want."

"How come?"

"I guess I've gotten too used to you guys... Lassila actually called a couple weeks ago and offered me a lieutenant's post, but I wasn't really interested in property crimes."

A brief flash of memory flickered through Huusko's mind, but vanished as quickly as it had come. He repeated Susisaari's words silently to himself, but couldn't recall what had triggered the memory. Huusko knew that the only way to capture it was to leave it be, and let it come to him later.

He dug a pad of Post-its from his pocket and jotted down a note, "Lassila, property crimes division." Then he stuck it on the dashboard.

"Dementia's setting in," he said.

* * *

Customs Inspector Alanko worked in Erottaja, in an ornate building just across from Diana's Park. The

105

building housed several other departments in addition to the Customs monitoring and inspection offices.

Alanko met them in the lobby, and led them to his office, a small room crowded with bookshelves, the shelves brimming with binders. Alanko's desk was covered with stacks of papers as tall as the span of a hand.

"You can see what kind of work I do. Shuffling piles of paper from one place to another."

Alanko was in his mid-fifties, but in good physical condition. His graying hair was cropped short and he was dressed in a youthful blazer, faded jeans, and a pair of Docksides.

"Who told you it was me investigating the Finnair case?"

"Kempas."

Alanko sat down behind his desk and invited them to sit.

"How can I help?"

"We're investigating a double murder in Oulunkylä. One of the victims was a flight attendant with Finnair, and we found at least five thousand euros worth of stolen tax-free stuff in her apartment: headphones, sunglasses, perfume, expensive whiskey..."

"How is this linked to the murders?"

"We got an anonymous tip claiming that this flight attendant had threatened to blow the whistle on the theft ring," said Susisaari.

"Why?"

"She was a drug user. Maybe she seemed unpredictable...and therefore risky."

Alanko briefly considered Susisaari's words.

"I must admit it was a pretty big case. Much bigger than anyone thought. But we didn't really make any progress because it seemed like the whole firm was conspiring against us. Documents and evidence would just disappear. Hard drives would suddenly be erased. Based on what we found out, they were hemorrhaging upwards of a million euros worth of goods annually."

"How'd they cover up the losses?" Huusko asked.

"All written off as operating losses. Broken bottles, spoiled food, damaged goods, etc. It was all spread out over a long enough time span that no single theft attracted that much attention, even though some of them were pretty big. High enough revenues can cover up some pretty big losses."

"So quite a few people got scared when the issue came to light."

"That's right."

"You think this stewardess could have known something that would have raised some hackles if it came out?"

"Not sure. How long was she with the company?"

"About ten years."

"It's possible, especially if she was involved. But you say she was a drug user?"

"She used coke at least, and smuggled it, too," said Huusko. "We found two ounces of cocaine in the lining of her purse, and she had just gotten off a flight from Spain. The drugs would have had to have been on her during the flight."

"Don't you think it more likely that the murders had something to do with drug trafficking?"

"Yes, and we're already covering that angle. We just wanted to look into every possibility."

"Well, while we were investigating the thefts, we were also following the airline's baggage handling and personnel. One interesting fact became clear. When the planes landed, there were always unauthorized people on the tarmac."

"What does that mean?" said Susisaari.

"When a plane lands, the baggage trains are waiting there to meet them and unload the cargo. Afterwards, they fuel up the plane, and it's cleaned and serviced if necessary. Everyone who sets foot on the tarmac carries an ID badge, and the entries and exits are tracked by computer. According to the data, there were employees on the tarmac who weren't supposed to be there. People who weren't on duty."

"Did you figure out what was happening?"

"We tried, but the firm said that the data disappeared, and then told us it all had been due to a programming error. For us, it just went to show that outsiders have access to the airport. Just think of the opportunities that would present for drug traffickers. Even large shipments of drugs can be smuggled through the back door without ever going through customs."

"But that's all speculation, right? You didn't get any concrete evidence?" said Susisaari.

"No, we didn't."

"Where's the case at now?" said Huusko.

"Cold. We nabbed a few small-timers who'd stolen some goods off the conveyor belt in the warehouse. We tried to plant an undercover in there, but the company was like a mafia, one big family. Our guy was completely shut out. Anyhow, I'm pretty sure it leaked and everybody knew who he was."

"How big do you think the players were who were involved in these thefts?"

"Pretty big. Otherwise they couldn't have thrown wrenches in the gears from the very get-go."

"In other words, the upper level of the organization was protecting the lower, and taking a larger share of the winnings?"

"That's what it looked like to us. And they were protected from outside of the organization as well."

"What do you mean?" asked Susisaari.

"There're some big names on the board of directors at Finnair, current and former politicians. They weren't used to the police sniffing around. So we got several nasty phone calls, and I know that even this agency was bullied to some degree. But I can look myself in the mirror in the morning, and say with confidence that we didn't fail as a result of the bullying. The opposition was just too strong."

Huusko was filling in the lines of his notebook with a ballpoint pen so that they formed a sort of vague pattern.

"You think the organization is tough enough that they would kill if someone said too much?"

"They already have…at least we think so," said Alanko. "We busted one truck driver for theft after finding a few grand worth of stolen goods in his apartment. Instead of pressing charges, we agreed to drop charges if he helped us with the case. The guy had been with the company for over twenty years and knew everything, but after his wife ran away with a pilot, he started to drink too much… We agreed that he would go on as if nothing had happened, but would keep track of all the thefts, and record conversations with the others. He managed to give us a little information before he went with some co-workers to party at the company's seaside villa and drowned."

Susisaari looked skeptical.

"What did the autopsy show?"

"That he drowned. With a blood alcohol level of nearly point three. Before he drowned, he called me from the villa and told me he felt like the others were onto him. Someone had joked about it. He was afraid something was gonna happen to him, and he was right. I think he was drowned."

"Wow," said Huusko.

"Tough bunch."

"You think the same people are involved with the drug trafficking?" said Susisaari.

"I don't see why not."

"If that's the case, you think they were worried that the stewardess was gonna blow the whistle on their smuggling?"

"It's possible, but why would she do that if she was involved herself?"

"Maybe they couldn't trust her anymore. She went nuts a few times, and if she got busted she could've squealed. Junkies are never completely trustworthy... What sort of security measures did they have?"

"Hardly any. Random searches every now and then, but if airport personnel are in on it, it's easy to alert the smugglers. Then they can just leave the stuff on the plane or put it with the baggage and collect it later. I'll give you a tip, though. Get in touch with Pekka Kallio. He's a former Finnair security officer and a former cop as well. He's the only reason the investigation ever got started. And it cost him his job."

"Where can we find him?"

Alanko scrolled through the directory in his phone.

"He's a farmer in Degerby nowadays...inherited his childhood farm."

Alanko wrote the name and number on a corner of his notepad and tore it out.

"Here. Tell him I said hi. And keep me posted. I'll reopen the investigation the moment I get more evidence."

* * *

Huusko and Susisaari were exiting the Customs building when Huusko's cell phone rang. The call was from the Hotel Marski.

"You had inquired about two guests who stayed with us back in May?"

"Yes. What'd you find out?"

"Well, you asked us to look for South Americans, and we didn't find any."

"Really?"

"That's right. But we did find two Swedish nationals with Hispanic names. According to the address they live in Gothenburg. Does that help?"

"Who were they?"

"Pedro Bolivar and Santos Ramirez."

"And they're Swedish citizens?"

"That's what it says in the hotel registry."

"How reliable is your registry?"

"We verify our guests' IDs...driver's licenses etc., but Scandinavians don't need to show their passports. Can I tell you anything else?"

"Absolutely. Everything you know from the mini-bar to the porn channels."

"They didn't use the mini-bar."

"What about the room phone?"

"No. Only the por... pay-per-view channels and the lobby bar. They paid their bill in cash."

"How long did they stay?"

"Three nights."

"Could you fax me copies of their registration forms and everything else you have on them? Did they rent a car, make restaurant reservations, things like that. We're interested in anything you have."

"What have they done?"

"We don't know yet."

Huusko hung up the phone.

"With a little luck, we'll have their names, addresses, *and* photographs. According to the hotel, they're Swedish nationals. What do you think?"

"That we should've gone to get the registration forms ourselves—it's only a few blocks down the street."

"That's what technology is for."

"Well, it'll be easy to find out, anyhow. I know a couple of Swedish cops from that course in Copenhagen."

"Always the cosmopolitan, aren't you?"

"Nothing wrong with that. I'll send them the info. Even if the names are false, it's still possible they live in Sweden."

"But there's no guarantee they're actually the same guys that the neighbor saw in front of Liljeblad's building."

"We'll need somebody to confirm it."

Suddenly, Huusko remembered something.

"You remember when Kempas mentioned that last spring they were trailing two South Americans on a tip from Interpol?"

"The ones that saw that lawyer? Saramaa?"

"Exactly."

Huusko searched his cellphone directory and brought up Kempas' number.

"Hey, it's Huusko. Listen, at the meeting you mentioned a couple of South Americans that were in Finland last spring. Would you happen to have their names?"

Huusko waited for a moment. "Pedro Bolivar and Santos Ramirez... Just happened to run across the same guys... The Valiente family? I'll keep that in mind, thanks," said Huusko, and he hung up.

Huusko thought for a few seconds.

"Well?" said Susisaari.

"Hard-core mafia guys. They're with the Bolivian Valiente crime family. They run a cocaine operation in Scandinavia, along with the Russian mafia. Not easy to nab guys at that level."

"Hernando must have been working for them."

"What use is a lowly produce worker to a Bolivian cartel?" said Huusko.

"South America exports a lot of fruit, especially bananas. You could easily send some other things along with the fruit."

"Cocaine?"

"Just one example."

As they were climbing into the car, Susisaari changed the subject, "What do you think of Kempas?"

"How do you mean?"

"I mean as a boss. If I went to work for him in Undercover."

"Gruff, but professional. I might be tempted to do the same myself, if Saarinen takes Tuomela's place."

"What do you have against Saarinen?"

Huusko glanced over at Susisaari with a wry smile.

"One time Malmberg and I were out all night on a tough murder case. The victim was a celebrity at the time, and we were working our asses off because the bosses were fielding calls from the media all day, and had nothing to say but 'no progress.' In the morning the case finally started to unravel, and we zeroed in on the perp. The guy was known to be violent, so we called in some backup. So Saarinen and some beat cops came along. Everything went smoothly, and we arrested the guy. So all three of us headed back to the station in the same car, but Saarinen hopped out in front of the building, claiming he had to take care of some pressing business. Malmberg and I spent about fifteen minutes returning the car and what not. When we got back up to the station, Saarinen was sitting in the captain's office with a cup of coffee, bragging about how beautifully he cracked the case. Then he spotted us and piped up, 'These boys helped out a bit, too.'"

Susisaari shook her head.

"Can you take Fredrik Street? I gotta get something," said Huusko.

At the corner of Rata and Fredrik, Huusko asked her to stop.

"From the Security Police?"

"Won't take more than a couple minutes."

Huusko got out of the car and disappeared into a store. Susisaari glanced at the clock. Six minutes passed before Huusko returned with a large plastic bag.

"What, you go shopping?"

Huusko reached into the bag and took out a pink tutu laden with sparkles.

"Pretty, isn't it?"

"Very cute."

"Not for me, though," he added. "It's for Lea's little girl—ballet starts tomorrow."

Huusko pulled out a pair of white slippers.

"Those are pretty, too," said Susisaari, and she started the car. Then her eyes fell on the note Huusko had left on the dash.

"How long are you gonna leave that there? 'Lassila, property crimes division.' What's to remember about that?"

"Take the route through Sörnäinen," was Huusko's only reply.

* * *

Kirstilä, the CEO of the produce warehouse, appeared somewhat surprised.

114

"I thought you said you were investigating the murder, not the burglary."

"Tell me about the burglary anyway."

"It happened a week ago, so Wednesday night. I'm not sure how, but the burglars entered the warehouse without breaking any locks or doors. Then they broke into the office by busting the lock."

"What'd they take?"

"There was nothing valuable in there besides the computer, and that's what they took. They ransacked everything else…left a mess. Tore apart the archives and shipping records. Luckily, we had backups of everything."

"What was on the computer?" asked Susisaari.

"More or less the same information, shipping records, customer records, orders, for example."

"Did Hernando have a key to the warehouse?"

"Yes. He worked a lot of evenings, and sometimes the night shift if we were busy."

"But not to the office?"

"No. You don't think it could have been him, do you? What could he get there that he couldn't get otherwise? The computer wouldn't be worth anything to him."

"You said you have backups of everything. Could you send that information to the police?"

"Why do you need it?"

"That remains to be seen."

"I'm not so sure we have an obligation to do that. We're talking about confidential business information."

"If you really prefer, we can execute a search warrant for your offices. We're dealing with the murder of two people. There's no time to nitpick."

Kirstilä softened.

"Of course, we'll cooperate. I just don't understand…"

115

"Leave that for the police to worry about."

"If you don't mind waiting for a bit, I'll get you copies right now."

"Thank you. We can wait."

Kirstilä left Huusko and Susisaari to themselves.

Huusko looked over at Susisaari and said, "Lesson number one: that's how you crush a defiant dickhead. The man's gotta learn that we beareth not the sword on our logo in vain."

* * *

Jansson was almost startled at the change that Tuomela had undergone in barely a week. He was pale and thin, and his health had clearly taken more than one turn for the worse. His pallid skin hung loose on his face, and he moved with difficulty, though he had always kept himself in shape.

Tuomela was dressed in gray Dacron pants and a burgundy smoking jacket. Beneath the jacket, he wore a baby-blue dress shirt with a collar that seemed loose around his dwindling neck. Otherwise, everything was tip top. Tuomela was a distinguished enough gentleman that even in sickness he looked fashionable.

The man lived in a classic apartment building in the lavish Töölö neighborhood with his lecturer wife, and their cat, a fifteen-year-old Persian named Rafu. Jansson and Tuomela were sitting in his office, which was furnished with vintage glass-door bookshelves and a desk with a dark green, nickel-accented typewriter. Every object in the room was a relic of a bygone time.

Tuomela lived on the very top floor, with the treetops in the park across the street visible through the window. Steep stone stairs descended to a playground in the park.

Tuomela lifted a British teacup.

"I felt a lot better in the hospital a year ago, but they still say I'll be back to work soon."

"You just rest as long as you need," said Jansson.

"I suspect that rest won't help me anymore," said Tuomela with a weary smile. "Not that I'm asking for pity, least of all yours. That wouldn't be fair to you. I suppose it comes from being a cop for almost forty years and learning to accept the truth, no matter how cold. There's no room in this line of work for rose-colored glasses. I hear that Hakala's grooming Saarinen for my spot."

Jansson stared at his own knees, "Hakala can groom whoever he wants."

"You mean to say you're out of the running?"

"What running? I only filled in for you because you asked me to. Then I realized the job wasn't for me."

"You know you have the support of the entire team."

"Maybe, but I've decided to be selfish and do what's right for me. I'm a better case manager than a department manager."

"Sometimes I wonder if I should have done the same. Too much accountability is a hell of a burden, at least at my age. I should've pushed back, but I didn't have it in me. I'm a product of a post-war upbringing: steady, gloomy, and reliable. I suppose the country needed those types then."

"Those types are always needed," said Jansson.

"I feel like time has passed me by all too many times, and it just hasn't occurred to me to hop on for the ride, or off for that matter. So what's new at the station?"

Jansson told him about the double murder and their theories.

"Drugs are involved in almost every case these days. When I joined the department, there were about three hash addicts in all of Helsinki. Only veterans used the hard stuff because they got hooked on morphine during the war. Why is it that the world never seems to change for the better?"

"The TV shows are better. And Finland has made strides in hockey and soccer," said Jansson.

Tuomela smiled.

"You're right. Just like an old man to grumble about the good old days. Even the ancient Romans were no exception... Anyway, getting fingerprints for those foreigners would take us far. You might be able to find them on Interpol's database."

"I'll try to bug them, but you know how it is. If you bug them about every case, they won't take you seriously."

"I know, but you can't just wait while the case sits idle."

"Fortunately, things aren't quite that bad yet. We still have a few leads, but the drug connection looks to be the best."

"Looks that way to me, too," said Tuomela. "But you've got enough experience to know that the motive could be so simple that you'd never even think of it. On the other hand, it could be so bizarre, that you'd never even imagine it. I'm sorry that I can't give you anything more than these hollow platitudes. It's nothing new to you."

"No...good to be reminded."

"Somehow it all seems to revolve around this woman. If she was as bad as it seems, then she had a lot of enemies. Her behavior shows that she was unable or unwilling to control herself. Maybe it was due to the drugs, or maybe she was just too confident. If it was the latter, she could've been blackmailing somebody who was initially protecting her. Perhaps she went too far. An unpredictable person is always a threat, especially when they know too much, as she likely did."

"Likely so."

Jansson glanced at his watch. "Huusko's apparently found a new lead. We'll have to have at least one more meeting today."

"When duty calls, duty calls."

Tuomela walked with Jansson into the front entry, which smelled of clothing fresh from the attic. Tuomela always prepared for winter well in advance. A mink fur hung from the coat rack alongside an old-fashioned overcoat with a Persian lamb's-wool collar. Hanging on the top of the rack were a black silk-banded fedora and a silver-gray bomber hat. A pair of old galoshes lay on the shoe rack.

Tuomela held out his hand.

"Thank you for coming…my friend."

"See you soon," said Jansson.

Tuomela seemed to want to say something, but he settled for, "Alright."

"Send my greetings to Kaarina."

"I will. She would have wanted to see you."

"Some other time."

"Some other time."

Jansson took the elevator, an ancient contraption with hardwood paneling, an accordion door, and cables that jangled like a loose-strung harp, all the way down to street level. Only once back in the shadow of Pasila police headquarters did Jansson feel completely free of Tuomela and the quiet charm of the bourgeois.

* * *

"The burglary's got to have something to do with the double murder. Otherwise what's the point of breaking

119

into a produce warehouse? To steal bananas?" said Huusko.

Jansson looked to Susisaari, "What do you think?"

"I agree. Lots of fruit comes from South America. It'd be easy to stash something more valuable in there and have people along the way guide the drugs to the right place. Suppose Hernando was responsible for directing the drugs, and made a mistake. Then they broke in to find out where it went. That's why the burglars were interested in the shipping records and the computer. Hernando was killed to send a message."

Jansson nodded.

"I want you to get in touch with the Swedish police and ask about the men from the hotel. Call Interpol, too. Let's see if that nets us anything. And Huusko, why don't you call the downtown hotels and ask if the men stayed there. They had to stay somewhere."

"If the guys are even the same ones," Huusko noted.

"We'll find out soon. Anyone else?"

Lehto had brought his notepad; Malmberg trusted his memory.

Lehto began. "The Land Rover isn't registered in Finland. I've tracked them all down, rentals included. Since they didn't drive it here all the way from Bolivia, it must have come from one of our neighbors, Sweden, Russia, or Estonia."

"And nobody's seen it?" said Jansson.

"Nope. We have a nationwide APB out on it, but nobody's seen it. We searched the traffic camera footage in Oulunkylä, but nothing there either. I'm still working on the data from the border patrol, but there's just too many vehicles."

Jansson shifted his gaze to Malmberg.

"I've been at the airport all day, interviewing Liljeblad's co-workers. It seems she wasn't a very well-loved woman. The things we heard earlier about her relationships with management were corroborated—she had friends in high places. She could do basically anything she wanted without consequences, including passing out on a flight three months ago and being unable to fulfill her duties. The pilot filed a complaint with the company's HR director, but nothing came of it."

"Why not?" said Susisaari.

"According to the HR director, Liljeblad became ill, and was in no way under the influence of drugs. He acknowledged two complaints, and apparently she was given warnings for those. I asked everybody about the individual that Liljeblad drove home with, but got nothing. I still haven't gotten hold of all her co-workers, though. That's all for now."

"Good," said Jansson. "I just received the preliminary autopsy results. At the time of his death, Hernando had a blood alcohol level of point one, and had also used cocaine. The cause of death was what it looked like, a stab wound to the heart. The cause of the woman's death was heart failure as the result of an overdose of cocaine. She had also engaged in sexual intercourse shortly before her death."

"How did he manage to fuck her with all her clothes on?" said Huusko.

"Not with Hernando," Jansson went on. "The pubic hairs on her were different from his. Also, Hernando had slept with somebody else before his death as well."

"What kind of soap opera is this?" exclaimed Huusko. "Everyone sleeping around before they die. A regular Don Juan tale."

"We also found fibers on both of them that we should be able to cross-compare. We should be able to make some headway with this new information."

Huusko looked sullen. "I shoulda known. Just when I thought we were on the right track, with the best and most exotic theory we've seen in a good long while."

"The new information means that we have two additional suspects: their lovers. Either of them could have done it. We need to find out who was in the car and who was in the apartment."

Like a model student, Huusko raised his hand, "Maybe it happened just like we initially thought. She walks in to catch the guy in bed with his lover, stabs him, and then has a heart attack. The third wheel flees the scene and doesn't dare call the police."

Susisaari looked at Huusko, "Do you remember that tip?"

"What tip?" asked Jansson.

"Yesterday we went through the eyewitness tips we've gotten. According to one, a red Mazda was seen near the Oulunkylä ball fields around seven-thirty on Sunday evening. A blonde and a man were observed in the car. According to the witness…having sex."

"Using cocaine can increase your libido," said Lehto.

"So she snorted a bunch of coke and got horny, then drove to the ball fields and got it on with the guy," said Huusko.

"Can't we get DNA from the sperm?" said Susisaari.

"The man used a condom, and so did Hernando," said Jansson. "They did find some fluids on Hernando, which are being examined, but we don't have the results yet."

"So where's the condom, then?"

"Good question," said Jansson. "Hernando probably flushed it down the toilet, so it's likely in some pipeline, floating off to the sewage plant. We didn't find anything in the Mazda, either. At least no used condoms."

"Somehow I doubt she put it in her pocket," said Huusko. "Maybe she tossed it out the window by the ball fields."

"Good point. You and Sanna can go look for it today. Bring the eyewitness along so you know the exact spot. It hasn't rained, so there might still be something there."

Huusko glanced over at Susisaari.

"Alright," said Huusko. "But I bet you our backseat Romeo is one of the staff from the plane. Maybe the pilot or co-pilot, and he doesn't wanna contact us because of the sex. Scared the wife will find out about papa's shenanigans."

* * *

Osmo Lepistö was a seventy-year-old ruddy-faced outdoorsman, and so eager to help that Huusko and Susisaari had to struggle just to keep up with him. Lepistö stopped just beyond a small grove of trees on the far side of the fields and pointed with his finger.

"The car was right there."

"Which way was it parked?" said Huusko.

Lepistö used his hands to show where the nose and tail of the car were.

"I was right over there by the tree."

The tree he pointed to was just over thirty feet away, much closer than Lepistö had initially described.

Huusko glanced at the ground. The soil was sandy, the short grass interspersed with plantain.

"Well, I guess let's start looking."

Huusko and Susisaari pulled on some latex gloves and began to scour the ground.

"What are you looking for?" asked Lepistö.

"Hard to say just yet," said Huusko. "Anything that might have come from the car."

Lepistö began to look around, too.

"Did anything stand out to you about the man? How he was dressed, hair color, anything like that?" Susisaari asked.

"It was pretty dark already, which is probably why they thought they could come here to mess around. Seems like the guy was dressed in dark clothes...short hair...maybe even balding."

"Where were they sitting in the car?" said Huusko.

"The front seat, with the back rest reclined a little and the woman was on top... Looked a little crowded in that kind of car, as small as it is. No shame, I tell ya... There's people around here, walking their dogs and what not..."

Susisaari dropped a half-smoked cigarette butt and a match into a re-sealable plastic bag. Lepistö bent down to pick something up.

"Please don't touch anything!" said Huusko. He came over to see what Lepistö had found. A miniature bottle of cognac lay on the ground.

"A mini-bottle of cognac. The kind they sell on an airplane."

Huusko put the bottle into a plastic bag, and the bag into his pocket.

Lepistö was pleased to have found something, and redoubled his search. He crouched down nimbly and began combing the ground with his eyes.

They searched for more than half an hour without finding anything else of interest. Finally, Huusko broadened the area of his search and walked over to the edge of the thicket. He bent the grass carefully aside and inspected the undergrowth. Susisaari followed suit, ranging further away from the area Lepistö had shown them. Lepistö stayed put.

After a few minutes, Susisaari found something. She picked it up and showed it to Huusko: a blue plastic wrapper. As he drew nearer, he could see that it was a condom package.

"Good material for fingerprints," said Susisaari.

Lepistö came up from behind.

"So that's what you're looking for. Are you interested in the contents as well?"

"What do you mean?" said Huusko.

"It's hanging in the trees over there... You should've told me what you were looking for."

They found the condom, sealed with a knot, on a low-hanging branch of a squat shrub, just where Lepistö had pointed.

Huusko was tickled, "Pre-packaged DNA evidence. Very kind of him."

Susisaari examined the condom.

"Same brand as the package."

Huusko looked at the sky, "Thank the Lord."

9.

In recent years, Raid had been buying his weapons from an Estonian man who lived in Sweden. The man had served in the supply operations of the Soviet army, and his old connections allowed him access to any gun that Raid might need.

But this time, Raid had to enlist Uki's help, regardless of how much he didn't want to get him involved. Raid knew that Uki could get weapons from a certain gunsmith who dealt black market guns from the estates of the deceased. This gunsmith also built and repaired weapons himself. After listening to Raid's story over the phone, Uki was silent for a long time before asking, "What sort of an arsenal do you want?"

Raid already had a pistol and plenty of ammo, but he needed a rifle with a telescopic sight and a silencer, as well as subsonic cartridges. A few hand grenades would also be good to have.

Uki was familiar with the equipment, and needed no further directions.

"Tell me the time and the place."

"Juva, 6 P.M. It's about sixty miles from here."

"That would put you in the heart of Savo. Are you at Nygren's old place?"

"Yes. Can you make it?"

"If I hurry. You need backup?"

"No."

"So just target practice, huh?"

"Exactly. How's Raili?"

"Better than I. Always fussing over Merja's wedding."

"Merja's getting married?"

"That's what I hear, but I'd say it's mostly wishful thinking on Raili's part. When an only child gets married, it's a big deal for mom. Especially when you're dealing with an only daughter."

"True."

"We can chat some more when I deliver your order."

"Alright."

* * *

Raid passed a sign advertising an upcoming rest stop, bathrooms, and a café selling fresh, smoked fish. The road skirted the shore of a lake, which bore the reflection of the gray skies, the forest, and the rocky hills along the shore. In the middle of the lake was a small, lush island. A couple of mallards swam out from among the reeds along the shore and headed toward open water, dragging fine ripples behind them.

For all its enduring beauty, the countryside displayed a shade of autumn gloom, which required centuries of acclimation. A city slicker accustomed to the teeming populations of central Europe would suffer panic attacks within days in these parts, and soon, likely withdraw to a nearby cave to put himself out of his misery.

But the locals soldiered on alone, year in and year out, from one century to the next, miles away from the nearest neighbor, with whom they were always feuding over property lines, dock space, and politics. In these parts, the Center Party warred constantly with the Social Democrats over every milk house and acre of farm land. If the Center Party swept elections in any given year, the

Social Democrats would reclaim power the next time around.

Not even the dark furrows of the clay-heavy fields looming in the autumn twilight, nor the frosty silence of winter, discouraged these people. Two buses arrived daily—one at the break of dawn, the other at dusk. One took them to the nearest town and its liquor store, the other brought them back. After the bus ride, there were two miles of fighting the wind, dragging bags through the squeaky snow, and finally, the lights of home, looming in the darkness. A few whisks of a broom on snowy boots and then in through the breezeway, on with the television, on with the thrift store house coat…and on with the sauna.

Small comforts would suffice, as long as expectations weren't too high.

Raid was born here in the country, and he knew these people, though he had lived most of his adult life in Sweden.

His Mercedes covered the miles quickly, and the rest stop came up so suddenly that Raid had to slam on the brakes. As he was well ahead of schedule, he decided to stop for coffee. One car was already parked in front of the café, and just as Raid got out, a third pulled into the lot, a brand-new Saab station wagon.

Raid took a glance at the Saab and set off toward the café, a log-home-style structure. The door to the Saab slammed shut, and the sound of hurried footsteps approached from behind. Raid's hand dipped beneath his coat, and he turned to look as he walked.

"I *thought* that was your Mercedes."

The man was about thirty years old, thin, and stood as tall as Raid. His blond hair hung to the nape of his neck, and he wore a denim shirt that was tucked into a tight-fitting pair of jeans. On his feet were a pair of red, black, and white tennis shoes.

Raid knew the man. Not well, but he knew him. The last time they had met, the man had been working as a bodyguard for a Finnish gangster in Stockholm.

"You on vacation, or…?" the man asked.

"Yup."

"Same here. My folks live in Savonlinna, so I figured I'd stop and visit if nothing more important comes up. You never know."

The man laughed at his own comment.

"The old man's retired, which means bored and lonely. Never had much use for me before, but now he keeps calling and telling me to visit. Promised to warm up the sauna and cool down the vodka. It's like a scene right out of my sixth grade school play…the return of the prodigal son."

The man laughed at his joke, but when Raid was unresponsive, his laugh faded.

"You from around here too?"

"No."

"Where you headed?"

"Wherever the road takes me."

"Don't you figure that in advance?"

"Sometimes yes, sometimes no."

The man glanced at the Mercedes.

"Nygren left you his car."

"He did."

"And the house, too. At least so I hear. Whereabouts is it?"

"A long ways from here."

The man nodded toward the restaurant.

"I'll buy you a cup of coffee."

"I only stopped to stretch my legs."

"Then let's stretch our legs together. I wanted to chat with you…since we happened to meet. The world's a small place for two old vagabonds."

Raid stopped at the edge of the parking lot. Behind the café was a small sandy beach, bordered by a rocky cliff, and beyond the cliff was a sparse pine forest. He could smell the scent of the smokehouse next to the café.

"Anyway, I might have some work for you."

"I got plenty of work. Too much."

"Lucrative work."

"I'm pretty picky."

"So I've heard. Why don't we step over here and chat."

"What kind of work are you talking about?"

"For the Russians. They need some muscle to protect against the Yugoslavians. Looking for someone who's got a foot in a lot of doors. The second I spotted you I knew you were the man. Besides, you've worked for them before, right? You took care of Nikutjev and his bodyguards in Imatra."

"Really?"

"I heard it from the Russians."

"They never paid me."

The man laughed.

"Heard about that, too. I can guarantee that they regret that. It never had the bosses' blessing. What do you think?"

"Not interested."

"Let's not make a decision just yet. I got some twelve-year-old whiskey and a case of beer in the car. Let's talk, okay? Your place or mine?"

"Neither."

The man looked at Raid and nodded.

"Then I guess that's that. Some other time."

"Maybe."

"I guess I'll hit the road, then. The old man wouldn't wanna heat the sauna all alone."

"Hit the road, then."

* * *

Uki was already waiting with a cup of coffee and a sandwich when Raid arrived. He took a sip of coffee and looked Raid over.

"You look tired."

"That's because I am."

"Who was it that said you were human after all?"

"You."

"I reckon I did. Alright if I finish my sandwich?"

"Take your time."

Raid got himself a cup of coffee and came back to the table. He stole a glance at Uki, who had clearly aged since they last met, though that had been only six months ago. His hair was speckled with gray. The lines in his face were deeper than before, and his cheeks were slightly sunken.

"You said your last job was your last. You kept your promise?" said Raid.

"For the time being. The money's safe under the mattress."

"I just ran into someone I know."

"Do I know him?"

"No. A Finnish thug from Stockholm. He's got a contract to kill me."

"Is that why you need the guns?"

"No."

"What for, then?"

"A few Bolivian pushers."

"I see you've had an exciting vacation."

"Right."

131

"So how come this guy's stalking you?"

"I killed a Russian boss. They hired a Finn because they heard I was in Finland."

"So whatcha gonna do?"

"I guess I'll have to get rid of him."

"Aren't there any less serious alternatives?"

"He's already taken a payment, so he's gotta act or he'll end up on the hit list himself. To me, killing him is more humane than a wheelchair for the rest of his life. Those are the alternatives."

"I've always admired your pragmatism. Does he know about Nygren's house?"

"I would have to assume so."

"I'd like to check it out sometime," said Uki.

"Sure, sometime."

"But not now?"

"No."

Uki finished his sandwich and the rest of his coffee. Then he stood up.

"Let's get down to business, then."

Uki followed Raid's Mercedes to a remote forest road. Raid pulled over, and Uki parked his rusty Fiat next to the Mercedes. Uki opened the trunk, took out a hard plastic case and opened it.

The rifle was a Tikka .308 with a silencer that wrapped around the barrel so it didn't add length to the weapon. The sight was high-quality, with plenty of magnification.

"Three grenades enough?"

Uki pulled out a fabric bag and opened it. The grenades were dark green with Russian letters engraved in them.

Raid drew a wad of bills from his pocket and paid.

"You should come see Raili and I before you leave the country."

"Maybe."

"So you won't."

"Say hi to Raili, though."

"No. She'd be hurt if she knew you were in Finland and didn't come see her. I can say hi to Merja if you like."

Raid nodded and walked back to his car. The dashboard clock read twenty minutes till eight. Dusk was beginning to fall.

10.

Eila Tuuri favored public transportation—the subway from Itäkeskus to Herttoniemi, and then a bus to Roihuvuori. Huusko spotted her stepping out of the rear door of the bus with a shopping bag and a girl of about six. José Hernando's ex lived in a red-brick 1950s apartment building with staircases that never seemed to end.

"There she is with the little girl," Huusko said to Susisaari.

They got out of the car and stood waiting. At thirty feet off, the woman noticed them, and stopped momentarily before continuing on.

"Hello," said Huusko. "This is my partner, Officer Susisaari"

Tuuri didn't seem pleased. "What do you want?"

"Do you have a moment?"

"How long is a moment?"

"If the issue gets resolved quickly, a moment is a moment. If not, it can go on forever."

"My girl is hungry."

"We won't stop you…let's talk in the kitchen," said Huusko.

A few children were in the yard playing on the swings.

The woman turned to the girl, "Heidi, why don't you go play with Elsi and Lotta for a little while. I'll call you in later. But you stay by the swings. Is that clear?"

"Yes."

The girl's hair was dark, a sure sign of her father's genes. Huusko and Susisaari followed the woman to the second floor. The apartment was on the small side, with only two rooms, and decorated on a shoestring budget, though tastefully so. Much of the furniture was clearly thrift store material.

Huusko felt a vague sense of restlessness. He had awakened many times in such apartments. Once, a little boy had shaken him awake and asked excitedly, "Are you my new daddy?"

Occasionally he had been greeted at the breakfast table by some angst-filled teenager calling Mom a whore for once again dragging home some creep. Huusko tried to steer clear of such situations by slipping out at night or in the wee hours of the morning, depending on whether he needed a place to sleep that night.

Eila emptied the contents of a plastic grocery bag into the refrigerator: two cartons of skim milk, a package of margarine, two tubs of yogurt, a bag of carrots, and a carton of juice. Once the bag was empty, she filled a pot with water, set it on the stove, took some potatoes out of the fridge, and began to peel them.

"Well? Ask away."

"Last time we talked, you mentioned that you hadn't seen or heard from your ex in two weeks."

"Yeah?"

"According to the phone records, you called him several times over the course of those two weeks, the last time on the same day of his murder."

The woman's face stiffened and she suddenly began to sob. Huusko had seen this reaction many times before.

"Just tell us the truth. We don't want you getting into trouble... You have your girl to think about," said Susisaari, in a comforting voice.

The woman wiped her eyes with a paper towel and blew her nose into it.

"I never considered doing otherwise... He...José didn't come to see Heidi when he was supposed to...which was the second time in a row he let her down. How could a father do that to his own child? She gets so excited to see him that she can barely sleep..."

"So what did you do?" said Susisaari.

"Called him and yelled at him. I was furious, and I..."

The woman fell silent.

"But I didn't do it."

She dropped three potatoes into the pot, and water splashed onto the tiled walls. Then she continued peeling.

"A woman was there on the day of the murder," said Huusko. "Was that you?"

"Absolutely not."

"Then why did you lie?"

"I didn't want to get mixed up in anything."

"You claim you broke off the relationship when he cheated on you. But you continued to call and threaten both him and his new girlfriend."

The woman launched into a second bout of weeping and abandoned the potato peeling. It took a moment for her to collect herself.

"I just thought if he could see how stupid he'd been...that this woman was worthless, no better than a whore. Even when the private detective was following her, she was cheating on him. I wanted to tell him everything. Our relationship was fine before she came and ruined everything."

"How did José get to know this woman?"

"At some restaurant."

"You also called the woman," said Susisaari.

136

"And rightly so. She ought to be a little nervous. That doesn't mean I did anything to her."

"So what did you tell her?"

"I told her I knew what a whore she was, and that I'd tell everybody."

"And what did she say?"

"She laughed. But I know she was afraid I'd tell José."

"Where were you on Sunday?"

The woman thought for a moment.

"You'll find out anyway... I took Heidi to a friend's house. She lives very close... I thought about going to see José and trying to talk things through. I called him and suggested we meet, but he didn't want to. On the way there, I realized what I was doing and turned back."

"So you didn't go at all?" asked Susisaari.

"No."

"How did you know where the building was?"

"The address is in the phone book."

"If you didn't go to Oulunkylä, then where did you go?"

"I took the subway downtown and went for a walk to cool down. Then I went home... And I stopped at the store to buy some bread."

"What time was that?"

"Right around four o'clock."

"Do you have a receipt from the store?"

She thought for a moment. "Probably. I'm pretty sure I do."

She went into the entry, took a thick wallet out of her bag, and dug through it till she found what she was looking for.

"Here it is. It says ten after four."

Susisaari examined the receipt.

"So what time did you get home?"

"At five. You can ask my friend."

"Did you continue your sexual relationship with José after he left you?"

The woman turned to look at Susisaari. "Absolutely not!"

"José had sexual intercourse with somebody right before his death. It wasn't Liljeblad. Do you have a guess as to who that might have been?"

She appeared not to have understood the question. Finally, she said, "You mean there was somebody else in that woman's apartment?"

"Yes."

She buried her face in her hands.

"I don't know. I really don't."

Huusko had left the intimate questions for Susisaari. Now it was his turn.

"You mentioned that you knew Liljeblad had cheated on José. How did you know that?"

"The private investigator told me."

"Aho?"

"Yes."

"What did he say?"

"That he'd been following her, and she'd driven to Haukilahti and left the car in some secluded place by the seashore. Some guy had driven there for a rendezvous and they had sex in his car."

"Aho was supposed to follow José, not Liljeblad."

"Maybe he thought she was gonna meet José, but some other guy showed up."

"What did you do with the report?"

"I told you, I burned it."

"Did Aho show you any photographs?" asked Susisaari.

"Of the woman and this other guy?"

"Yes."

"No. I only wanted to know what José was doing."

"But with pictures you could've shown José what kind of woman he was keeping company with."

"I don't know if Aho took photos of them."

"That's what you say now, but why should we believe you?"

"If you don't believe me, ask him."

"How did you find him? He doesn't advertise in the yellow pages."

"Online. He has his own website."

Huusko suspected she was lying. Her reply had been preceded by a pause, for which there was no reason. Then she had turned away to stare at the potatoes in the pot.

"Where did you two meet when he turned the report over to you?"

"We met for lunch by my work."

"Whereabouts was that?"

"Once it was in the library coffee shop in Itäkeskus, the other time at an outdoor coffee shop. Other than that, we talked on the phone a few times. That's it."

"So you don't know where he lives?"

"No, I don't."

"I hope you're telling the truth."

"I am."

"Then you won't have any objections if we take a DNA sample from you?"

Susisaari's suggestion startled the woman.

"Now?"

"At the hospital. As soon as possible."

"Do I have to?"

"No, but you just said you're telling the truth. A little DNA sample shouldn't be any problem. Otherwise, we'd just get a warrant for it and search your home while we're at it."

"Take the sample. I haven't done anything to be ashamed of."

* * *

On the way to the car, Susisaari looked pensive.

"I hope she's not involved. The girl would wind up in foster care. It's already enough that her dad is dead."

"I don't think she is, not much, anyhow. But I think she was lying when you asked her how she found out about that private eye."

"Strange. I thought the same thing. But what reason would she have to lie about that? Especially when it's so easy to check."

"Maybe she knew Aho better than she let on. The guy's a dyed-in-the-wool ladies' man…least he used to be. Suppose she went to the bar to drown her sorrows and happened to bump into our king of the dance floor. Aho plays it cool at first, but then he slowly lets on what a world-renowned private eye he is. How he single-handedly cracked the mystery of the Marquis of Zanzibar's itchy balls. So she gets swept off her feet by Aho's tales of a thousand and one nights, and hires him for her own job."

"It's possible. She seemed ashamed about something."

"I would be too, if I woke up in the same bed as him."

Susisaari laughed, "Single parents have to get their kicks when they can."

"What's even more interesting is that this private investigator didn't tell her who Liljeblad's lover on the side was, though as an old cop, he well knew how important that information would be."

Susisaari unlocked the car doors with the key fob, and Huusko hunkered down into the passenger seat.

"Maybe he's a double agent selling information to both parties," said Susisaari as she turned on the ignition.

"What would he have that Liljeblad would want to pay for?"

"His silence. Not telling Hernando what he saw."

"That fits his style, but what reason would he have for keeping that information from us?"

Both detectives realized the same thing at the same time, but Susisaari managed to say it first, "Because he's blackmailing Liljeblad's lover from the seashore."

"You took the words out my mouth. Time to drag the dirty cop out of his hole and put him through the wringer. Not a good idea to lie to the police. Especially not to me."

* * *

Finding Aho was easier said than done. As Eila had mentioned, he did indeed have a webpage, but he didn't respond to email, nor answer his phone. His registered address was not current. He had leased his car, and the address registered to him at the Department of Motor Vehicles was the same as that at the Address Office: wrong.

The phone ultimately did the trick. Huusko's former girlfriend worked at one of the cellphone service providers, and managed to acquire the billing address connected to his account. It was in an old industrial building on Päijänteen Street.

Huusko hopped in his car and drove straight there. The staircase was in the courtyard, and the names of the businesses in the building were listed on the wall in the lobby, but Aho was not among them. Beneath the listings was a row of mailboxes. Huusko scanned the names and found the one he was looking for. On one, just beneath an engraved badge for *Print Brothers Inc.* was a piece of masking tape that read: *Aho Detective Agency.*

The throbbing of the printing presses could be heard from the stairwell, and the smell of ink and cleaning chemicals lingered in the air.

On the third floor landing was a pair of metal doors, one of them ajar, and Huusko stepped inside. The thousand-square-foot room housed two printing presses, both active. One was a newer-looking green go-getter, the other, old-fashioned and ornate. With clock-like precision, the latter contraption thundered away, all the while looking so fine that Huusko could almost picture it as a fixture in the corner of his living room. A man of about fifty, dressed in overalls, was standing next to the old machine. Huusko waved him away from the din.

"There's a name of another company on your mailbox. Who can tell me about that?"

"Ask the boss. Over there in the office."

The boss was sitting in the office, inspecting a print layout. Huusko nudged open the door, and the man turned to look. Huusko introduced himself.

"There's a name of another company on your mailbox, Aho Detective Agency. Does he operate out of this space?"

"Does it look like he does?"

"Not really. So what gives?"

"I gave him permission to use our postal address. Is he a criminal?"

"Not to my knowledge. Where can I get hold of him?"

"Don't ask me. What's he done?"

"Scooped out his toe jam in public. When's the last time he was here?"

"A few days ago."

"To do what?"

"He had a moving box here he had to pick up."

"Containing?"

"Some old stuff from his police days...newspaper clippings. Probably stuff for his investigations, photos and what not."

"When's he coming back?"

"No idea. Sometimes he comes once a day, sometimes once a week, depending on whether he's expecting mail. He gets mostly bills."

"How do you know this guy?"

"He's from my hometown. We grew up together."

"But you don't know where he lives?"

"The last few years he's been kind of a drifter. Spent a few nights in the shelter, and every so often he sleeps at some broad's house."

Aho's lifestyle sounded surprisingly familiar to Huusko.

"Disgusting. At his age, he should be settled down and taking up Nordic walking."

The print boss laughed.

"That's what I always tell him."

"What's the best way to get a hold of him? I'm looking for maybe a girlfriend's name or address."

"Can't help you there...that's over and done with. But if you leave your name and number I'll tell him to call you next time I see him. Or you could leave a letter in the mailbox."

"I think I'll do the opposite. Did he get any mail today?"

"I haven't checked."

Huusko held out his hand.

"The key."

"Isn't that mail fraud?"

"Not today. I'm in a bad mood."

"I'll come with."

The man took a key out of his desk drawer.

The mailbox contained some junk mail and four letters to Aho, which Huusko snatched from the man's hands.

Three of the letters were addressed by hand. The fourth was in an envelope from an east Helsinki locksmith. Huusko opened one of the handwritten envelopes. From the first lines it was clear that the writer was responding to an advertisement in the personals section entitled "Sun Child." Huusko refolded the letter and opened another. That, too, was responding to the same ad, as was the third.

"How many of these does he get?" asked Huusko.

"A couple dozen. I asked Aho about them, but he didn't tell me anything. Just said he's laying the groundwork for retirement."

The fourth letter was a bill from a locksmith for installing a deadbolt. The meticulous biller had even included the installation address: Lumikin Street 4, stairwell C.

"In Roihuvuori," Huusko said aloud.

"What is?"

"Nothing."

Huusko wrote down the address and handed the letters back to the man.

"When you see Aho, tell him to contact me ASAP, or he won't be a sun child for long."

* * *

144

The building on Lumikin Street was a couple of hundred yards away from Eila Tuuri's apartment, where Huusko had just been that morning.

And surprise, surprise, the mailbox for the apartment was in Aho's very own name. The sticker above the mailbox read, "No Ads." Huusko rang the doorbell relentlessly, but nobody answered. He inspected the deadbolt, which appeared to be brand new, went back downstairs and found the maintenance man's name on the notice board. He called, stated his case, and the maintenance man promised to be there in fifteen minutes.

To burn time, Huusko called Lea, who was at the flower shop.

"You busy?"

"Not right now. You?"

"Just waiting for the maintenance guy to come open the door. I miss you."

"Did you have time to pick up the tutu?"

"Of course. I know my priorities, right?"

They continued to chat for about five minutes when a customer walked into the flower shop, and Lea had to cut it off.

"I got a sitter for Saturday," she whispered. "So we'll be all alone. Any requests?"

"How 'bout a bubble bath for two and some champagne?"

"I'll take care of the bubble bath, you get the bubbly."

"Deal."

Huusko waited another ten minutes before the maintenance man arrived.

"You lucked out."

"How's that?"

"The tenant had a deadbolt installed last week, and wasn't going to share the key. I just happened to walk by, so I made him give me a spare. Just the rules. We need access to every apartment in case of emergency."

Huusko acknowledged his stroke of luck while the maintenance man fished out the right key and opened the door.

"I'm sure you have a search warrant," said the man.

"Of course," Huusko lied, and marveled that the man didn't ask to see it.

"Just let me know when you're done."

The apartment was a spacious studio with a kitchen nook. The main room featured a plush but dirty light-brown leather sofa and matching recliner. Between the set stood a glass coffee table. On the opposite wall was a chipboard shelf veneered with mahogany that housed a long row of porn films betraying a special preference for Asian women, along with some trophies and medals. A brief scan told Huusko that Aho had been a decent cross-country skier in his younger days, a fact that seemed hard to believe.

In the corner of the room was a 28″ TV beneath which stood a collection of movies. Several more porn tapes were stacked on top of the videos. Huusko perused the titles, then let his gaze wander the room. His eyes paused on a massive oil painting of a Finnish spitz that hung above the sofa.

He searched the closets and drawers, but it appeared that Aho had gone on vacation. There were few clean clothes, and no suitcases or bags. In view of Aho's lifestyle, such things would be essential, especially considering the old torn-off baggage ticket in the trash—he had traveled to the Hotel La Plaza in the Canary Islands. Another thing missing was the camera with the telephoto lens that Aho had used to snap the photos of Liljeblad and her trysts.

Huusko searched the apartment for another half an hour, but found nothing more of interest.

He wondered where Aho kept his work files, as there weren't any in the apartment. On the other hand, aside from the trophies, the apartment contained nothing of any personal significance—no photos, no diplomas, no army paraphernalia.

Huusko went back to the kitchen and noticed two keys on a nail over the counter. He slipped them off the nail and went up into the attic, which stretched the length of the building, and was surprisingly tidy. Huusko could hear the rustling of pigeons on the roof. One of the keys fit the lock for an attic closet walled with chicken wire, but he didn't bother to open it. There were only a pair of skis, poles and four kitchen chairs.

He went downstairs into the basement and wandered the hallways for a while until he found a row of storage units. The building was old, and the storage closets— originally intended for vegetables, potatoes, and berries—had sturdy hardwood doors.

Huusko tried the second key in one of the locks, and it opened. He could still smell the earthy scent of root crops from seasons long past. A mummified potato lay on the ground, a pale sprout the length of a hand jutting from its side. The potato looked as if it might turn to dust under the mere weight of his gaze. On the wall were a few wooden shelves, and for the potatoes, a bin with corn crib siding that now held only a plastic tub with a lid.

Huusko lifted the tub out into the hallway. The lid was tight, and he had to use some force before it finally opened.

The contents of the tub were a disappointment. There was a policeman's hat, a belt, and two thick folders full of yellowing newspaper clippings of various sex

147

scandals and prostitution cases. The oldest of them was from the early seventies, and the most recent, from the eighties. Huusko guessed that Aho had had to leave the department in '85 or '86. A few black-and-white photographs were also mixed in, one showing a beautiful girl of about twenty sitting naked on the edge of the bed, trying to conceal her breasts with her hands. In the background, an older man was frantically pulling up his pants. There was something comical about the picture that made Huusko smile, and he guessed it had made many others smile as well. The pictures of police raids had probably been squirreled away for Aho's own titillation.

Huusko scanned the clippings and recalled one of the cases. Because it had involved two politicians, a few CEOs, and a well-known prosecutor, it had garnered a lot of attention. The case had been handled behind closed doors, and the names had never been revealed. Of course, the press found out, but none of the local rags had dared to print the news. Apparently, Aho had been involved in the investigation.

Huusko continued on until he happened upon a blank sheet of paper. Some glue residue was evident, and a strip of paper was missing where something had been torn off. All the other clippings were intact.

Huusko searched the floor again and climbed onto the storage bin so he could see onto the topmost shelf. Empty.

He was just climbing down when he noticed a few crumbs of concrete in the corner of the shelf. He glanced up. At the ceiling juncture was an old-style vent that could be opened by pulling on a string. Huusko grabbed the ring where the string was supposed to be and pulled. The vent opened with a clang and a pile of garbage, pigeon shit, and a few feathers tumbled out. It was too high up to see into, so Huusko stuck his hand in and struck upon a glossy piece of paper. He removed what turned out to be a black-and-white photograph of the same raid as the one with the man pulling up his pants, but with a different subject. In this photograph, a younger man was getting busy with a woman kneeling on all fours in front of him. The picture had been taken from the rear, and the man's face was not visible. His hair was short and dark.

Huusko wiped the dust away from what appeared to be a broad U-shaped spot on the man's right buttock. He looked more closely. It was a birthmark.

* * *

Huusko was already on the way to Pasila police headquarters when his cell phone rang.

"Where are you?" said Susisaari.

"On the way back from Aho's apartment."

"You find anything?"

"Nothing special. Looks like the weasel packed his bags and took off somewhere."

"Well, come back to the station right away. The meeting starts in half an hour. I guess we got some new leads."

"What leads?"

"Don't know, we'll find out then."

"Put some coffee on for me."

Despite the pounding rain slowing the pace of traffic on the East Highway, Huusko made it back to the station in just over fifteen minutes. Driving against the flow of rush hour traffic, the roads had been free flowing all the way back.

He stopped by his desk and had time to check his email before the meeting started. A former co-worker had invited him out for a beer on Saturday, but Huusko didn't feel like going.

The conference room was in full swing—even Kempas had come. Jansson stood, his way of giving emphasis to his words.

"Forensics has brought forth some new and significant information, which means we need to reevaluate the case. Up to this point we've been following several different leads, which have yielded some results, but now it may be necessary to concentrate our efforts in one track. I'd be more than happy to hear your thoughts."

Jansson picked up a bottle of mineral water and took a sip.

"Forensics has analyzed the fingerprints found on the condom package from Oulunkylä. We haven't received the DNA results for the semen yet, but there's little doubt of what that will be."

Jansson took a brief pause, during which he gazed off into the distance.

"The fingerprints belong to private investigator Aho, which would seem to indicate that the contents of the condom belong to him as well."

A wave of surprise swept through the listeners. Huusko was the first to find words.

"No surprise that he took off, then. The guy's a regular energizer bunny."

"Has he gone somewhere?" asked Jansson.

Jansson's expression hardened as he listened to Huusko's findings from the apartment, "We'll have to put out an immediate APB on him. I'd suggest that at least for now, we focus on him and the woman who slept with Hernando... Could it be that she and Aho have been working together?"

"Why would that be?" said Huusko.

"I don't know. Aho surprised us once. Maybe he's involved in drug trafficking."

Kempas straightened his back and crossed his arms like an Indian chief sitting around a campfire. "I've known Aho for long enough to know what kind of rat he is. I can think of two reasons right off why a woman like Liljeblad would stoop to working with Aho."

"We're all ears," said Jansson.

"Reason number one. Liljeblad had something to gain from Aho, either financially or otherwise. Maybe Aho was involved in the drug trade, or maybe he was protecting her from something. Drugs are a dangerous business. Reason number two. Aho knew something about Liljeblad and was blackmailing her into sex. It seems to suit him. A guy like that isn't bothered much by his conscience. Those types only change for the better when they're six feet under."

"So you think it's possible that Aho would dare get involved with drugs?" said Jansson.

"He's had persistent financial problems, and he's deep in debt. In that situation, he'd be tempted by money regardless of where it came from."

"Why do you think he met Liljeblad at the airport on Sunday evening?" said Malmberg. "It had to have been him on the footage. She didn't change passengers mid-trip."

Kempas wrinkled his broad brow. "Maybe she was afraid something was going to happen that night, and so she asked for protection. On the way home, not surprisingly, Aho asks for an advance, and she pays him in the parking lot."

"Maybe even gave him a cash bonus, too," laughed Huusko.

Malmberg had thought it out further.

"Liljeblad had her man waiting at home. Why didn't she ask Hernando to come to the airport if she was so scared?"

"Maybe she was scared of him...or his South American buddies," said Kempas.

Huusko raised his hand. "Okay, let's assume that Aho was acting as her bodyguard, which seems credible to me, and yet the woman was killed. So where was Aho when it happened? We know he was with Liljeblad in the Mazda at the Oulunkylä ball fields. That's like a five-mile walk to his place in Roihuvuori, so he wouldn't have jumped out there. So he had to have been in the car all the way to her apartment. She was killed as soon as she got home, so either Aho is the killer, which doesn't seem probable, or he was nearby when the victims were killed. In that case, he had to have seen something."

"Maybe that's why he's running...he saw something and got spooked," suggested Lehto. "Figured he wouldn't live long with the cartel on his ass."

Jansson nodded with satisfaction. "So does anyone have a theory as to who Hernando was having sex with?"

Susisaari raised her pen. "Could be Tuuri, Hernando's ex. She lied to us once, and when we cornered her, she admitted to having intended to go to Liljeblad's apartment on Sunday to confront him. She's also threatened Liljeblad. Another thing is that she lives in Roihuvuori, just a couple hundred yards from Aho, so it's possible that Aho and Tuuri know each other. I think we need a DNA sample from her."

"Might she have killed them both?" said Jansson.

"I doubt it. It's possible she could have killed Liljeblad in a rage, but it's hard to believe she would have killed Hernando. I think she still loved him. Plus, they had a child together. It's more likely that she went to the apartment to have sex with him, and left before the killer got there."

"Get a DNA sample as soon as possible, but the results will take a few days, in any case. In the meantime, we need to pursue other avenues."

Kempas looked at Jansson. "So what's the division of labor?"

"Narcotics and Undercover will be joining the investigation. Kempas will head up undercover ops for us, and Karila will run the case for Narcotics. They'll focus on the drug angle, we'll concentrate on the murders. The case is now being investigated as a double murder. I realize the cases will overlap somewhat, but I think we'll be fine if all the departments are kept updated, and we keep the competition and jealousy in check."

"Who said anything about competition?" said Huusko wryly.

Lehto and Malmberg laughed. Huusko glanced over at Kempas, who was sitting just as stiffly as before, staring straight ahead—a man clearly beyond reproach.

* * *

After the meeting, Huusko invited Susisaari over to his desk and pulled a photograph from one of his desk drawers.

"What's this?" she said.

"I found it in Aho's cellar. He'd stashed it in a vent."

"What's so special about it?"

"There's a U-shaped birthmark on the man's right butt cheek."

"And?"

"Nothing special about it otherwise. You follow me?"

Susisaari glanced at the back of the photo where someone had penciled a date and the initials AK.

"No. May 7, 1984. AK."

"The cops were investigating a big prostitution case at that time involving some big names. Aho was one of the detectives."

"Somebody else must've taken the picture."

"Right...this AK. I'll have to find out who that is."

"Who's the guy getting his rocks off?"

"Don't know, but the birthmark is a good clue...which must be why Aho hid the picture."

"We're talking ancient history here. Why would Aho be worried about it now?"

"He removed a box of stuff from his office a few days back. Why? Maybe he remembered something and wanted to check it out. Or maybe he picked up the box for no particular reason, and while he was going through the files, he noticed something that made this photo seem important."

"And what might that have been?"

"This is just a guess, but I think a good one. When's the last time Aho snapped a photo of a bare ass?"

Susisaari thought for a moment before answering.

"In Haukilahti. When he was trailing Liljeblad."

"Bingo. So I'd be interested to know if that ass had the same birthmark as the one in this photo."

11.

Kempas was confident that beneath Saramaa's hard shell lay a cowardly man. Saramaa's courage was the same as that of a little boy who pokes fun from a safe distance, but bursts out crying as soon as his safety is in jeopardy.

Kempas intended to rid Saramaa of any notion that he was safe behind his shield of success and connections. He would shake that ivory tower so hard that Saramaa would topple out to join the mortals below.

One look at Saramaa's offices made it clear that the man had made a mint off of his legal practice. The reception area was furnished with timeless classics, and the walls with expensive art. Three other lawyers were employed there, along with an assistant and a secretary. The secretary was no nail-filing high-schooler either, but an adult woman radiating with professionalism.

Kempas looked at the clock on the wall. Ten o'clock sharp. Then he glanced at his watch: three minutes past. It was still running far too fast, though Kempas had already brought it to his favorite watchmaker twice. He decided to bring it in for service a third time, and also swap out the stretchy metal band—his arm hairs usually got pinched in the gaps. Style always came with a price.

"I'm Lieutenant Kempas. I've got a ten o'clock appointment."

The woman looked up from her computer screen. "If you could wait just a moment, Mr. Saramaa will be with you shortly."

Kempas took a seat in the waiting room chair, and began paging through a *National Geographic* featuring an interesting article on some mummies discovered in the Andes. Kempas became so engrossed in the story that he nearly forgot where he was. Only when the secretary called his name did he snap out of it.

"Counselor Saramaa will see you now."

"Counselor," as far as Kempas was concerned, was the height of overindulgence. Saramaa was a scoundrel and a knave, not a counselor.

Kempas stood and walked through the door as the secretary held it open. Saramaa got up from behind his desk and came to greet him with an open hand. Kempas gave it a strong squeeze. Saramaa pulled his hand away and looked at it.

"You must lift weights. Please, sit."

Kempas sat down in a leather chair with a frame made of steel tubing. The cushion felt as though it had been filled with air that slowly leaked out as he sat on it. Kempas looked it over, and Saramaa took notice.

"We prefer Danish classics."

"So do I," said Kempas. "But I'm not so sure we're talking about the same thing."

"I have half an hour at the most, and then I have to meet with another client. Shall we get started?"

"Sure."

"Is it okay if I record our conversation?"

"No."

"Then this must be unofficial business?"

"Very much so."

Saramaa took out a notepad and pen. "Then I'll just take a few notes if you don't mind."

Kempas was undeterred by Saramaa's antics. He knew that the lawyer was trying to make a point that he should watch his words…and he always did.

"Pedro Bolivar and Santos Ramirez. You could almost mistake them for a couple of Colombian coffee farmers. I'm sure you recall them?"

Saramaa's only response was to raise an eyebrow.

"Currently Swedish citizens residing in Gothenburg. Both convicted murderers and drug dealers from the Valiente syndicate."

"I'm sure you've heard of the Western notion that convicts start with a clean slate after serving their sentences?"

"I'm sure you've heard the saying, 'God has mercy; I do not?'"

"I'm sure you've been reading too many trashy mysteries."

"And I'd recommend them to you, too. You'll find all kinds of fitting quotes for all of life's quandaries."

"That sort of language would hardly be suitable for my profession."

"On the contrary, it'd be perfect. You lawyers already have too much of an affinity with snakes. Come on out from behind your gray suits and speak like regular people."

"Like yourself, I suppose?"

"Something like that."

"If you're asking for donations to the fraternal order of the police, you can speak with my secretary."

Saramaa glanced at his watch, which boasted a snakeskin wristband and a rectangular watch face. There was no doubt of its expense. "There went five minutes."

"You met with Bolivar and Ramirez in May. I'd like to know what they wanted."

Saramaa flashed him a smile. "You can't possibly think I would answer that."

"Both are suspects in a double murder that's connected to a large-scale drug dealing case. You know that gives us a fair amount of latitude."

"Latitude for what?"

"Home searches, phone taps, arrests and interrogations, to say nothing of what goes on off the record. I could give you an enema with a six-inch garden hose, if I wanted."

"I think I'll record this conversation after all. Your colorful language deserves to be documented for posterity."

Saramaa reached for the tape recorder on his desk.

Kempas got up, snatched it off the desk, opened the window and looked down. The building's roof was being repaired and a dumpster full of debris was parked in front of it. Kempas took the shot and scored.

"If you think that…"

"Shut up. The clock is ticking."

Saramaa fell silent.

"Let me tell you a little more about these two Bolivian coffee pickers. Both are suspects in at least three murders, which have been linked to drug trafficking throughout Scandinavia. The twosome have now started a partnership with the Russian mafia, so a boatload of new bad guys is entering the picture, each of them willing and able to kill, rape, and chop up anyone without ever ruining their appetites. Are you sure you know what you're getting into?"

Saramaa was silent.

"I know a lawyer from Gothenburg who didn't. He handled the Valiente family's affairs for two years and got in so deep that he hung himself from the porch roof of his summer cottage."

Kempas took a photograph out of his jacket pocket and slid it across to Saramaa.

"Kind of idyllic, actually. A nice touch, hanging himself amid the splendor of the Värmland lakes."

Saramaa glanced at the photograph and swallowed.

"The Valientes' other lawyer sold everything he had, packed his bags, and moved to Portugal. Haven't heard whether he's still alive... You really think you can just skim off the top and pick and choose the jobs you like? Maybe to start with, you can, but they'll have you doing the dirty work in due time. A family member will go to prison for murder—as he should—and you'll end up being their little pageboy, ferrying notes in and out of the pen. Then you'll start toting suitcases full of cash to some offshore bank in Gibraltar."

Kempas looked at Saramaa at length. "You married?"

Saramaa nodded.

"Children?"

"Two."

"Let's pick up where we left off with the suitcase. You'll bring it where you're told, even if you risk winding up as cockroach food in some Spanish prison. If you don't, your wife will have an 'accident' and break her leg, or your cabin will burn down, or your kids will go for a little ride on their way home from school."

Kempas let his words sink in. Then he looked at his watch and stretched out the band. His arm hair had gotten stuck in the band and it was pinching his skin. How the hell had he made the mistake of buying a metal wristband?

"Only fifteen minutes left," said Kempas.

"I'm a corporate attorney, they wouldn't use me for criminal cases."

"To them, one lawyer is the same as the next. If they tell you to sing an aria, that's what you'll do, and they'll enjoy the show. And no matter how loyal you are to them, or how hard you work, at some point they'll start to think that you know too much. That's when they'll invite you to Bolivia for a visit and bury you in the jungle or feed you to the piranhas or an army of fire ants.

Or do you really think they'd just say 'tsk, tsk,' cut up your silk tie, and kick mud on your shoes?"

Kempas was quiet, and looked absent-minded.

Saramaa wiped his forehead and said dryly, "Go on."

"That's it. Just wanted to tell you what'll happen if you work with the Valientes."

"So what do you want?"

What seemed a simple question revealed his willingness to negotiate. Saramaa's ivory tower was beginning to crumble.

"I don't think you're too far along yet, you can still back out. But the further you go, the harder it will be. If you help us, you'll have a good chance of freeing yourself of the Valientes and putting this whole thing behind you. If not, prepare for the nightmare."

"What do you mean by 'help?'"

"Why'd you meet with those two thugs?"

"Do you promise that my statements won't be used against them in court?"

"Yes."

Saramaa paused, and Kempas shook his tower once more.

"Look at the photo. You got a cabin?"

Saramaa glanced reflexively at the photo.

"They're interested in either purchasing or founding their own produce wholesaler."

"In Finland?"

"Yes. I was to search for a suitable business and make a bid on their behalf. And if something suitable wasn't available, to start a new one and take care of the paperwork."

"Why are they getting into the produce business?"

"It's not my call to ask why my clients want something. I simply do everything I can to ensure that they get it. That's what I'm paid for."

"I'm sure you're smart enough to have given the question some thought."

"I figured it might have something to do with ordinary money laundering."

"Money laundering is ordinary?"

"Money abides by its own laws. In capitalism, that's acceptable."

"They must have told you something about themselves."

"Just that they're working for an investment firm in Sweden, and the firm wants to invest in the food industry."

"So, in your judgment, they looked like businessmen?"

"I don't judge my clients by their appearance."

"Did you find them something suitable?"

"Not yet."

"Any bids?"

"Two."

"Does 'Southern Fruits Inc.' mean anything to you?"

"That's one of the companies I approached with a bid."

"But they weren't interested?"

"It's a family business, and they already have a successor."

"Was it you who found this business, or did they suggest it?"

"They had heard that it might be for sale, and asked me to find out about it."

"How did they react when they found out it wasn't for sale?"

"I don't really know... I suppose they were a bit disappointed."

"How long are your clients willing to wait before they start their own?"

"I've already received the go ahead to launch the company."

"When?"

"Just over a week ago."

"By phone?"

Saramaa stared at his desktop with arms folded.

"They came to Helsinki."

"Are they in Finland right now?"

"I don't know. I haven't been in contact with them since."

"Where did you meet?"

"At the Hotel Kämp…where they were staying."

"Is there anything else?"

"The last time we met, they asked me to find out about Southern Fruits' distribution channels...how they distribute the produce to stores."

"Why'd they wanna know?"

"So they'd know what kind of competition to expect and what kind of business they're getting into. Effective distribution and logistics are of interest to them."

"So what have you done about it?"

"Nothing. I told them that it was impossible to find out, at least by legal means."

"And what did they say?"

"That I can use whatever means I have to, as long as I find out."

"Very generous of your clients to give you such free rein."

Saramaa looked at Kempas. His cheek twitched, and his eyes betrayed their fear. "Is there anything else?" he said.

"I was wondering the same thing."

"I've told you everything."

"Did you hear any names, or observe them meeting anybody?"

162

"No, but they apparently had a friend in Helsinki. My understanding was that he was a compatriot of theirs...a Bolivian, I mean. I know a bit of Spanish."

"Could you elaborate a bit?"

"I don't know who he was."

"Did they mention a woman? A Finnish blonde, for example?"

Kempas could see that his guess had hit the mark.

"Somebody called one of them to set up a meeting while we were at lunch... He told the caller something along the lines of 'Don't bring the blonde along.'"

"Did they mention a meeting spot?"

"No. It was a short phone call. He said he'd call back."

"Did these clients arrive by plane or boat?"

"Plane."

"Are you sure?"

Saramaa consulted his desk calendar. "It's right here. Flight from Stockholm, arriving 10:25 A.M."

Kempas jotted the time down in his notepad.

"How do you intend to get in contact with them if you have something to tell them?"

"I have a nu..."

"If I'm not mistaken, you were about to say you have a phone number."

"I can't reveal it. They'll find out."

"No, they won't. I need that number."

Saramaa slid open his desk drawer and took out a phone directory. He looked up the number and read it to Kempas.

Kempas stood up. "Thanks for your cooperation. I expect you to contact me if you hear anything more."

Saramaa stood, too. He smoothed the breast of his suit coat nervously.

"You promised I wouldn't get dragged into anything… I'll continue to help as best I can."

"Thanks for offering. Many hands make light work," said Kempas.

Saramaa's new client was waiting behind the door, a slim, gray-haired man, clutching a black briefcase to his chest. The man looked warily at Kempas.

Kempas strode into the hallway and pressed the button for the elevator. He felt content, and not the least bit bothered by the fact that he had had to exaggerate a bit to gain Saramaa's cooperation. The fire ants and piranhas had been a nice flourish. Nor was he bothered by the fact that his photo of a "Swedish attorney" was actually a civil engineer who had hung himself on the porch of his cabin in eastern Finland.

Kempas was a firm believer that sometimes the end justified the means.

12.

"What do you mean missing?" said Joseph Espocio with a foreboding tone in his voice. Diego's uncle was known for his short wick, even within a family with as hot-blooded a reputation as theirs. If he sensed that someone was about to tell him bad news, he would raise his hands as if to swat it away, and say with a smile, "Is there a problem?" Diego could imagine his uncle's black eyes hardening, like two iron nails.

Bearing the brunt of Uncle's gaze was no fun if you were behind on your debts or had screwed up a job, even if you happened to be Espocio's nephew, and even if he had nicknamed you "Popo."

Diego knew his uncle, and had thought long and hard about when to make the phone call, and how to break the news. He had decided to speak frankly, and to ask for advice. His aim was to paint a picture of a dutiful nephew in dire straits, in need of guidance from his experienced uncle.

"We caught up with them, but one of the kids had a piece and shot me in the leg. Rafael killed him, but the other one got away. I told the others to go after him so me and Simon could ditch the body."

"So what's the problem?"

The problem. Diego felt his stomach turn. There was that word. And that tone of voice.

"No problem. I'm just trying to tell you what happened."

"Get on with it, then. And quickly, I'm busy."

"We waited for them so we wouldn't get separated. It was a pretty remote area."

Diego considered what to say next and his uncle grew impatient.

"Go on."

Diego told him about the Lopez brothers going missing.

"Are they still missing?"

"No, we found them. But someone shot them both in the shoulder…"

"You said there wasn't a problem. That sounds like a problem."

The edge in Uncle's voice was sharper now.

"I thought you told me that place is no bigger than a cow pie. How does someone capable of getting the better of the Lopez brothers just happen to be in the middle of the woods like that? They might not be the brightest, but they're still pros…"

"Well, I've been thinking about it…"

"That's great, Popo," Espocio hissed. "Why don't you tell me all about it."

"Well…maybe that shipment wasn't sent here by accident like José claimed."

Diego let his words sink in.

"You mean it was stolen?"

"Yes."

"By who? The Russians?"

"Maybe. Or maybe José himself. He could've recruited some help."

"No way. He wouldn't dare steal dirty socks, much less betray the family."

"What about the Russians."

"I've been negotiating with Kirilev myself. He knows the business won't run without us. Why would he do

166

that? Our partnership is worth millions to him. He's not stupid."

"What about someone else, then? Say one of Kirilev's men that knew about the shipment."

Only the sound of Uncle's hoarse breathing came from the receiver. The man was a lifelong smoker.

"What do you want me to do, Uncle? We've seen a doctor… We're here in the hotel room now…"

Diego was pleased by his use of the word "you." It spoke to his desire to involve his boss in decision making, and at the same time, it put the ball in his uncle's court.

"You're asking me what to do?"

"Yes."

"You're there and I'm here, and you're asking *me* what to do? You think I have a crystal ball or something? Didn't I put *you* in charge of this operation?"

"Yes, you did, Uncle."

"And did I force it on you, or did you volunteer for it?"

"I volunteered for it, Uncle."

"You're my dear sister's son. I held you in my arms when you were hardly two hours old. You asked for the opportunity, and I gave it to you."

"I know Uncle, but…"

"I'll speak with Kirilev. You take care of problems on your end, Popo. You know how I and everyone else will react. It's as much a matter of principle as it is of money. We wouldn't want to lose either."

Diego listened to the sound of the dead line for a moment, then set the phone down in his lap. He felt the same way he had as a child, when his father had taught him to swim. Thrown him into the pool and watched him thrash and flail over to the edge.

Diego grimaced as he bent down and touched his leg gingerly. Manolo Perez, the Spanish doctor, had known how to treat it, but even more so, he had known how to bill for it. Altogether, Diego's and the Lopez brothers' billing statement had come to more than five thousand euros. Perez had justified his price by the fact that he had come to the clinic late in the evening, almost at night. And by the fact that he had endangered his medical license by not reporting the gunshot wounds to the police.

The antibiotics, a couple of bottles of powerful pain meds, and spare bandages were on the house. As the patients had filed out of the office, Diego had overheard Perez ask Simon.

"What war are they fighting?"

"Finland versus Bolivia. Finland's leading one-zip."

Later on, Simon had got them some rooms at a nice downtown Helsinki hotel, and ordered some dinner and drinks from room service. Diego had taken his pain medication and fallen asleep almost immediately.

He had awakened to the alarm clock on his phone at eight-thirty in the morning, carefully washed himself so as not to wet the bandages on his leg, and gotten dressed. Then he had taken a deep breath and called his uncle. In this land, mornings never started out right.

Now Diego took another deep breath and padded off quietly to the hotel dining room for breakfast. His partners already had their plates brimming with food from the buffet. Diego didn't have much of an appetite.

The younger Lopez dangled a filet of smoked salmon from the end of his fork.

"Try this with some scrambled eggs. Sooo good."

Simon was more interested in Diego's plans than food.

"You call your uncle?"

"Why should I?" he lied. "It's four of us against one man and a kid. What's the problem?"

"I can ask a couple friends of mine for help," said Simon.

"Four's plenty," said Diego, his foot aching in spite of the pain medication. "Have you figured out who shot these two?" he asked Simon.

The elder Lopez turned to look at Diego. "A professional, that's for sure. You think he could've taken us otherwise?"

"What's a professional doing in the middle of the woods?" asked Simon.

The elder Lopez stuffed half a boiled egg into his mouth. "Still a professional."

"Don't speak with your mouth full," Diego snapped. "Even if you are a pig, you don't have to make it so obvious."

The younger Lopez swallowed his food before speaking, "When he saw we had Swedish driver's licenses he started speaking in fluent Swedish. Pretty sure he's lived in Sweden before."

"Describe him," said Diego. "You saw him in the daylight."

"Maybe forty years old. Fairly tall. Messy hair. Seemed like a bit of a bum, but fit. Light on his feet, moved fast as hell and shot straight…as you can see. His gun was a nine-millimeter Beretta. My brother's right; he's a pro. Ordinary hicks don't strut around with Berettas stuffed in their belts."

"You think it was just a coincidence that the boy led you there?"

The younger Lopez looked at his brother. "What do you think?"

The elder drank the remainder of his juice. "Seemed like a coincidence to me. When this guy appeared, the boy looked just as surprised as we did. Besides, the kid fell in the yard, and he might have kept going if he hadn't."

"Quite a stroke of luck for the little shit," said Simon. "I'd bet that guy was the only person within a hundred-mile radius besides the cops who could've helped in that situation."

Diego's sour mood persisted, and his tone became sharp and demanding, "If the guy's a professional, and lived in Sweden, then our guys gotta know him, or at least of him. That sort of guy doesn't just appear outta nowhere. He's gotta have a past, a record, some jail time, that sort of thing. I want every one of you to ask your friends. And ask the Russians, too. And that means right after breakfast."

"Got it," said the elder Lopez as he got up to fill his plate again.

Diego pointed his fork at Simon, "And you. You think we can find out who owns the house? Say from a local property information database?"

"I can try to find out."

"Get going, then. I wanna know who we're up against."

Simon got up, and Diego watched with irritation as he left.

"I'm pretty sure he got a slice of that fucking doctor's bill."

"That's for sure," said the younger Lopez as he poked at his teeth with a toothpick.

Diego glanced at the table in front of him. "Your knife and fork!"

The younger Lopez looked at his silverware. "What about them?"

"Put 'em at five o'clock! How the hell is the waiter supposed to know you're done?"

The younger Lopez looked at Diego. The boss had been on edge ever since Hernando had lost the shipment. And no wonder, he thought. The boss would become the late boss unless the shipment was found.

* * *

The men had gathered in Diego's hotel room at two in the afternoon. Simon looked at ease, confident that he had done the best of the three. He had found the name of the property owner in a database. The owner had died the previous fall, and the new owner hadn't yet registered the property. Nevertheless, with the help of a former police officer he had managed to find a lead. The officer had contacted an old co-worker who had said Nygren had been a career criminal, and his nephew had taken the house. According to the police database, this nephew lived at times in Sweden, at other times in Denmark, and was considered to be an extremely dangerous and violent criminal.

Diego opened the mini-bar, took out a bottle of beer and opened it. The Lopez brothers looked longingly at the bar, but Diego ignored their ogling. He sat down on the sofa, took a swig from the bottle and eyed the others.

"Well, who's going first?"

The brothers glanced at one another, then the elder spoke up.

"I called everyone who knew even a little bit about anything. The only good tip I got was from the Russians, who're looking for the guy who shot Zetov in Stockholm last spring. According to a tip they got, the hit man was a Finn. They were hunting him down, but he left Sweden, probably for here."

"Did you get this guy's name?" asked Diego.

"Not his actual name, but he has an alias."

"Which is?"

Lopez looked to his younger brother for help.

"What was it again?"

"Raid. You know…like the roach killer. You remember those funny animated ads where…"

"Simon? How 'bout you?" said Diego.

Simon told what he knew, and Diego's expression softened a bit.

"Sounds like the same guy."

"Either way, he won't catch us off guard again," said the elder Lopez.

"You forgot one thing," said the younger.

"What?"

"That the Russians paid some crazy Finnish hit man to kill the guy. Two hundred thousand krona on his head, and the hit man already got fifty of it as an advance."

The elder Lopez perked up. "I'm their man. May as well fork over the money now…I'll even give 'em a discount."

"First we get the boy, then we have some fun," said Diego. Finally, despite all of the adversity, it felt to him like the tide might be turning in the right direction.

13.

The car was parked beneath a tall birch, and plastered with hundreds of fallen leaves. From a distance, it appeared to have been splattered with yellow paint.

The car was at the end of a partially overgrown forest road, at a small clearing. Through the patchy blanket of fallen leaves, the tire ruts in the road were barely visible. It had been raining all day, and the soil was soft and damp.

In the afternoon, the rain had died down a little, and the leaves in the trees and the boughs of the spruces were filled with raindrops that bulged and bulged, until they finally fell to the ground.

The forest was largely a mix of old birches and spruces, interspersed by a few young, scrubby, speckled alder trunks. Anyone walking through these woods focusing only on the trees could easily imagine themselves to be deep in the wilderness. But in reality, the highway was only a few hundred yards away, its constant drone occasionally punctuated by the roar of some noisy truck.

A flash of yellow flickered from among the trees, and an elderly woman in a mustard-colored raincoat appeared on the far edge of the clearing. On her head was a felt beret; on her feet, low cut rubber boots; and in her hand, a basket full of mushrooms.

She stopped to pluck a family of chanterelles from their secluded hideout beneath the leaves and twigs. Only once the entire golden brood was in the basket—father, mother, siblings, and cousins—did she continue happily on her way. She could scarcely imagine anything better than chanterelle soup or a creamy chanterelle sauce. And what was more, these delicacies were free, no small matter for a woman on a state pension.

As she emerged into the clearing, a raven burst noisily from a birch, and when she saw the car, she stopped. It was almost new, a silvery gray, and dappled with yellow birch leaves.

She hesitated briefly before crossing the glade.

In the center of the glade was a weathered bench cobbled together from two stones and a plank of wood. Off to the left were the rear axle of an old car, a rusted-through muffler, and an old battery with its lead-acid cells peeking out from beneath the cracked housing.

She continued on across the glade, stopped a few yards away from the silvery-gray car and listened briefly, then set the basket on the ground and approached the vehicle. It occurred to her that maybe the car had been stolen and left in the woods after a joyride, and that the owner or the insurance company would offer a reward for its return.

An open suitcase was lying on the ground behind the car. Clothing was strewn on the ground as if somebody had been frantically searching for something. The woman looked around and spotted a dark brown wallet next to the rear tire. Rain and moisture from the earth had soaked through it, and a yellow birch leaf had fixed itself onto it like a sort of emblem.

The billfold was empty, as were the credit card slots, but there was a driver's license in the transparent plastic sleeve—the man in the photo appearing to be in his fifties. His dark hair was thinning on top, and his facial features were imbued with a heavy sense of melancholy.

The woman searched the wallet and found a couple of unused postage stamps and a few business cards, all bearing the same name: Henri Aho. Beneath the name, it read: "Private Investigator, Detective Services, 30 years of experience," and then a telephone number.

She looked once more at the driver's license—the name matched the business cards.

Then she went to the driver's side door, wiped the rain off the window and glanced inside. Her heart sank.

In the driver's seat was a man, and in his temple, a small, red hole.

* * *

"It's Aho, alright," said Susisaari as she studied the cab card from the glove box.

"About to take a trip somewhere," said Jansson, nodding at the suitcase lying on the ground.

Susisaari glanced around the interior of the car. A broad-brimmed fedora lay on the back seat, nothing more. Then she pointed to the blood spatters on the driver's side window and door.

"He was shot by someone in the passenger seat with a small-caliber weapon. The bullet just barely pierced through the skull, but didn't have enough energy to break the window. So he was either forced to come here or he met someone here. In any case, the car is his."

"Was he armed?"

"If he was, not legally."

Susisaari stepped aside as the Forensics techs assembled an aluminum frame and tent around the car.

Jansson's old friend, Lieutenant Pajula, stepped out of a Vantaa squad car. Once Pajula had realized that the Helsinki PD had an APB out on Aho, he had called Jansson immediately.

"Well, what do you think?"

"Yep, we'll take it," said Jansson.

"Connected to your case, then?"

"Appears so."

"Good. Our forensics team will take care of the crime scene, but we'll send the results to you. I'm too busy at the moment anyhow."

Jansson knew that Pajula was investigating a drive-by shooting in Tikkurila, where two Vietnamese immigrants had been killed in front of their home. The press had been reporting on it for several days now, portraying it as yet another example of the arrival of hard-core racism to Finland. Both neo-Nazis and right-wing radicals had been mentioned.

"So I heard."

"Well, don't believe everything you read in the papers. We're not talking about a couple of Boy Scouts. Both had previous drug convictions. Probably a turf war or something."

"Well, you focus on that—we'll take Aho. If we find anything interesting, we'll be in touch."

"I'll make sure you guys get all the tips, if we get any," said Pajula.

"Thanks."

"I'm gonna have a look around," said Susisaari.

Pajula watched her leave, then turned to Jansson.

"I spoke to the woman who found him, and I released her. She hadn't seen anything…just happened to find the car while out mushrooming. Older woman. The car's been here at least a day, maybe longer."

"Looks that way," said Jansson.

"You have any idea what this is about?" asked Pajula.

"A few theories. Did you find anything interesting on the body or in the car?"

"Only thing interesting to me is that he didn't have a cell phone or a passport, even though he appears to be going somewhere. Otherwise, his suitcase was packed with all the typical things, including toothpaste and a shaver. The suitcase was lying open on the ground. Same with his wallet. So either the killer was looking for something, or he tried to stage the scene to look like a robbery, but how would we know if it was or wasn't."

"How do we ever know," said Jansson. "Aho's just not the type of guy to have a lot to steal, least not in the traditional sense."

"So what's it about then?"

"I dunno."

Jansson spotted Huusko driving up in an old white Golf.

"Wasn't he a former police officer working as a PI?" said Pajula.

"That's right."

"Did you know him?"

"I met him, but I never knew him."

"This is a pretty remote spot," said Pajula. "Which begs the question: how'd the killer get out of here? Did he bring his own car beforehand or did he have a partner in another car?"

"Good question," said Jansson.

"At least the time of death looks pretty clear, even without an autopsy," said Pajula as he held up a receipt in a plastic bag.

"He bought some gas at the North Helsinki Shell at 2:20 P.M. yesterday. The tank must've been near empty, since he bought eleven gallons. The gas gauge is still at full, so he probably came straight here. Forensics can confirm that once they find out how much more gas they can fit in the tank. The trip from the station to here is about four miles, so we oughta be able to figure the time of death pretty accurately. I doubt the killer spent much time chit-chatting."

"I doubt it," said Jansson.

Pajula held out his hand and Jansson squeezed it, then Pajula climbed into his squad car and drove off.

Jansson walked around and opened his umbrella. Susisaari came out of the woods and headed over to him, as did Huusko.

"You reap what you sow," said Huusko.

"Look at all the underbrush. And the nearest road is over there, almost a mile away. I doubt the killer went crashing through the thicket," said Susisaari.

"And he sure didn't call a cab out here either," said Huusko. "But what are we doing in the rain? Let's get in the car."

Jansson plopped down in the passenger seat out of sheer habit—he always made Huusko drive. Susisaari sat in the back seat.

"If we assume that the same people that killed Liljeblad also killed Aho, then the South Americans don't really fit the picture," said Jansson. "If he had seen them at Liljeblad's apartment and wanted to keep it a secret, he never would've told you that they were at the Hotel Marski in the spring. Aho wasn't dumb."

Huusko agreed.

"But it looks to me like Aho was expecting to get a big chunk of change. Here he couldn't even afford to pay his own phone bill, and he was planning to travel abroad. You find out if there're any tickets in his name, and start looking into his phone records," Jansson continued.

"Will do."

"In other words, it seems to me that Aho got overconfident and got bit. Maybe he thought his clients weren't dangerous or he could keep things under control. So he met the killer somewhere, picked him up, and the guy pulled a gun and told him to drive here. And this spot wasn't chosen by accident. We'll have to go over Aho's apartment with a fine-toothed comb. If the murder has anything to do with his past, we might find some leads there. As a private investigator, he's bound to have some kind of archives."

Huusko glanced about, then spoke them, "Forgive me Father, for I have sinned."

Jansson regarded him for some time. "Confess your sins, my child. You'll feel better."

"I searched Aho's apartment yesterday."

"I commend the initiative, but the search was probably illegal. At least I don't remember signing the warrant."

"Partly legal."

"Which part was legal?" said Susisaari from the back seat.

"I called Aho's cell, but got no answer. Nobody answered the doorbell either, so I figured something must've happened to him."

"So you were just doing a welfare check, then?" said Jansson.

"Precisely."

"And the illegal part was the fact that you searched the place even though Aho wasn't there and you didn't have a warrant?"

"I intended to get the warrant later."

"Good intentions. Your sins are forgiven, insofar as I have any say in it."

"I promise to make amends."

"So what did you find in the apartment?"

Huusko told them about the search, and about the photograph stashed in the vent. Jansson listened intently. When Huusko was finished, Jansson was quiet for a moment. Then he asked.

"What do you think it means?"

"Sanna and I were thinking about that. Maybe Liljeblad's killer and our mysterious boy toy from the car in Haukilahti are the same person. So Aho was staking the apartment, saw and recognized the guy, and started blackmailing him. That's why he lied to me and neglected to tell us about the photos of the guy."

"So why does he need that old photo, and why now?"

"Maybe it's just more ammo for extortion. The wife probably wouldn't like it if she knew the guy had been sleeping around for all of twenty-five years. Something reminded him of that old photo and that's why he picked up the storage box and started working on the mystery man's identity. There was no camera in Aho's apartment. Maybe he'd pawned his camera along with the film, and had it developed only after recovering the camera. Once he saw the picture, he noticed the same birthmark and started to connect the dots."

"We could always ask the pawn shops—they've got everything on the computer nowadays. But there's another possibility... Let's say Aho's been blackmailing the guy for many months, threatening to send the photos to his wife. After the guy kills Liljeblad, he realizes that the photos could incriminate him because they connect him to her. The killer and his victim, in other words. So he went ahead and took care of his problem, as we see here."

Huusko had yet another theory.

"What if Aho couldn't really see the guy's face when he took the pictures of the sex scene in the car, or didn't recognize him. It'd been a long time since the last incident, after all. So when he picked up the storage box, he started going through the photos for old time's sake and struck upon the birthmark. That's when he connected it to the one in the car. So he figured out the

180

name and started blackmailing him. The ending's the same as yours... Maybe we should give the photo to the newspapers and have a 'name that ass' competition."

"Not a bad idea," said Susisaari.

Huusko struck his palm against his forehead. "I forgot about the deadbolt and security latch."

"Say what?"

"Aho had a deadbolt, hinge pins, and a security latch installed just a few days before his death...which would indicate that he knew he was treading dangerous waters."

"One of you should go to the North Helsinki Shell," said Jansson. "We found a receipt in the car showing that Aho gassed up yesterday at 2:20 P.M. There should be a security camera there."

"I can go," said Susisaari.

Ström, the medical examiner, pulled up in his own car, and Jansson stepped out to meet him.

"Hello," said Jansson.

"Hi, what brings you all the way out here?"

"Just a little friendly cooperation with Pajula. Make sure to send the autopsy results to us."

"Fine by me," said the coroner, and as he opened his bag, the rain seemed to pick up again.

* * *

"Sure I remember him," said the service station cashier as he studied Aho's driver's license. "Had on a wide brimmed felt hat...a real eye-catcher. Figured he was trying to hide his bald spot."

"Was he alone?"

"Yup. I checked out his car outta curiosity...just to see what kinda car a guy with a hat like that would drive.

I figured he'd have a big ol' Chevy, but it was just a run-of-the-mill rice burner."

Susisaari glanced at the surveillance camera over the register. Behind the counter was a monitor.

"We need the video footage."

"All of it?"

"Everything that he's in."

"Okay."

"Did he buy anything other than gas?"

"Yep."

"What?"

"Breath mints and a pack of condoms."

14.

The attic was tall enough for a man to move about completely upright. A mixture of pine shavings and sawdust served as insulation, some of it exposed, some hidden beneath floor boards. The attic had been used for storage, and there were still some odds and ends blanketed with dust: furniture, window frames, bottles and jars, doors, and stacks of yellowed newspapers.

The fine dust hanging in the air made Raid want to sneeze, but out of sheer habit he cut it short by squeezing his nostrils shut.

His eyes searched the space for a good hiding spot for the guns and grenades he'd acquired from Uki. Ordinarily, he would never keep such things in his own house, but since he expected to use them shortly, an exception was in order. If worse came to worst, he could always claim not to have known about them, that they were part of Nygren's estate.

Two light bulbs lit the attic space. They and the wires leading to them appeared to be rather new, probably installed by Nygren, though Nygren had owned the property for many years.

Raid pried up a couple of floorboards, dug out a long furrow in the insulation and lay the rifle in it. Then he covered it up, put the boards back in place, and finished up by sweeping any stray insulation away from the hiding spot.

Raid was just leaving when he noticed an old, scratched up, faded-brown suitcase next to the wall. What was certainly once an expensive suitcase bore almost a dozen hotel stickers from decades past: the Pohjanhovi, Kalastajatorppa, the Hotel Aulanko, the Hotel Torni, and several other exclusive Swedish and Danish hotels.

Raid stared at the bag. He remembered where he had seen it last—more than thirty years ago. Then the suitcase had been lying on the back seat of a red Porsche owned by his uncle Nygren, who had returned to his home town to recount his stories of good fortune. During that visit, his uncle had showered Raid with gifts: Canadian hockey skates and sticks, a leather shirt, jeans and a wristwatch, among other things. All of these treasures were imported items that weren't available in Finland at the time, and nearly all had been in the same leather suitcase, which had then been brand new.

Raid could remember vividly the moment when his uncle opened the case and began to dole out the presents, one after the other, into his arms. Nygren, his uncle and godfather, had then risen in his eyes to a status second only to God.

As Raid picked up the bag, he could feel that something was inside. He clicked open the nickel-plated latches and opened it up. The smell of old paper and musty fabric wafted out.

Inside was a cardboard picture album and a stack of letters bound together with a rubber band.

Raid lifted the album to the light. The photos were black and white, and judging from the outfits, taken in the '50s and '60s. He recognized the smiling young Nygren, sitting on a bridge railing in his hometown, his hair oiled back, and a bolo tie reminiscent of the Wild West tied round his neck. In another picture, Raid's grandparents were sitting on the front steps of their home with their brood spread out before them. The picture was taken sometime during the final stages of the

Second World War. Raid recognized his own mother sitting next to Nygren—she was around seven, and Nygren a couple of years younger. Raid's mother, dressed in a checkered frock and apron, had a hand-drawn cross above her head, as did her sister, Irja. Irja had then been about twenty, and married. In her arms she held her infant, who, soon after this photo had been taken, became an orphan of war.

Raid closed the album and placed it back into the case. He went downstairs with the stack of letters and sat down at the kitchen table to read.

According to the postmarks, the letters had been sent in the '60s and early '70s—they constituted the correspondence between Nygren and Raid's mother. Nygren must have recovered his letters from his sister's estate.

Raid opened a letter from Stockholm in the spring of 1962. In it, Nygren carried on in his rather boastful way about how well he was doing.

For the past two months, business has been good and I've made some money...and spent it, too. I bought a car, a two-year-old Triumph. Perfect for a summer drive in the country, and for camping. I'm renting in Söder, while I look for my own place. Finns aren't always all that popular here, but if you work hard, you do fine.

Try to hang in there back home. How's my godson getting along? Tell me if he needs anything and I'll bring it next time I come. I can get almost anything here...stuff you can't even get with big bucks in Finland. I think I'll visit soon, maybe at midsummer. I guess it depends how Dad feels about it. And don't be so worried about me, sis. Guys like me know how to take care of themselves, which is something I've had to learn the hard way.

Your drifter brother, Risto

Nygren didn't return to Finland that summer, nor the next. Raid knew that he had served his first prison sentence in Sweden at that time, a year and three months for grand larceny.

And indeed, the following letter came from a Swedish prison, dated September of 1962.

I am a disgrace. There, I said it...as difficult as it is. But what's even more difficult to say is whether I'm a disgrace because of my own stupidity for trusting the wrong man, or because I got involved in that sort of thing to begin with.

I'm sure Dad will get plenty of firepower out of this if he finds out. Which is why I'm asking you not to tell him or anyone else (except your husband, of course, who always knows to mind his tongue). If someone finds out through the grapevine, then there's nothing we can do about that.

Prison's not as bad as I thought it would be, so don't worry too much. And a year will be over in no time...it's really not that different from the army. I guess I'll have to figure out what I'll do once I grow up. Write me if you find the time. In here, time tends to drag on, though they do have a library. Send my greetings to your husband and the boy. Fine choice picking your tramp brother to be your son's godfather, sis.

Inmate 2217/62

The next few letters were also sent from prison to Raid's mother. She had written back about half a dozen times. His mother's crisp, flowing script drew Raid in immediately.

Poor little brother. I don't mean to wag my finger all the time, though perhaps there's good reason. You're a grown man, with your own deeds, and only yourself to blame for the results.

I haven't told anybody about what you've done, except for Arvo. He said that he wouldn't tell anybody else. You know him well enough to know that he's a man of his word. Although he never says it, I know that he feels sorry for you. He sends you his greetings, and hopes that you can persevere there under such difficult circumstances. He hopes, as I do, that you take this as a lesson, and that the first time will be the last. And I haven't lost hope that you were indeed the best choice to be my son's godfather. I even had a dream about it, and I believe strongly that there is a higher purpose for everything.

If you can't find a place to live when you get out in the summer, you can live here temporarily. I spoke with Arvo about it, and he thought that that would be fine. Maybe you could even find work here.

Your still hopeful sister, Hanna

Raid looked through a few more letters. The last was dated 1972. In it, Nygren responded to a fretful letter from his sister, in which she mentioned Raid's yearning to follow in his uncle's footsteps.

I wouldn't worry if I were you. The boy is only twelve, and that sort of admiration will have plenty of time to fade once he gets some sense in his head. I promise to do all I can to ensure that that happens as soon as possible. I can have a little man-to-man talk with the little hardhead next time I come to visit, and if necessary, I can spank him.

I must admit that I feel a little guilty about all my strutting and swaggering when I have come to visit, but I guess it's human nature to want to show folks back home that you've succeeded in the larger world, even if your ass got burned in God knows how many fires. And maybe I've been trying to make it up to the boy recently for all the years I wasn't able to visit or give any Christmas or birthday presents. Maybe my last visit was a little overboard. I promise to leave the Porsche at home next time. I'll come in my old Volvo junker. Send my greetings to Arvo, and tell the boy that unless he behaves, his big bad uncle's gonna jump on the next plane and come set him straight.

Risto

Raid folded the letter, slipped it back into the envelope, and the envelope into his pocket. Then he went outside, sat down on the stairs, and gazed off into nothingness.

15.

Within two hours, Huusko had solved the mystery of the initials: AK. Right off the bat, he had gone into the police database and queried the birthmark with as thorough a description as he could, but the computer didn't spit out a single individual with a U-shaped birthmark on his right buttock.

Since the shortcut hadn't worked, Huusko would have to go the long way around, and so he looked in the vice squad's old staff directory. The initials AK were common enough that he found three matches. One had died in a car accident a year back, another was retired, and the third had transferred to Järvenpää.

He called the Järvenpää station and got hold of one Lieutenant Ari Kuosmanen, who wasn't the photographer, nor did he know any other cops with the same initials. Arto Karvinen, the retiree, was in physical rehab, and also declined to take credit for the photo—he hadn't been involved in the case, nor taken the picture, and he didn't know anybody else with the initials AK.

"Do you remember anything unusual about the case?"

"This is all rather sudden," said Karvinen in a weary voice. "What do you mean by unusual?"

"There were a lot rumors about the case."

"As always."

"Was there any basis for them?"

"The vice squad at that time was headed up by Captain Huoponen, who I knew well. He was a stiff, war-hardened, hothead. Not the kind of guy you jerk around."

"Maybe he didn't know."

"Then that's a completely different thing. I'm not gonna speculate on anything. To me, a rumor is a rumor."

Karvinen hung up the phone.

Huusko was at a loss for a moment, so he called a friend of his from Undercover and explained the situation.

"Aren't you investigating that double murder in Oulunkylä?" the man asked.

"Yes."

"Just having trouble seeing how an old prostitution case would have anything to do with it."

"That's what I was hoping you could tell me."

"That's a pretty tall order."

"Well, I'm just trying to find out who all got away."

"Not an easy task either...I do remember it was an embarrassing ordeal for the bosses. All hush-hush and smoke and mirrors, and Aho was stirring the pot behind the scenes. I heard several of them paid Aho...bought their way out. It's possible there were other palms being greased, too. And it wasn't just about money, either. It was about the credibility of high-level officials. I seem to recall a few prosecutors flopping around in the net with our own guys, too."

"You recall any names?"

"The deputy chief of police was mentioned, and the head of the police division of the Interior Ministry, but this was all hearsay. Or at least their roles in the case were never investigated."

"Is there somebody with the initials AK that could have taken any photographs?"

"I don't know. Any cop could have snapped them. Plop a camera in their hand and tell 'em to push the button."

"These are high quality."

"Then a hobbyist. One thing did occur to me, though. Back then, there was no such thing as the Criminal Intelligence Division or Covert Operations. We all just called it the I-team. Remember?"

"Yup."

"The guys on the I-team got to play around with a lot of cameras and other technology, and some of them got to be quite the shutterbugs. A lot of their work used to turn up at the department's Christmas parties, and some of it was very revealing."

* * *

After he hung up, Huusko thought of yet another way to make some headway, and if not headway, then at least it was the next sensible step.

He phoned the library at the police academy, where the police recreational periodicals were in circulation. Huusko introduced himself to the librarian.

"Does the police department have a camera or photography club?" he asked.

"Yes, it does. Guess what the name is."

"The Police Camera Club?"

"How'd you know?"

"Could you tell me who the president is?"

"One moment."

The librarian was away for just over a minute before returning, "Hannu Reimarla from Espoo."

Huusko took down the number and thanked her. He then dialed the number and Reimarla answered.

Huusko told him that he was searching for a Helsinki police officer, a photographer with the initials AK.

Reimarla hardly skipped a beat. "Antero Kero, former vice president of our club. He retired a couple of years ago. Used to take photos for a lot of criminal cases. We even had an exhibit featuring his work.

"Where can I get hold of him?"

"He lives in Vartiokylä, east Helsinki. He's listed in the phone book."

"Is he in good health?"

"Yes, at least last I heard. We bumped into each other about six months back; he looked pretty lively then."

* * *

Within half an hour, Huusko was at Kero's front door. Before leaving, he had called to make sure that he had the right guy.

Kero was a thin, white-haired man with a crutch tucked under his arm. He exuded an air of police professionalism, though Huusko couldn't work out just how.

"Sprained some ligaments on a sailing trip," said Kero.

He led Huusko through the living room and into the kitchen where he had some coffee waiting. Huusko stole a glance at a large photographic print hanging on the living room wall that had been made to look like a painting. The subject of the photo was a beautiful blonde who appeared to be in her forties. Oddly, there wasn't a single photograph of a child or grandchild on the bookshelves.

Four rather awkward-looking ham-and-cheese sandwiches lay on a plate on the kitchen table. Outside the kitchen window was the backyard, where a yellow indian canoe was perched on sawhorses near a greenhouse and gardening shed.

"I should say right off that I've been waiting many years for one of you to come visit."

"Why?" said Huusko.

Kero poured the coffees from a thermos.

"Because it's high time for the truth to come out. There're only a few of us still alive who know exactly what happened, and Aho was one of them."

Huusko took a pen and a pad of paper out of his pocket and set them on the table.

Kero swallowed a bite of his sandwich, gulped down some coffee, and began, "I just happened to be with the case from the very beginning, even though back then I was on the I-team, and Vice was handling the case. It all started with this woman...a prostitute...who was raped at the Hotel Torni. I'd interviewed her once in a gambling case, and for some reason, she trusted me. Anyhow, she called and wanted to meet. I picked her up and we drove around town for over an hour while she told me everything she knew. And that was a lot... More coffee?"

"Thanks."

Kero poured Huusko a full cup.

"The woman was working as an escort for a certain high-powered businessman, when the guy ran into a few buddies at the hotel bar. These guys had come to the hotel to play poker in another room, but the guy who'd invited them never showed. So the businessman invited them to his room, where they played cards and drank all evening. Finally, the lady got bored and wanted to leave, but the poker players wouldn't let her. They tied her to the bed with a belt and gagged her so she couldn't shout for help. At least four men raped her, one after another. To top it off, one of them hit her so hard she lost a tooth. They kept her in the hotel room all night, and let her go in the morning... The woman went straight from the hotel to the station to file a report. Then she waited for a couple weeks, but started to wonder when she didn't hear back. When she called, they told her they couldn't find any record of her complaint—it was missing. She called me and told me the whole story, so I looked into it. Somebody working the front desk remembered that a report had been filed, and that somebody had promised to take care of it, but they couldn't remember who."

Huusko couldn't resist asking, "Did you get to the bottom of it?"

"I did. When I told the victim that the report had vanished, she went ballistic. She told me she'd turned tricks at an upscale brothel in Töölö, whose clientele included the interior minister, a couple of high-ranking officers, two prosecutors, and a few other big shots. The captain of the Vice Squad at the time was Teuvo Huoponen, a respectable, but crotchety old cop who was well over sixty at the time. I told him what had happened, and he ordered me, Aho, and one other cop who's now dead to look into her claims. So we staked out the brothel every night for almost two weeks."

The postal carrier rolled into the yard on a yellow bicycle. Kero looked at the clock.

"Half past one. The mail used to come at eleven every day, at the latest."

"So you staked out the brothel…"

"Right… And right away, it became clear that the situation was even worse than we had thought. On the second night of the stakeout, the interior minister waltzed up with the chief of staff from the Ministry of Justice. And the very next night, the deputy chief of police and a bigwig from the Interior Ministry came calling. I took photos of every one of 'em. Our informant even kept a wire in her purse a few times. She got so excited about playing detective that she told us about another place…an old villa in the backwoods of Espoo. That's where the hard stuff happened, or so we were told, which is why it was in such a far-flung place. A real king's feast, you know, leather whips and that sort of thing. This woman had worked there a couple of times, but found it revolting enough that she quit. So we staked out the villa for a few days, and saw the same familiar crowd come knocking. One evening, we watched as one of the country's most notorious white-collar criminals came bouncing up to the door with a metro area police chief. Then came one of the local drug lords, followed by a well-known pop singer. I'm sure you understand what kind of dynamite we were dealing with."

Huusko felt a little dizzy, but he nodded.

"Huoponen did, too. But he was a stubborn ass, as usual. We pulled together some backup beat cops and raided the place one Saturday night, but for the first time, not one cop or prosecutor showed up. Obviously, our cover was blown, but we tossed about twenty johns and a couple dozen girls in jail. After that, Huoponen had to inform the higher-ups, and that very same night, the phone started ringing off the hook. The big cheeses upstairs were up in arms about us scrapping the force's hard-earned credibility because of some trivial case. The next day, Huoponen was forced to forward all the case files upstairs, so they would have time to prepare. Then, one day later, Huoponen called all of us detectives in for a meeting. Huoponen was white as a sheet—he said right off that the case had to be whitewashed or the department would be dealing with the consequences for the next ten years. Then he told us he'd been in contact with… Well, his daughter had gotten mixed up in a drug trafficking case. We all knew that Huoponen's daughter was an addict, and apparently so did somebody else. So Huoponen had been told that his daughter's fate was in his hands. She could either get the book, or we could soft-pedal the case so much that the dogs would never smell blood. All they wanted was for it to be downsized to 'manageable proportions.' Huoponen told us we could do whatever we wanted, but that he had decided to comply."

"So what did you do?" asked Huusko as Kero paused.

"We deep-sixed it. Eventually, of course, it did come to court, but it was a ghost of its former self. One guy got charged with pimping, and a couple of girls for prostitution and the sale of illegal alcohol."

Huusko took the photograph out of his pocket and handed it to Kero.

"Who is this man?"

Kero inspected the photo carefully. "I remember taking the photo, but I don't know."

"The photo was taking during the raid. You must have written down his information."

"I just snapped the photo and rushed into another room to take more. Altogether, I shot two rolls of film. Aho's the one who took down everyone's information, but most of their names disappeared before the investigation ever got started. Apparently, this guy's included."

"What about the woman?"

"I don't know her."

"What about your informant? Was she working then?"

"We tipped her off about the raid, so no."

"Is she still alive?"

Kero paused for a moment. "Yes."

"I need her name."

Kero looked hesitant. "I think she's already done her share in this case…more than her share. I doubt she wants to get mixed up in it again."

"Let's let her decide," said Huusko.

"Right...it should be her decision. Her name is Helena Kangas; that's her maiden name. She's a salesperson at a women's boutique downtown."

Kero gave directions to the store, and Huusko thanked him.

"You should know that she's a wonderful woman...truly wonderful."

Kero's attitude made Huusko wonder, but he promised to keep that in mind. Kero was silent for a spell, while he gazed out the window.

"So what happened to Aho?"

"He was shot."

"And you think it has something to do with the past?"

"Why else would he have hidden the photo now?"

Kero got up and hobbled into his office. He came back with a loupe, sat down at the table, and began studying the photograph.

"It's a unique birthmark...a good means of identification."

"That's why I think she might remember him."

"You think this guy's at it again?"

"It's possible. The picture was hidden only a few days ago."

"That would indicate that Aho was afraid someone would find it. And you don't find anything without looking. So the guy with the birthmark must be looking for it?"

"I dunno."

"Could he have some other reason? A visit to the whorehouse twenty five years ago would hardly seem all that important now."

Huusko considered it for a moment, then decided to tell him the whole story—Kero might be useful again.

"Quite the case," said Kero after hearing the story. "His ass pops out of the archives at the moment this lady lover gets knocked off. Sounds like just the kind of case for Aho to get mixed up in. But you don't kill someone to avoid getting caught for sleeping around. You think this is about something else? Say the guy's afraid this photo would connect him to the woman that he killed?"

"It crossed my mind."

"Aho did have a tendency to make a mess of his affairs."

"Did he resign like they say he did?"

"I never saw him after he left. He claimed they wanted him to resign because he knew too much, but he told me he wasn't leaving for free. I'm guessing he squeezed some money or favors out of some people before he left. Aho was too sly to be a cop, and had too much of a fondness for women."

"What happened to all the photos in the case files?"

"Disappeared. Some into Aho's album, it seems. I still have the negatives, though."

"You do? All of them?"

"Yep."

"How'd you manage that?"

Kero laughed, "Once I realized what game they were playing, I decided to play too. I told them the negatives had been stolen from my office. When I threatened to file a police report for the theft, they deemed it best to leave it alone."

"So there's no other photos of this man?" Huusko asked.

"What, you don't trust me?"

"I'm sorry."

"Hey. I was young and ambitious once, too."

Huusko stood and extended his hand. Kero took it, and they shook.

"Could you do me a little favor?"

"What's that?" said Huusko.

"Could you get my mail for me?"

* * *

Huusko parked his car just in front of the shop and slapped a police emblem onto the dash.

One glance told Huusko that the garments in this store weren't intended for people on government assistance. The price tag on one crimson dress had four numbers before the decimal, and the first was not a one.

No customers were in the store when Huusko stepped in. In short order, a woman dressed in an ivory-colored pantsuit breezed out of the back room, and when Huusko got a look at her face, he stopped. It was the same blonde whose giant photograph was hanging on Kero's living room wall. Huusko knew she had to be close to fifty, but she looked like she was still in her thirties. Upon closer inspection, however, her face revealed the subtle clues of an arduous life.

When Huusko introduced himself, the woman knit her forehead, and her eyes grew hard.

"The police? What is this?"

"I got your address from another officer. He thought that maybe you could help us with an important matter. I'd be grateful if you could."

The woman scrutinized him. "It'd better be important. Some memories are dreadful enough that I don't care to recall them."

"I understand."

"And I don't have a very high regard for the police."

"I don't always, either. But the world has changed a lot since then."

"Some things never change."

Huusko looked at her face. A thin scar was visible near the corner of her mouth, and another along her temple. The "occupational accident" Kero had mentioned, Huusko concluded.

"Well, I'm a good cop. Even if I don't look it."

The woman flashed a little grin. "Well, let's make it quick, before a customer walks in."

Huusko took the photo out of his pocket and handed it to her. Again, her eyes went cold.

"What's this?"

"Do you know who this man is?"

"It wasn't very often I saw men from this perspective," she said without the slightest trace of irony.

"He has a rather unique birthmark...in the shape of a U."

She handed the photo back. "I remember him. The girls called him Mr. U. because of the birthmark. I never knew his real name. He wasn't my customer."

"Whose customer was he?"

"She died some time ago. Almost all of them have...didn't know to quit while they were ahead."

"Do you remember anything about him?"

"He came around pretty often, and not always as a customer. He was usually there as kind of a procurer...you know...well, the pimp."

"Clearly, he got caught with his pants down here, but there's no record of him in any case files. Do you know how he managed to slip through the cracks?"

"Because he was usually there as the pimp. Plenty of people were indebted to him, and he knew too much. People like him almost always get away with it."

"If he was the pimp, who did he work for?"

"Some big construction company; he was some kind of marketing executive. I don't really know why he was involved in this stuff," she said with a cheerless laugh. "Maybe that's just the kind of man he was—a lover of whores—and he found a way to unite passion and practicality through his work. I was one of five girls that they ordered for a party at the construction company once. We had to service guests, customers, officials, and anyone else invited to the party...all night long. We really had to earn our money that night, too—when a man gets a free fuck, he doesn't hold back. And these weren't your ordinary pencil pushers, either. They were high-level officials."

"What was the name of this construction company?"

"Solar. At the time, it was one of the country's bigger construction firms, but it went under in the early nineties when the Soviet market ran dry."

"Did you ever work at the Bembôle villa?"

She nodded.

"What went on there?"

"What went on in Sodom and Gomorrah? Use your imagination...I mean the dirty half of it."

"I've got a lousy imagination."

"Some sick stuff. I only went there once, and that was enough. Even some of us hookers have a little self-respect, you know... Not a lot...but a little."

"Did Mr. U. frequent the place?"

"Yes."

"Apparently some police officers, as well?"

"Yes... I recall at least one, a short, pudgy guy. Looked more like a banker than a cop."

"Do you remember anything else? Anything that comes to mind?"

"He never paid us, and never tipped. To me, that says a lot about a person. Can I ask you a question?"

"Go ahead."

"Why is this coming up now? Just four days ago, some private eye came by—a former cop—asking about the same stuff. And he had the same picture you do."

"Was his name Aho?"

"Yup. That's the guy…former vice cop. Used to badger me back in the day. I heard he was involved in this case back then, too."

"Did he tell you why he was interested?"

"No, and I didn't give him the opportunity. I don't have fond memories of him, so I told him to leave. So maybe you can tell me."

"I'm trying to find out if Mr. U. is involved with a recent crime."

"A serious crime?"

"Very."

"Well, I hope you find him then… And if you do, don't let him get away this time."

"I won't."

"And I'm sure you understand that I don't want to get involved in the case in any way. I've got my life together now, though I never would've believed it… I own half of this store…"

The door opened, and a young, beautiful woman appeared in the vestibule. Huusko had seen her in the tabloids before.

"You should probably go now."

Huusko thanked her, but he lingered at the counter. He knew it would bother him if he didn't ask, and so he did, "How well do you know Sergeant Kero?"

"As well as a wife would know her husband after twenty years of marriage."

16.

"Heel!" Jansson commanded as he stopped at the foot of the stairs in front of Pasila police headquarters. The dog stopped and glanced back. "If I let you inside, there'll be no marking your territory or any other such nonsense. Do I make myself clear?"

Jansson took the dog's friendly whimper as a yes, and they headed inside and took the elevator upstairs. It was early evening, and the station was quiet, though many of the offices were still lit. The more eager workhorses were still slogging away on their cases.

The meeting had been set for 6:30 P.M. Jansson had stopped at home because his wife had called to say that she'd be working late. The dog had looked so forlorn and miserable that Jansson had brought it along.

Over the course of his career, Jansson had attended thousands of meetings, and had never liked them, but he understood their necessity. Any new information had to be shared and analyzed at regular intervals in order to keep the case moving in the right direction, somewhat like checking compass bearings in the wilderness. Jansson had the most complete picture of the Liljeblad case, and could sense that something pivotal was about to happen, but as to where and how, he couldn't tell.

The others were already waiting—even Huusko—and Jansson was even a few minutes early.

In addition to Susisaari and Huusko, Lieutenant Kempas, the coroner Tykkylä, and Narcotics Lieutenant Kamppari, sometimes referred to as "Campari," were in the room. Kamppari was a rather portly man, a shade over forty years old, who wore his hair in a crew cut. He was dressed in a snug, checkered golf sweater and brown corduroy pants. Broken blood vessels dotted his cheeks and nose, reminders not only of his nickname, but also of his fondness for liquor. Everybody took notice when the dog walked in.

"You trade in the Benz for a pooch?" said Kamppari.

Susisaari brought him up to date on the dog, and turning to Jansson, said, "You know if it's a boy or girl yet?"

"It hasn't said."

"Then it's a boy," said Huusko.

"Ha! You just gotta watch how it pisses," said Kempas. "If the leg goes up, it's a he. If it squats, it's a she."

"I haven't looked. Real gentlemen look the other away."

"How could you not notice something like that?" said Kempas.

"Easy," said Jansson. "Least for me."

The dog settled down at Jansson's feet, as if homicide meetings were a daily occurrence.

"We've received some new information that links the case to drugs, which is why Kamppari is here from Narcotics. Kempas can tell us more."

Kempas cleared his throat, "It appears that a Bolivian cartel operating out of Gothenburg is using a fruit import business to smuggle cocaine. They're buying produce wholesalers, or starting their own, and smuggling drugs in with the fruit. Which is why they met with Saramaa, the attorney. Apparently, they already tried it with Hernando, but something went wrong and a large coke shipment got lost somewhere in Finland."

"We're working with the Swedish police to figure out just how the cocaine is being smuggled here," said

Kamppari. "Whatever the case, we're dealing with hundreds of pounds, only a fraction of which is intended for local markets."

"So Hernando was killed because of drugs?" said Susisaari.

"It seems that way. Something similar happened in Gothenburg a year ago. A woman working in the cargo terminal was supposed to redirect a crate with a shipment of cocaine, but she inadvertently let it through. She was found a month later, floating in the harbor."

"Do you know where the lost shipment is?" said Huusko.

Kamppari shook his head. "We're working on that."

Jansson spoke up, "We've gotten some lab results back from Forensics. Most of the fingerprints they found in Liljeblad's apartment had no matches in the database. In the Mazda, they found Aho's and a few other unidentified ones."

Huusko raised his hand, "I've been thinking about this and wondering…what if Aho's killer was somebody other than the one who killed Liljeblad and Hernando?"

Kempas wasn't convinced. "Too much of a coincidence. Especially when the only motive we have for Aho's murder is his connection to Liljeblad."

"Coincidences happen. What if the motive for offing Liljeblad and Hernando was drugs, but Aho was killed for blackmailing one of Liljeblad's lovers."

Kamppari looked skeptical.

"I found out who took the photograph that Aho hid," Huusko continued. "A retired sergeant by the name of Antero Kero. Aho was apparently asking around about the same photo."

"Asking Kero?" said Jansson.

"No, his wife."

Huusko told them about his conversations with Kero and his wife.

"I dug up an old annual report from Solar Construction. We should be able to find the guy in there."

"And what then?" said Kempas.

"I'm sure there's something else we don't know yet. If he's got the same ass as the guy who was banging Liljeblad in Haukilahti, then that's something to look at."

"His ass?" said Kamppari.

"Exactly."

"I couldn't care less what his ass looks like. I'm more interested in the Bolivians," said Kempas. "They were seen at the scene of the crime; they had a motive, a means and an opportunity to kill. So what's keeping you from…"

Jansson raised his hand in an effort to quiet Kempas. He looked at Tykkylä, the medical examiner.

"Thanks to Tykkylä's efforts, the forensics investigation is also coming along nicely, and has yielded some new information. Despite his busy schedule, he agreed to provide a summary of the results in person. I assure you it will be very interesting."

Tykkylä wore a pair of thin, frameless glasses, which made him seem like an absent-minded professor, particularly when he peered over the tops to compensate for his near-sightedness.

"Let me start with the DNA results, which show that the sperm found in the condom near the car was indeed Aho's, something we were already reasonably confident of based on the fingerprints. Likewise, we've confirmed via DNA that the condom in question was used during intercourse with Ms. Liljeblad. The cause of Aho's death was just what it looked like—he was shot in the head with a .22 caliber firearm at close, but not point-blank, range. I won't bother with an in-depth description of the injuries. The bullet is being analyzed at the lab. At this point, we know that the murder weapon was a Ruger semiautomatic pistol. Rugers are fairly common mid-priced consumer handguns. Aho was killed in the same car where his body was found, between twenty and thirty hours before it was discovered."

Tykkylä peered over his glasses at Jansson. "I suppose you have a more exact estimate based on the gas station receipt?"

"Correct," said Jansson. "The murder occurred yesterday, around five o'clock."

Susisaari spoke up, "I stopped at the station where he bought the gas, and found out that he also bought some breath mints and a pack of condoms... Which makes me think the killer is a woman."

The others reflected on the idea for a moment.

"Maybe he picked up the rubbers for later," offered Kempas.

"The car was in the middle of nowhere. He could've easily picked that spot anticipating a little liaison. But we didn't find any condoms—so what happened to them?"

"Do you have a theory?" said Jansson.

"Suppose this woman was leading him on, so Aho pulls out the condoms. She then kills him and takes the condoms with her because they'd reveal the sex of the killer."

"Seems logical," said Jansson.

Tykkylä cleared his throat. "One more thing about Aho...we found a bite mark on his right leg.

All eyes turned to Tykkylä.

"A small dog's bite mark."

Jansson beamed. "And you all underestimated him," he said as he scratched the dog's ruff.

"That little dust bunny bit Aho?" Kempas marveled.

"Yup. We measured the spacing of the teeth. There's no doubt of it."

"So Aho *was* in Liljeblad's apartment," said Susisaari.

"Yes," said Jansson. "It's likely he saw the murderer. The dog was in the back room, which had a separate exit. So Aho had to be running from something, because he used the back door. He'd be our top suspect for the murder if it weren't for the fact that he was murdered himself."

"That complicates things," grumbled Huusko. "So what do we have on the table? Aho saw the killer—or killers—in Liljeblad's apartment. Aho was murdered in his car. It's possible Aho was murdered by a woman, which means that Liljeblad and Hernando could also have been murdered by a woman. Since we know Hernando had been having sex in the apartment shortly before his death, we have reason to suspect that his sex partner and killer are one and the same."

"Tykkylä's not done yet," said Jansson.

"Let's move on to Liljeblad and Hernando. No surprises on the cause of death for either. Hernando died of multiple stab wounds, and the woman died of a heart attack brought on by a cocaine overdose. I understand you've deduced the time of death by other means, and my conclusions are not in contradiction with yours. What's still unclear is who killed who? The blood on Liljeblad's hands and clothing was Hernando's, but the forensic evidence shows that the events did not occur the way they were made to appear. It's not my job to speculate on whether Liljeblad was framed or not, I'm just giving you the facts of the forensics investigation."

208

"Is it possible that Liljeblad was forced to take an overdose of cocaine?" asked Susisaari.

"Yes, that's possible. If her mouth was forced shut, she'd have to breathe through her nose. Cocaine could then be blown or poured into her nostrils. But that's not something that could be done by one person...unless she was unable to resist for some reason."

"So murder isn't out of the question?"

"No. Although this is Finland's first death due to a cocaine overdose, that's only due to the fact that cocaine is rare here. Cocaine deaths are relatively common in the United States, so yes, murder is a possibility."

Tykkylä waited briefly to see if there were more questions, but there weren't.

"I suppose it's your turn then, Eero."

Jansson stood. The information he had received that afternoon had made him uneasy. Now it was time to pass it on to the others.

"As Huusko reminds us, Hernando was having intercourse just shortly before his death. But not with Liljeblad. That possibility was eliminated based on the time that Liljeblad left work. So some other woman was in the apartment, either shortly before the murders, or during them. Unlike Huusko, I wouldn't just put two and two together and say that she's the murderer, but it is possible. An even greater possibility, however, is that she knows something about the murders."

"Did we get the woman's DNA?" asked Kamppari.

"Hernando used a condom, which was never recovered, but Forensics found some material containing the woman's DNA. They also found her pubic hair on his body, and in the bed."

"So all we gotta do is find the woman, right?" said Kamppari.

"Yes, but we do have something helpful in that regard...look for a close relative of the female victim. According to the lab, their DNA sequences have so many commonalities that nothing else could explain it."

"The sister!" Susisaari gasped. "It's got to be the little sister."

* * *

Erika Liljeblad was curled up in a Danish egg chair. She appeared to have a chill, and had wrapped herself in a shawl.

"Trust me, it was the first and only time. I didn't know him before that, and I regret I ever met him."

Huusko peered out the window, which opened onto a quiet side street near downtown. A street lamp loomed in front of the window.

"Why didn't you tell us?" said Susisaari.

"How would that have helped?"

"Tell us what happened."

Erika curled up a bit tighter, "I only went there to see Nina. I didn't know he'd be there."

"Why were you going to see your sister?"

"Mom wanted to sell her place in Helsinki and give the pre-inheritance to us. I just wanted to talk with her about it."

"Why didn't you call first?"

"She knew my number, and didn't always answer when I called... I just wanted to get it out of the way."

Erika fell silent and stared into her lap.

"So what happened when you got there?"

"He was there and answered the door... He'd just taken a shower, so all he had on was a towel. I'm sure he thought Nina had come back."

"What did he say when he saw you?"

"He was surprised at first. Then he invited me in. He told me he was there dog sitting, and that Nina would be home in a couple hours."

"Did he know who you were?"

"I told him."

"Why did you go in when your sister wasn't there?"

"I don't know."

"Go on."

"He asked if I wanted orange juice or something, and I said yes. I took the glass to the couch, and he sat on the chair and stared at me for a long time. Then he told me that I wasn't like Nina at all… He got up, came over, and pulled me to my feet…and then his towel came off."

She closed her eyes momentarily, then continued, "He brought me into the bedroom…and I didn't resist… I was like a sleepwalker."

"Were you sleeping when you did the deed, too?" said Huusko.

Susisaari shot him a reproachful look. "Sorry."

"Maybe…subconsciously…I wanted to hurt her. She'd always been the beauty of the family, and now her boyfriend wanted me. I guess it flattered me…"

She buried her face abruptly in her hands.

"But in reality it was just dirty and disgusting. I'd have never imagined I could do something like that."

"What happened then?"

"When it was all over and I was getting dressed, I heard a car pull up in front of the building. I panicked, and I think he did, too. I grabbed my jacket and shoes and went out the back door. I didn't put on my shoes till I was outside."

"Did you see who came?"

"No… I cut through the backyard to the driveway. I had left my car on a side street."

"Why?"

"Because Nina would recognize it. I figured she wouldn't open the door for me."

"Why not?"

"You just never knew with her. Sometimes she could act like a two-year-old. If she didn't want to do something, she didn't. It was as simple as that. If she didn't want to see me, she didn't."

"Did you see anyone outside?"

"There was a dark green SUV in front of the building, but nobody in it. There's a hedge along the road and some apple trees and shrubs in the front yard, so I couldn't see to the front door. I didn't wanna wait around, so I walked to my car and drove off."

"What time was it then?"

Erika Liljeblad thought for a moment. "It was just after five when I got there, and I stayed for just shy of an hour."

"So around six o'clock?"

"Right."

"You said that the SUV was green. Did you notice the make or model?"

"I don't know much about cars."

"Did you notice the plates, or anything else that could help us identify the vehicle?"

"I'm pretty sure they were Swedish plates, or Russian. They were longer than Finnish ones, anyhow."

"What did you do when you heard your sister had died?"

"I was horrified, but it never occurred to me that I might have something to do with her death... That only occurred to me after you mentioned that whoever came might've been the killer."

"Did Hernando say anything when he heard the car pull up?"

"No."

"He didn't seem afraid?"

"Maybe a little…"

"Where did you go, then?"

"Home."

"What were you wearing?"

"What difference does that make? Black jeans, a black sweater, and a leather jacket."

"Could we have them?"

"What for?"

"We'll need to bring them to the lab."

"You don't think I actually killed my sister and her boyfriend, do you?"

Susisaari looked directly at Erika, and said with deliberate calm, "You have a motive. Two, in fact. And you had an opportunity to do it."

"And what motive could that be?"

"Not only were you afraid your sister would find out about your fling with Hernando, but you also said yourself that the two of you were getting an inheritance. Your share just got bigger when your sister died."

Erika's lips began to quiver, and she burst into tears.

Susisaari and Huusko waited for her to calm down.

"Nina was my sister. I could never hurt her… I can't even imagine it."

"We have to take every possibility into account. Could we have the clothes now?"

"Am I under arrest?"

"Not until we're done with our investigation."

Erika calmed down a bit. She went to her wardrobe and plucked out a pair of black jeans and a black sweater, and handed them to Susisaari.

"Look closely, do you see any blood?"

"Have you washed these since you went to your sister's place?" asked Susisaari.

"No. And I haven't worn them either."

Susisaari took a clear plastic bag out of her pocket, unfolded it, and put the clothes inside.

"We'd like to take a look at your other clothes as well."

"Suit yourselves."

Susisaari began looking through the garments in her wardrobe, and Huusko examined those in the entryway.

"Did you meet anybody else, either before or after visiting your sister's place?"

"What do you mean?"

"Say a neighbor, or anybody else who could verify that you were wearing these clothes?"

"No."

"And did you go anywhere else either before or after your sister's place? A gas station, a cash machine, anything like that?"

"No."

"Where is your car?"

"In the lot. It's a white Audi."

"We'll need your car keys, and a spare key, too."

Erika got her keys from the entryway. Huusko reached into the inside pocket of his coat and slipped out Solar Construction's annual report. He opened it to a spread containing photos of the company's management.

"You mentioned that a week ago you saw your sister at a restaurant with an older man. Do you see that man in any of these photos?"

Erika Liljeblad examined the photos for a long time, then shook her head.

"No, I don't, at least I don't think so. The pictures are kind of old."

Huusko searched his pockets again, and handed her another photograph.

"What about this one?"

She looked at the photo and her face lit up.

"That's the one."

"Are you certain?"

"Absolutely certain. Who is he?"

Huusko looked at Susisaari, then back at the photo of Aho.

* * *

Huusko was quiet until they reached the car. "Seems like we find Aho under every rock we turn over. The guy was more lizard than PI…slithering around in the cracks."

"We already knew that Liljeblad and Aho knew each other," said Susisaari.

"But how could a woman like Liljeblad let herself be seen in public with Aho?"

"Maybe she had to. Aho was giving the orders."

Huusko glanced anxiously at his watch, and Susisaari noticed.

"You've never been in a hurry to get home before."

"Never had a home before…"

"So things are going well?"

"Yeah…long as I don't screw it up again. Which is my tendency…"

He eyed Susisaari tentatively. "Have you heard any gossip about me at the station?"

"What do you mean?"

"A cop living with the ex-wife of a criminal."

"I haven't heard anything. And I wouldn't have thought it'd make any difference to you anyway."

"I wouldn't have either."

"Don't even think about those things."

"I have to. Just look at Kero. The cop marries a prostitute turned informant. They've been happily

215

married for twenty years, or at least it seems so. Been thinking about that all day."

"Love conquers all. And it looks like you're really in love."

"Apparently so… I *am*…"

They drove for a while in silence. Then Huusko said, "I don't think the sister did it. She saw the SUV, she couldn't have made that up. We never mentioned it before."

"Well, if she did do it, or even if she was there during the murders, blood will be on her clothes or in her car."

"Drop me off at the train station, will you?" said Huusko.

* * *

It was already dark when Jansson left for a walk with the dog and his brand new retractable leash. His wife hadn't yet come home. The dog stopped near the poplar, sniffed around eagerly, and glanced back at Jansson. Then it lifted one of its back legs high in the air and left its mark at the base of the tree.

"A boy!" Jansson exclaimed.

The dog kicked up the dirt behind it and set off down the road. Jansson followed along at the other end of the leash. As he watched the little white creature trotting along in front of him, he realized that they were now friends, and that no amount of money could come between them.

17.

Raid suspected that the man in the silver-gray Saab was still after him. Too many Swedish criminals knew about Nygren's farm, and that Raid had inherited it, along with the Mercedes.

His suspicion was vindicated that very night, when the shopkeeper's son called.

"Some creepy looking guy with a mullet was just here asking about Nygren's place."

"What kind of car was he driving?"

"A silver station wagon…looked like a Saab. With Swedish plates."

"Thanks."

"Who was it?"

"I don't know. Did you tell him where the house is?"

"No, but the stupid fucking cashier did. I didn't have time to tell her not to. Is that bad?"

"Hard to say."

Raid checked his pistol, loaded it, and slipped it into his waistband. He grabbed a pair of binoculars, walked across the yard into the barn and climbed into the loft, where a window on the gable end provided a view of the road and the forest. Raid lifted the binoculars and studied the road. Though it was already getting dark, he could see well through the lenses.

Even so, the man almost surprised him. He had come along the shore, rather than through the woods, as Raid expected. Now he approached the house under cover of the barn. At a hundred fifty feet from the house, he began to crawl, using the tall grass as a blind.

Raid didn't see the man until he emerged from the grass only thirty feet from the barn. The man slunk along the barn wall toward the house with a pistol in his hand.

Raid climbed swiftly down, opened the door quietly and skirted along the opposite barn wall. When he came within a few feet of the corner, he stopped and waited.

Soon he heard the soft padding of the man's footsteps in the grass. The man stepped out from behind the corner, peering toward the house.

"Hello!"

The man stiffened and whirled around. Raid smacked the butt of his pistol into the man's gun hand, and the gun fell. Then he jerked the man's arm so violently that the elbow popped, and the man screamed out loud. Raid threw him face first onto the grass and pinned his shoulders down with his knee.

"What do you want?"

"I just forgot something."

"What, that you were supposed to kill me?"

The pain had to have been great, but the man struggled to speak in a normal tone of voice.

"That hurts like hell...can you ease up on my arm a little?"

"Why?"

"This is all a big misunderstanding."

"How'd you find me?"

"Somebody was here with Nygren and knew the place. Took me a while to find it. A very nice place... Ease up on my fucking arm!"

"How'd you know where I was?"

"The arm!" he screamed.

Raid took some of his weight off of it and the man breathed a sigh of relief.

"The Bolivians called their guys in Sweden and were asking everyone about this guy they had a run-in with in the Finnish countryside... The guy laid out four of theirs and spoke good Swedish. I figured it was you... Nobody else could..."

"Are you here alone?"

"Yeah. Figured I'd try to make it before the Latin boys... They're coming, too..."

Raid looked at the man, who made an attempt at a smile.

"I fucked up...come on...let's just forget about it. I'll make it up to you. You can have the money, and I'll tell 'em I couldn't find you. Deal?"

Raid didn't reply. He slipped a folding knife out of his pocket and opened it with one hand. The man heard the blade snap open, and made one more attempt to flail himself free, but to no avail.

"Fucking kill me then!" he cried.

Raid plunged the blade into the hollow at the nape of the man's neck, first lightly, then he muscled it in.

He wiped the blade clean, and put it back in his pocket.

Raid pulled the corpse into the barn by its hands and emptied the pockets. Then he climbed up to the attic and found an old rug, and in the shed, a rusty cast iron stove. He loaded the body and the stove into a wheelbarrow, wheeled them down to the shore and dumped them into the boat.

He tied the two tightly together.

It was nearly dark as Raid pushed the boat into the water. A couple of birds burst from the reeds, scolding loudly as they flew off across the lake. They would have to find another place to sleep for the night.

Raid rowed into open water and let the boat glide to a stop. The lake was lush with the smell of earth and rotting plant life, and a light breeze brought in a trace of the scent of fresh autumn forest from the shore, now

219

barely visible. The lights in the yard of the farm were his only landmarks.

Raid grabbed the corpse and heaved it into the lake along with the stove. As the stove sank, air bubbles from the interior gurgled up to the surface momentarily. Then, the lake became just as placid as before.

When Raid returned to shore, he saw the shopkeeper's boy drive into the yard in the store's van. The boy waited there timidly with the engine still running.

"So who is he?"

"A Finnish gangster who lives in Sweden."

"I saw his car back there on the road. What'd you do to him?"

"I haven't seen him. Probably got lost in the woods… City boy."

"Why's he after you?"

"For money."

"From who?"

"The Russians."

"Seems like you got enemies all over. If I were you, I'd leave for a few months. The Greek islands, or something."

"Maybe later…but not yet."

"Later might be too late. What should we do with the car?"

"Why would we do anything with it?"

"I just thought…"

"If you want, we can drive it further down the road."

The boy drove Raid to where the Saab was parked.

"You follow me," said Raid, as he unlocked the car doors.

"Where'd you get the keys?"

"Don't ask questions."

Raid sat down behind the wheel and started the car. He drove it for about three miles and left it at the edge of a forest. Then he climbed back into the van. The boy drove off down the pitted road toward town, glancing occasionally at his silent passenger.

"It wasn't easy, but I finally got the old man to realize the stakes—he took a trip to Germany. I promised to call as soon as it's safe here."

"Good."

"Seems to me like things are going in the wrong direction. Fine time for this Finnish gangster to show up."

Raid didn't reply.

"What're we gonna do?"

"I'll tell you tomorrow."

"Why not now?"

"Because now I'm going to sleep."

* * *

Officer Similä, from Mikkeli police department, provided the tip that put the dark green SUV back on the radar. Two days ago while on vacation, he had spotted the vehicle in a gas station parking lot as he exchanged the propane tank from his cabin.

After returning to the office, Similä had been browsing through the past week's memos and noticed that the Helsinki PD was hunting for a green Land Rover Freelander, probably driven by a Hispanic-looking man.

This last detail was the very reason the vehicle had even stuck in Similä's memory. The driver had looked exactly like the coffee pickers on the sunny slopes of the Andes in a recent TV commercial. The same handlebar mustache and droopy eyes. Similä had almost laughed aloud, but had concealed his smile by wiping his mouth with the back of his hand. The man in the passenger seat had the same look, but slightly younger. In the back seat had been two more men, but the sun had glared off the windows so that Similä was unable to make out their features. The car had had Swedish plates.

Officer Similä was positive this was the car and the men in question. He read the APB in more detail. Toward the end, it emphasized that the men could be armed and dangerous. The contact people were Lieutenants Eero Jansson and Simo Kempas, and detectives Hannu Huusko and Sanna Susisaari.

Similä mulled over the names for a moment, then decided to call Huusko. He would rather talk with a fellow officer than a supervisor, and with a man rather than a woman. Women and supervisors spoke a different language than he did.

He was already punching in the number when Officer Arjola walked in holding a cup of coffee. Arjola was a tall, wiry man, an endurance runner and rower, and in the winter, a long-distance cross-country skier. For years, he'd been trying to convince Similä to partake in the Sulkava rowing race, an annual competition spanning roughly forty miles, but Similä had so far managed to evade it with one excuse or another.

"How was vacation? Any fish?"

"Good. A few," said Similä, matching Arjola's brevity.

"You get the sauna done?"

"Just about."

Similä had been remodeling the floor of his old log sauna, as well as replacing the worn-out stove. Arjola took an interest in such projects, and had been giving Similä plenty of pushy, unsolicited advice, all the way down to the brand of the stove.

"Anything new and exciting around here?" asked Similä, before Arjola could ask about the stove. He had settled on a different brand that cost less, one well-rated by *Tekniikan Maailma*, a leading technology magazine.

"The summer vacationers are keeping us busy. Two drownings and a stabbing, but that's the worst of it."

Ever since a bomb exploded in a bank robber's car in front of Mikkeli Town Hall one summer, Similä had been afraid that he'd miss out on some nationally significant incident while on summer vacation. During the explosion, Similä had been in Lapland, and hadn't heard about the incident, which had shocked the entire nation, until three days later.

This was Similä's opportunity to shine by bringing up the APB.

"I saw that SUV while I was on vacation."

Arjola looked doubtfully at Similä. As far as he was concerned, Similä was overeager, and prone to rushing to conclusions. When tackling a crossword puzzle, the younger officer always penciled in the first word he could think of that fit the space, no matter how many other options there might have been. And when Arjola saw the puzzle, and starting making corrections, it always wound up quite a mess.

"The Land Rover Freelander," Arjola guessed. "Was that the make?"

"That's the one. And dark green, too, just like it says, a metallic green."

"How can you be sure about the make?"

"Come, on…I know my SUVs. I had a Rover myself once."

"That thing was ancient."

"Still. I'm a connoisseur. And I read the magazine reviews. Besides, the guy behind the wheel looked

Hispanic, and had a big mustache. Same with the guy in the passenger seat."

"If Helsinki's looking for it, what's it doing here?"

"It's a nationwide APB. Maybe the driver's heading north to cross the border into Sweden... Oh yeah, and it had Swedish plates."

"Was that in the APB?"

"No."

Arjola hemmed and hawed. "Weeell...if I were you, I'd think twice about it. Respect is hard to earn, but easy to lose."

Annoyed by Arjola's arrogance, Similä turned his eyes away. In his own way, Arjola was a decent cop, but as far as Similä was concerned, he should concentrate more on his work than his sporting endeavors. The moment he finished one marathon, he began plans for another, and he spent a good portion of his days calling training partners, poking around for cheap rental cars and good hotels, and looking for sponsors.

"I'd think twice," Arjola muttered again, and sat down behind his desk. He dropped a sugar cube into his coffee, and began stirring it with a plastic spoon.

"There's no doubt in my mind... It matches the description perfectly... The make, the color, the driver..."

"Don't you think someone else would've seen it? You can't just drive halfway across Finland in a wanted car without getting noticed... And what would a bunch of South American gangsters be doing around here anyway? If you wanna get to Sweden, it's a lot faster to take the ferry from Helsinki. Anyway I can't imagine professional criminals giving the police time to catch up with them after murdering two people."

"Well, it just occurred to me that..."

Similä trailed off, knowing that Arjola wouldn't be able to resist the bait.

"You should finish your sentences. What occurred to you?"

"That it might affect the Mikkeli PD's reputation if I didn't say anything and those guys turned out to be the murderers."

Arjola eased up a little.

Before long, his excitement began to show, and Similä could guess why. If the car and the men were found on the basis of this tip, Arjola, too, would get to bask in the glory of a rare triumph for such a small town. He could sit around the break table and brag that the murderers were found because of *our* tip, and that Helsinki was just cherry-picking off of *our* hard work.

Arjola took out a notepad, and dug a pen out of his breast pocket.

"Let's go through all the details once more before you call, so we don't forget anything. What gas station was it?"

Similä told him.

"And the date and time?"

"Tuesday, sometime around one in the afternoon."

"Thirteen hundred hours, Tuesday," repeated Arjola as he wrote it down. "A dark green SUV, Swedish plates, anything else?"

"You mean plate numbers?"

"Yeah…or anything. You know, bumper stickers, scratches, dents, fancy accessories."

"I don't recall any," said Similä hesitantly. He didn't especially want any help.

"Where exactly was the car? At the gas pump, in the parking lot?"

"In a parking spot."

Arjola pointed the pen at Similä and asked a question, which he immediately answered himself, "Why would a driver stop at the gas station? Either he needs to fill up, or he wants coffee, lunch, or both."

"Maybe they wanted to buy a tabloid," smirked Similä.

"That's possible too," said Arjola with a straight face.

"Or needed to piss."

Arjola glanced at Similä disapprovingly. "Hey, you started this, take it seriously. The gas station has a security camera. I'm sure the men and the car are on the tape. Let's see this through."

Arjola slipped the pen back into his breast pocket and sprang to his feet.

"Here's what we'll do. We'll go straight to the gas station and confiscate the tapes. Once we've watched them, we can call those detectives in Helsinki."

* * *

Within two hours, Arjola's excitement was so palpable that he could all but feel the lieutenant stripes on his shoulders.

Luckily, the tape was almost new, so the picture quality was crisp—the car's model and license plate were clearly visible. The image of the driver paying at the register was also clear. The best picture, however, was of Similä leering out the window at the car.

"Did you really have to stare like that?" said Arjola.

"Of course. How else would I have been so sure it was a Freelander?"

"With Swedish plates."

"My point exactly. Rewind."

Arjola rewound the tape to the spot where the SUV pulled up to the gas pump. Two men got out, one of whom removed the gas cap and went to the pump. The other headed for the store. He stopped briefly, flicked his hand, and then continued on.

"What was that?"

Arjola rewound it again. This time, he pressed pause repeatedly to show the image frame by frame.

"He's got something in his hand. Pause it."

Arjola stopped the tape. The image flickered a bit at the top, but otherwise, it was sharp.

"A coke bottle. He's tossing it in the garbage."

Arjola peered out of the back room toward the register, where the station owner, a man in his forties, was sitting.

"How often do they pick up the trash here?"

"Whenever it fills up."

"When's the last time?"

"Three, four days ago."

"Could you come over here for a minute?"

Arjola showed him the car and the men on the tape, "You remember these guys? The SUV, and the two Hispanic-looking guys?"

The man looked at the frame with a wrinkled brow.

"Yeah...must've been the day before last. That guy's mustache is hard to forget. Looks like something out of a comedy sketch. I had to take over for the one of the girls... She was running errands."

"You remember what they bought?"

"Ten gallons of gas, some tabloids, chocolate bars and chips, and two bottles of diet coke."

"Did they pay by cash or plastic?" said Arjola.

"Cash."

"Damn!" said Arjola. "Coulda got the name with a credit card."

"So how come you're so interested in these guys?" said the owner.

"Too early to say. But we'll have to confiscate the tapes for the case."

"Do I get a replacement?"

"That reminds me," said Arjola. "The Mikkeli PD running club is registering for the Stockholm marathon this year. We'd be grateful for any donations. We publish a sports journal with a free ad for every sponsor... Why don't you just think about it while we have a look around."

Arjola and Similä fetched the garbage can and carried it into the empty half of the service garage. In the other half, a young man in coveralls was changing the shocks on a Nissan compact. Similä spread some newspaper out on the floor and Arjola dumped the trash out on top of it.

The trash can had been nearly full, but they found the coke bottle quickly. It was the only one in there. Arjola held it up with a cheeky grin, and put it in a plastic bag they'd gotten from the cashier.

"*Now* it's time to call Helsinki."

Similä dug the printout out of his pocket.

"I got four numbers here."

Arjola snatched the paper and looked it over.

"I'll call this Kempas. I've met him. He did a lecture on undercover work with us once. Knows his stuff."

"I was thinking maybe Huusko."

"Nope. Kempas," said Arjola with an authority afforded only by his seniority. Similä thought it best to comply.

18.

"I'm gonna find out who this Mr. U. is, and what he's up to nowadays," said Huusko. "If his picture's in the annual report, I know someone who can pick him out."

"You mean the ex-cop's wife?" said Jansson.

"Yep. Then I'm meeting with that former Finnair security officer. The one that runs a hobby farm."

"You still think the murders could be connected to Liljeblad's work?"

"Well, what I *don't* think is that the South Americans killed Aho. Maybe Liljeblad and Hernando, but not Aho."

Jansson took a swig from a one-liter bottle of mineral water.

"After you talk to the cop's wife, come back and pick me up. A little fresh air in the countryside would do me good."

* * *

Huusko had to wait outside the shop for ten minutes while a customer quibbled over her garments. When she finally came out the door, he slipped inside. Kero's wife recognized him immediately, and didn't look pleased to see him.

"Did you find him?"

Huusko shook his head and dug out the annual report.

"I need a little favor."

"I thought you were gonna leave me alone."

"You mentioned that this Mr. U. worked for Solar Construction. Well, here's a copy of the company's annual report from back then. Can you show me which one of these suits is him?"

She fetched a pair of eyeglasses from behind the counter. Clearly embarrassed by them, she slipped them on.

Huusko furled his brow. "You didn't have any trouble seeing without glasses last time. That birthmark was pretty small."

"I didn't see any better. You described it for me."

She began scanning the photos, and abruptly put her finger on one of them. "This one here. That's him."

Huusko looked at the photo she had pointed out. "Tom Hietama, vice president of sales. Doesn't ring a bell. Mean anything to you?"

"No more than last time."

Huusko looked at the photo again. It was twenty-plus years old, so the thirty-something man in the photo had to be over fifty now. His face was square, with a broad forehead. His dark hair was receding around his temples. The man stared at the camera with something akin to hostility.

"Have you remembered anything else since we last met?"

"No… Well…there's this one thing… I remembered that Ritva—the woman in the photo with Mr. U.—was laughing about something once…about the man right there being a candidate in the church council elections."

"The church council?"

"Yes. I remember it because right afterwards I saw his picture in some free newspaper. Sure enough, there he was, a candidate from the conservative party."

* * *

The countryside of Southern Finland was in all its autumn glory. Jansson gazed at the landscape with a pensive look on his face.

"I've never been much of a cabin man," said Jansson. "But maybe there is something to it."

"I got a hunch that all this fawning over rural life is a Farmers Party conspiracy."

"Well, I can't deny that it's beautiful out here."

"Maybe now, but you just wait till November, when the sleet starts coming down."

Huusko pulled over and looked at the map. Jansson cranked down the window to take in the aromas of the countryside.

"Shut the window," said Huusko. "Smells like shit out here. Must be a pig farm around."

Jansson took his time shutting the window.

"It does kind of smell. You figure it out?"

"A right after the gas station and head toward the sea till we get to a little bridge and a big red barn. From there, we should be able to see the greenhouses."

Huusko found the gas station, and then the barn. Ahead on the right were three large greenhouses, which stood in front of the sprawling old main building and a few other outbuildings. Huusko pulled up to the main building.

A youthful-looking man emerged from one of the greenhouses, waved, and shouted, "Come on over!"

It was warm and humid in the greenhouse, and only half of it was in use. Some kind of lettuce was growing in the beds. The man wiped his hands on the bib of his overalls and held out his hand to Huusko.

"Name's Kallio. My friend Alanko already called and warned me you might be coming."

"Did he say what it was about?" asked Huusko.

"Not much. So let's have it."

Huusko let Jansson do the honors.

"We're investigating a double murder. One of the victims was a Finnair flight attendant, and it's possible that the murders have something to do with her job: thefts of tax-free goods or drug trafficking. She was guilty of both."

"Then you're talking to the right man. I opened up that case. I suppose Alanko already told you?"

"Some," said Huusko. "But we'd rather hear it directly from you."

"Who was the flight attendant?"

"Nina Liljeblad."

Kallio recognized the name.

"Nina, huh? Not so tough after all."

"What do you mean?" said Jansson.

"Last time we met, she claimed she was untouchable. Well, looks like she wasn't."

"What did she mean untouchable?"

"Well, this was just after we busted her at work on drugs. And just before I left I interrogated her, and she laughed in my face."

"Let's go back to the beginning," said Jansson.

"Right. Well, it all started when a large amount of inventory was reported missing. I heard about it almost by accident from one of the warehouse guys. So I started looking into it, searched a few lockers, and found a bunch of stolen stuff. The head union rep called me and told me I'd been harassing the employees and violating their rights in the employment contract. But the most surprising thing was that the bosses were backing him... Next one of the warehouse guys gets pulled over for DUI. They searched his apartment and found almost twenty grand worth of goods stolen from airplanes and the warehouse. I discussed the case with the Vantaa police department and Customs, and they decided to start an investigation. I'm sure Alanko told you how that went."

"Alanko suspected their informant was murdered. Do you believe that?"

"Absolutely."

"It's that serious?" said Jansson.

"We're talking about the futures of dozens of employees. And not just workers, but bosses, too. If this racket had come to light, it would've triggered a bloodbath. Plenty of heads would've rolled."

"Tell me more about Liljeblad," said Jansson.

"Lord have mercy on that sly, devious, and beautiful woman. She was all of those."

"Over five grand worth of tax-free goods were found in her apartment."

"All part of her benefits package. But you said something about drugs?"

"We found two ounces of cocaine in her bag. An amount that large isn't for personal use. And she'd just gotten off a flight from Spain, too."

"Doesn't surprise me at all. She realized how easy it was, and decided to make a killing."

"Do you think she was working alone?"

"Maybe with the cocaine, but not the rest. Otherwise, it doesn't explain why they kept her on after all her stunts."

"Did she have a protector in the company?" asked Jansson.

"Probably several. She played her men like pipes."

"How high up were these protectors?"

"Way up...at least in the last incident."

"You're talking about the incident where she was high on the plane?"

"That's right. It happened on a flight from Tokyo to Helsinki. She wasn't able to perform her duties, and passed out in the bathroom. The co-pilot called it in during the flight, and I came to meet them at the gate. By that time, she was already awake, and somewhat coherent. She was the last one off the plane, but not alone—she walked off with both the CEO *and* the CFO. They'd been on a business trip in Tokyo. The CFO told me it was just food poisoning, and the resulting fatigue. He said straight to my face that it was best if I forgot the whole incident."

"Do you have any idea how she had such a hold on them?"

"Pulled 'em around by the berries—mile-high club and stuff like that. With that kind of allure, a little misstep could be forgiven, right?"

"Do you know what this business trip was concerning?" asked Jansson.

"Plane deals. The airline sold four planes to a Japanese investment firm and then leased 'em right back."

"What's the sense in that?" Huusko wondered.

"It's called a sale-and-leaseback arrangement. In certain situations, they can be beneficial for tax purposes."

"And in this situation?"

"One attorney I spoke with suspected it. And it raised eyebrows that ownership of the planes was transferred to a company based out of the Cayman Islands."

"Didn't you have any opportunity as a corporate security officer to find out what was going on?"

"Not really."

"Did you yourself suspect that something shady was happening?"

"When tax havens are in the picture, I'm always suspicious. The airline business is among the world's most corrupt, and if an off-shore company is involved, then it's twice as suspicious. Who can really say whether the executives are taking a little slice of the profits, arranging for a fraction of the lease payments to be wired to their own bank accounts in the same tax haven. No matter how honest they start out, the buyer might suggest such a deal to sweeten the pot. And something like that would be hard to turn down."

"Did Liljeblad stay the night in Tokyo?"

"Of course. It's standard procedure on overseas flights for the crew to stay the night."

"Was she in the same hotel with the CEO and CFO?"

"Likely. Typically all the employees stay in the same place."

"Do you recognize any of these men?" asked Huusko, and handed over the Solar Construction annual report.

Kallio looked through the photographs, "Hietama. He's the CFO I was talking about."

"The one watching out for Liljeblad?"

"Yep."

"Tell us a little more about him," said Jansson.

"He's been with the firm for almost twenty years, and kept tight reins on it from the very beginning. When the former CEO left, a lot of people thought Hietama would take his place, but the spot went to a Social Democrat. Hietama's with the conservatives. As long as the state owns a majority of the airline, politics will always run the show."

"Does he have a family?"

"God, family, and country. He's got all his ducks in order. Lives the good life in Espoo…wife's a manager at the Department of the Treasury…two kids. He's a lieutenant in the reserves and a member of the church council."

"And you still think he's a member of the mile-high club?" said Huusko.

"Rumor has it he's a wolf in sheep's clothing. That his wife can't keep up with his desires, and never has. A stewardess mentioned something to me once at a Christmas party, but the next day, after she'd sobered up, she recanted. She'd claimed that Hietama had accosted her in the middle of a flight and demanded sex or she'd lose her job."

"Did you believe her?"

"Why wouldn't I? She had no reason to lie. And she was genuinely afraid. Later on, I got an anonymous tip that Hietama arranged for certain stewardesses to work his flights and provide special services, either on the plane or in the hotel."

"Is he the one that got you fired?" asked Huusko.

"Well, he sure didn't fight it. But what does he have to do with Liljeblad's murder?"

"They had a relationship," said Jansson.

"That's it?"

"We're still looking into it. Do you think it's possible that Liljeblad was killed for work-related issues?"

"For example?"

"She was a cocaine user. Maybe they thought she was too big of a risk. Or maybe she got too bold and demanding."

"That would fit the picture. She *was* bold and demanding, the type to make off with more than she could carry."

"If that's why she was killed, who do you think could have done it?"

"I wouldn't really know. It's a tough bunch, though. Maybe they outsourced the job to the Russians or Estonians."

"What about Hietama?"

"You don't think *he* did it, do you?"

"Well, is it possible?"

"I just don't see why he would've. I don't think he was involved with the theft ring, even if he knew about it. He was playing for bigger stakes."

"What if his relationship with Liljeblad was revealed? It could've wrecked his marriage. And what if Liljeblad knew some other sensitive things about him."

"You think she was blackmailing him?"

"Somebody apparently was," said Jansson.

"Who?"

"You're a former cop, aren't you?"

"Vantaa PD. Ten years with the property crimes division."

"Well, a certain private investigator, also a former cop, was found shot dead in Vantaa. We think he was blackmailing Hietama. He had photos of Hietama and Liljeblad having sex, among others."

"Huh," Kallio muttered. "How'd he get the photos?"

Jansson looked to Huusko.

"The oldest of the photos are from twenty-plus years ago," said Huusko. "He was with the vice squad then, and got the photos while working a prostitution raid. At that time, Hietama was working for Solar Construction, where he was using the girls to help him produce business. He was also dipping in on the side himself. The more recent photos were taken when a woman suspected her husband of having an affair with Liljeblad, and hired Aho to follow him."

"Tricky case," said Kallio. "Never say never. Hietama's smart and aggressive. He could've ordered the hit, but he wouldn't do it himself. He's a very careful man, and committing murder would be too much of a risk."

"The social consequences to somebody like that could be more serious than we might imagine," said Jansson.

"Still. I'm the last one who'd want to defend him, but it's hard to believe he'd kill anyone."

Jansson's phone rang. "Excuse me," he said, and withdrew to the side.

Jansson recognized the voice immediately.

"Are you in Finland?" he asked.

"Yes."

"I presume you have something important to discuss?"

"That's right. I'd like to help with your crime prevention efforts."

"What kind of crimes are we talking about?"

"Drugs and murder."

"This is a bad time, but let's hear the short version."

"I'm at Nygren's old place. There's four South American drug dealers headed here now."

"South American? How do you know?"

"They were here before, and promised to return. They're looking for a big cocaine shipment that somehow ended up at a local grocery store in a banana crate. The grocer's kid got me mixed up in it. They already killed his friend, and I'll probably have to kill them, unless you get to them first."

"Were these South Americans driving an SUV?"

"Did you already know, or was that a guess?"

"I guess I knew."

"Then our interests overlap."

"Looks that way. Does the kid still have the cocaine?"

"I don't know."

"Well...I have to go. I'll call you later and we can talk more."

"When?"

"One hour."

"Okay."

238

Jansson approached Huusko and Kallio.

"I appreciate your help, but unfortunately, we've got to go."

"Won't you stay for coffee?"

"Some other time."

Kallio walked them to their car.

"To tell you the truth, they did me a favor by firing me. I'm starting to enjoy this life, and I get along just fine. My wife even got a job in town as an elementary school teacher."

Jansson looked around at the fields. "I don't doubt it. Almost makes me jealous."

* * *

Once the car was outside the gate, Jansson spoke up, "The South Americans were seen in a town called Pyhäsalo. A cocaine shipment was accidentally sent there."

"Where's Pyhäsalo?"

"In Savo."

"Does Kempas know?"

"Not yet."

"Who called?"

"Someone who does."

"Well, let's get cracking, then."

"Take it easy, though. Let's think carefully about how to proceed. I don't want anybody's life in danger."

"Yeah, yeah. What do you think about Hietama? Sure looks like Aho was putting on the squeeze."

"It's possible."

"Alright if I have a chat with him?"

Jansson glanced over at Huusko, who was trying his best to look well-intentioned.

"Concerning what crime?"

239

"No crime at all. Aho had a picture of him, and Aho died. Seems natural the police would ask him about it."

Jansson thought for a moment. "Alright. Just don't ask him to show you his ass. We don't have a speck of evidence against him. Let's play this by the book."

19.

Pyhäsalo? Now why did that name sound familiar?

Kempas leaned back in his chair and looked relaxed for a change.

Pyhäsalo...the little town in east Savo. But what had just happened in east Savo?

Kempas racked his brain with all his might, and finally, it came back to him.

"Nygren's house. It was in Pyhäsalo," he said aloud, though he was alone in his office.

Kempas had visited the house while tracking Nygren, who had been on his way to Lapland to die before his cancer could kill him in a more painful way. Nygren's nephew, known as Raid, and an even harder criminal than his uncle, had been along for the ride. He was the hit man who had inherited Nygren's house.

Two plus two. Raid was a gunslinger, and there'd been some shooting in Pyhäsalo. But who had shot at who? Had Raid shot the South Americans, or vice versa? Kempas didn't believe in coincidences—two and two was simply four.

He took a map of Finland out of the drawer and unfolded it onto his desk, and when he found Pyhäsalo, he circled it. The nearest large towns were Kuopio and Pieksämäki.

Kempas opened Nygren's file on the computer. He had once interviewed a farmer who lived near Nygren's place, and taken his number down. Kempas glanced at his watch: twenty after two.

What would a sixty-something farmer be doing at two thirty in the afternoon on an east Savo farm? Buzzing around in the fields on an old tractor, chopping firewood with a log splitter, chasing after the piglets in the pen, pulling up the nets in the lake, or lounging on the steps at the store, sucking down a beer. He certainly wouldn't be sitting by the phone.

Kempas was wrong.

"Väänänen."

"Hi. This is Lieutenant Kempas from the Helsinki police. We met once concerning your neighbor, Mr. Nygren, if you remember."

"You the scrawny guy? Dark hair?"

"That's right. Lean…dark hair."

"Flat forehead, bad skin?"

"Listen…"

"You were tryin' to find Nygren?"

"Yes."

"Who you doggin' now?"

"Nobody. I just want to ask a few questions… I was a friend of Nygren's."

"You sure didn't look it. Did he really shoot himself in Lapland?"

"He had cancer."

"But he went to there to die?"

"Yes, that's right."

"I reckon a guy would want some privacy when he faces death. What about the nephew… What happened to him?"

"That's who I wanted to ask about. Is he there now?"

The man considered his choice of words, and Kempas could almost hear him twisting them around like a true Savo man.

"Somebody is."

"Who is somebody?"

"Beats me."

"When did this somebody arrive?"

"The house's been heated since day before yesterday. I seen the smoke, but nothing else. Yesterday I went into town for the day."

"The police received a complaint about gunfire there. Did you hear any shots?"

"Here? Gunfire?"

"Yes. We received the complaint yesterday, but the shooting was heard the day before yesterday."

"I reckon I did hear something. Four shots or so?"

"That's what we heard. Where do you think the shots came from?"

"Hard to say."

"What's your guess?"

"Seems to me they came from different directions. Two from town, two from the lake."

"I'm guessing you know your guns. Can you speculate as to what kind of guns they were? Rifle, shotgun, pistol?"

"Nobody'd be shooting pistols around here. Shotguns and rifles, that's the local fare."

"Doesn't Nygren's house fall between the lake and your farm?"

"That's right."

"Could I give you my number so you can call me back after you've been over there?"

"Alright, let's have it."

Kempas gave him his number.

"One more thing. Did you see any Hispanic-looking men around there?"

"Not I, but someone at the store mentioned somethin'. Wondered what they's doin' around here. Didn't look like tourists."

"Who saw them?"

"The shopkeeper."

"The name, please?"

"Porola, Väinö Porola."

Kempas looked up Väinö Porola's information in the database. Born April 12, 1948 in Pyhäsalo. Divorced, with a twenty-two-year-old son, Matti. According to the database, Matti still lived at home. Kempas punched the boy's information into the computer. He'd been convicted on drug charges in Kuopio district court. His sentence of six months in jail had been suspended on condition of good behavior.

Kempas walked over to Kamppari's office. Kamppari was reading the newspaper and munching on salad from a plastic container.

"Yesterday, you mentioned a tip about a couple of country boys hawking off thirty pounds of cocaine in Helsinki."

"Yeah, but it didn't sound credible. More like an April Fool's joke."

"Who did it come from?"

"A small-time Estonian dealer."

"What else did he tell you?"

"That one of his buddies bought about an ounce from these kids at the Hotel Kämp."

"Don't you trust your informant?"

"Not this one, least not always. When he panics, he'll say just about anything."

"Did you check with the hotel?"

Kamppari munched on a black olive, spit the pit into his hand, and tossed it into the waste basket.

"What're you getting at? We got more important business, you know."

Kempas went back into his office, called the Hotel Kämp, and introduced himself.

* * *

Jansson shed his overcoat. Then he took off his gentleman's cap with the houndstooth pattern and set it on the backrest of his chair. The cap had been a present from his wife, but Jansson hadn't warmed up to it yet.

"You have a second?" Kempas asked from the doorway.

"I always have a second."

"A couple of days ago, Narcotics got a tip that a couple of country boys were selling off a big stash of cocaine at the Hotel Kämp. I checked with the hotel about it, and they said a young man by the name of Matti Porola had been there with a friend."

"The shopkeeper's son?" said Jansson. "From Pyhäsalo?"

Kempas gaped at Jansson. "How'd you know?"

"Informant. Go on."

"This Porola has a previous drug conviction, and his friend's been reported missing. A green SUV was seen sixty miles from Pyhäsalo, and soon afterwards, four Hispanic-looking men were seen in Pyhäsalo. We've also received reports of gunfire there."

"They were looking for a thirty pound shipment of cocaine that was hidden in a banana crate, but they didn't find it," said Jansson. "The shopkeeper's kid has it."

Kempas looked pained. "I don't know how I feel about fellow cops hiding key information from me."

"I just got the intel."

"Then let's call the local precinct there and have them take the kid in for safekeeping. I was thinking I'd go myself, too... And one more thing," said Kempas. "Pyhäsalo's the town where Nygren's place is. Nygren left the house to his nephew."

"You mean Raid?"

"That's right. And it's likely Raid is there right now. According to the neighbor, the gunshots came from the direction of that house."

"I'm coming with you," said Jansson. "And the dog, too."

20.

The façade of Finnair's headquarters looked rather pretentious to Huusko: all glass and aluminum. A guard on the security company's payroll sat in a glass booth in the lobby, reading a tabloid. Huusko knocked on the glass. The man put the tabloid away and slid the window open.

"I'm here to meet with Mr. Hietama."

"Do you have an appointment?"

"Yes."

"One moment."

The security guard closed the window and picked up the phone. He exchanged a few words with somebody, then opened the window again.

"Name?"

"Huusko."

"Have a seat. Somebody will be down shortly."

Huusko sat down on a leather sofa, and paged briefly through a magazine on the coffee table before his escort, a young woman in a pantsuit, came to meet him. She led him to the elevator, which brought them down three stories underground.

"We going to the bomb shelter?" said Huusko.

"To the gym."

"How many miles do I have to run before I'm allowed to meet him?"

The woman laughed. "Our CFO keeps himself in good shape. And he encourages all of his employees to do the same."

"Sounds like some Aryan."

The gym was well equipped. In addition to the exercise machines, three TVs hung from the walls, all looping the same music video. Hietama was sitting on the rowing machine, wearing a gray track suit with the company logo on the front. He was rowing hard, evidenced by the beads of sweat on his forehead. Hietama's hairline had receded a couple of inches since his time with Solar Construction, but otherwise, he looked the same. Time had had little effect on his chiseled features.

"Heli, get us some coffee," he said.

On the opposite wall was a small space with a table, a few chairs, and a thermos.

Hietama took a few more brisk strokes, then stepped off the rowing machine. With a wave of his hand, he indicated to the woman that she should leave, then he held his hand out to Huusko. Huusko guessed correctly that his handshake would be crushing. Most con-men had a firm handshake and good eye contact.

"How official is this meeting, Hannu?"

Huusko couldn't stand people who called him by his first name when they didn't know him. To him, it was a manipulative American way of cozying up to somebody.

"That depends on what we find out."

"What are you trying to find out?"

"I'm working on a murder case… Three of them, actually."

Hietama sat down at the table with a confident bearing. He dropped a sugar cube into his coffee and took a sip.

"Go ahead, then. I'm all ears."

"You're familiar with a private investigator by the name of Aho?"

"I am?"

"You mean you're not?"

248

"Tell me more. I'm in contact with dozens of people every day."

Huusko sat down opposite Hietama. "Aho is a former police officer. Among other things, he investigated a prostitution case when you were still the vice president of sales at Solar Construction. You yourself were involved with the case, don't you remember?"

Hietama shook his head. "I'm not involved with prostitution."

"Maybe not anymore."

Huusko slid Aho's photo across the table.

"This came out of the files for the prostitution case."

Hietama glanced at the photo, and his face went blank.

"This picture must be at least twenty years old."

"And it is. You recognize that rear end?"

"Should I?"

"I don't know how well a guy can recognize his own ass, but if I had a badge like that, I'd think it pretty easy."

Hietama didn't respond.

"You do have the same birthmark, isn't that right?"

"Is this how low the Finnish police have stooped? Do they really pay you for harassing people with these kinds of things?"

"First of all, it's not the Finnish police, it's just me. Second, for what little they pay me, this is what you get."

"What do you want?"

"Just to clear up a few facts. Is this you in the photo? Of course, I could ask your wife. Maybe she'd be able to recognize it better."

"Are you blackmailing me?"

"Just answer the question."

"Is seeing a prostitute a crime?"

"Does that mean it *is* you?"

"You can draw your own conclusions."

Huusko took the photo and put it back into his pocket.

"According to the case files, you were procuring prostitutes for your customers, and regularly soliciting them yourself."

"If I remember correctly, nothing ever came of that case. At least not anything that had any impact on me."

"This photograph came from Aho's collection. Now Aho's been found murdered in his car in Vantaa. Does the name ring a bell yet?"

"No."

"What about Nina Liljeblad? That mean anything to you?"

"Of course. She was an employee with our company. It was in the newspapers, and I can read. Very unfortunate."

"What about on a personal level?"

"What do you mean?"

"Have you ever been in a situation with Liljeblad that could have resulted in the same sort of photos as the one I just showed you?"

"No-o."

Hietama's response was somewhat hesitant.

"What if I refresh your memory: last summer, a car, and the Haukilahti seashore…bring anything to mind? Aho was following Liljeblad, and he had a nice camera along with a big zoom lens."

Hietama shook his head.

"And what if we search your car and find Liljeblad's fingerprints?"

"Go ahead."

That one smacked of confidence. Hietama could have traded in the car, or thoroughly cleaned it.

"Where were you on Tuesday?"

"Do you honestly believe that I could've murdered her?"

"Routine question."

"At that time, I was in Tallinn. I returned yesterday. You can check with my secretary. We probably had fifty witnesses on the plane. Is that enough?"

"Back in May, you were in Tokyo, negotiating the sale-and-leaseback arrangement for four airplanes. Was Liljeblad on the same flight?"

"Yes. You know that."

"And the same hotel?"

"Yes."

"And the same room?"

"No."

"Were you aware that Liljeblad was a cocaine user?"

"No, I wasn't."

"But she had had problems at work. She'd received several warnings, but was never fired because you were protecting her."

"She was a good employee. She'd been with us for over ten years. Sometimes we have to help solve our employees' problems, and firing them isn't always the best way to solve it."

"We found two ounces of cocaine in her bag, and five grand worth of tax-free goods stolen from airplanes in her apartment. Is that what you call a good employee?"

"I wasn't aware of that."

"Was Liljeblad blackmailing you?"

"No. And what could she possibly blackmail me with?"

"Your sexual relationship."

"We didn't have any sexual relationship."

"What about Aho? Was he blackmailing you?"

"No. I don't even know the man."

251

"We're currently analyzing Aho's phone records. If we found a call to your phone, what would you say about that?"

"Nothing. He didn't call me... At least not that I remember. I already told you I get dozens of calls every day. People applying for jobs, various companies offering their services. Maybe he called us to offer his services as a private investigator."

"Have you ever been to Liljeblad's apartment?"

"No."

"You've never driven her home?"

"No. Not that I remember, anyway."

"Are you married?"

"Yes, as you know."

"Children?"

"Three."

"That's nice."

"What is that supposed to mean?"

"That I'm happy for you. Lasting marriages are so rare nowadays."

Hietama's face flushed a bit.

"Where were you last Friday?"

Hietama thought for a moment. "Had I known how rudely you'd behave, I would've had my lawyer here. I'm more than willing to help the police, but this hardly qualifies as police work. This is harassment. I don't know what you have against me, but you won't get another opportunity to waste my time."

"That won't be up to you."

Hietama winced.

"Is there some reason you won't tell me where you were on Friday?"

"I was in London. I came back on Saturday."

"When you were in Tokyo, you sold four airplanes and rented them back. Was that very smart?"

252

"We're not the only company that does so. And I don't think you're qualified to assess those types of activities."

"Is it the state's position that doing business with tax havens is advisable?"

"The state is only one of our shareholders."

"But the largest."

"Times are changing for business…"

"Do you yourself have a personal bank account at a tax haven?"

"What do you mean?" Hietama growled.

"Just asking. Purely out of curiosity. Seems like something like that would be nice. Once a month, just squirrel away a piece of your paycheck in some tax paradise…in case of hard times."

"Hard times for you might not be as far off as you'd think. I know a lot of police brass as well as top officials at the ministry of the interior."

"I'd love to hear their names."

Hietama glowered at Huusko, but said nothing.

"How about just one?"

"Leave."

Huusko got up. Hietama hurried off to a stationary bicycle and began pedaling furiously.

Huusko stepped into the hallway with the feeling that the prostitute who'd been beaten and raped by Hietama's associates had gotten at least some restitution.

Just as he was climbing into the car, his phone rang.

"Huusko."

"This is Liuhula from the Print Brothers. You were here a while back asking about Aho?"

"That's right."

"You find him yet?"

"Yes. Dead."

"Aho's dead?"

"Yes."

"Murdered?"

"Yes."

"Then it's a good thing I called. Got some mail here."

"For Aho?"

"Yes."

"What sort of mail?"

"A thick envelope...photos, I think, since the sender looks like a photo lab."

"I'm on my way. I'll be there in less than half an hour. Don't go anywhere."

* * *

Huusko waited until he was back in the car before opening the envelope. The very top photo was the one he had been looking for. It had been taken from behind some birch saplings, and the subject was a silver BMW with its back door wide open, and a couple who were clearly trying to rid themselves of most of their clothing. Sitting on the backseat, the woman was pulling her panties down from beneath her lifted skirt. The man was next to the car, unbuckling his belt.

By the next photo, the dalliance had progressed: the woman was lying on the backseat with her legs spread, while the man crawled in. The photo was taken from a good distance, but the birthmark on the man's buttocks was clearly visible.

In the next photo, the man was pulling the car door shut behind him, and the following one showed nothing but the back of his head, but the rest was easy to imagine.

Huusko hurriedly scanned the rest of the photos, but the last one caught his attention. It was taken at the Linnanmäki amusement park. The photo showed a younger woman sitting on the carousel with her six-year-old daughter.

Huusko recognized the woman immediately. It was José Hernando's grieving widow, Eila Tuuri.

* * *

"Am I under arrest?" said Eila with a look of fear on her face. She was clutching her daughter closely in her lap.

"Pretty close," said Susisaari. "You've lied to us twice already. That's called obstruction of justice."

Huusko looked grim, which was easy for him. "It's all up to you at this point. If you cooperate with us, maybe we can work out a deal. If not, Child Protection will pick up your daughter, and you'll come down to the station with us."

Eila Tuuri almost burst out crying.

"Heidi, go play in your room."

The girl hopped down from her mother's lap and darted off to her room.

"It was all his idea. The whole thing. But I thought that Liljeblad should have to pay for her actions."

"What are you talking about?" said Susisaari.

"About blackmailing Liljeblad and her boyfriend with the pictures. The boyfriend was ready to pay, but she just laughed it off. In the end, Liljeblad managed to talk him into something else and everything changed."

Susisaari and Huusko looked at her blankly.

"She got him involved with another deal with a bigger payout."

"More blackmail?" said Susisaari.

Eila Tuuri nodded.

"She'd been in Tokyo with some of Finnair's bosses when they sold some airplanes to a Japanese investment firm and leased them back. They were celebrating the deal that evening when the CFO got drunk and told her too much. After he had passed out, she found the documents of the deal and made copies of them. The papers showed that three of the company's executives were getting an illegal slice of the sale proceeds, and a small share of the lease payments. The money was going into their personal bank accounts in the Cayman Islands. The documents had the account numbers and all the details. Liljeblad wanted to blackmail the execs, but she didn't dare do it alone. She promised Aho a share if he would help and protect her."

"So that's why Aho picked her up at the airport?"

"That's why everything went about as wrong as it could possibly go. Henri had to bring her home because she was completely high on cocaine. Liljeblad ended up finding José in bed with her little sister Erika, so she grabbed a bread knife and stabbed him several times in the chest and the neck. José died immediately, and she passed out on the floor. Then the doorbell rang, and Henri and the little sister went out the back door."

Eila Tuuri squeezed out a few sobs, but the sorrow she felt for poor José didn't seem too terribly deep.

"What then?" said Susisaari.

"Even after all that, Henri refused to let the deal go. He had copies of Liljeblad's documents, so he met with the airline's CFO and demanded a million in exchange for the documents. And he'd get the sex photos as a bonus."

"Did he get the money?" said Huusko.

"No. The CFO promised to pay on Thursday, and Henri was killed on Wednesday. That's all I know."

"Who was Aho supposed to meet on Wednesday?"

"I don't know. The last time I saw him was Wednesday morning."

"Do you have any of his things? His papers, for example?"

"No."

"Where are the documents from Liljeblad?"

"I don't know."

Huusko gave her a stern look. "We can get a search warrant at any point, you know."

"Go ahead, if you don't believe me. They're not here, and I don't know where they are. He kept all his things in a brown suitcase so he'd be ready to take off if things went bad."

"Are you positive there's nothing more?" said Susisaari.

"The phone call," she remembered. "On Wednesday morning, Henri called someone on my phone. I wrote the number down."

She hurried off to look for the number, which she found on the telephone stand in the hallway. She handed it to Huusko.

"Did you find out whose number it is?"

"No. I left for work and forgot the whole thing… I haven't done anything wrong except for not telling you about Henri. I just didn't want to get mixed up in anything… I love my daughter, and don't want anything to happen to her… She's already lost her father, isn't that enough for a six-year-old to bear?"

"We won't be nearly as forgiving the third time," said Huusko, and he and Susisaari marched out the door.

21.

"Just a couple hundred yards more," the kid said as he stepped up onto a moist tussock of peat moss. His boots sank halfway into the bog, and made a sucking sound with every step.

Raid followed the boy few feet back. The strong stench of mud and moss rose from the bog.

"Over there behind that little knoll," said the boy. "Not many people know this place. Not even the locals."

The pond, which was about a hundred yards long, and thirty yards wide, lay between two steep bluffs, which were covered by squat, ground-hugging pines with gnarled branches. On the far end of the pond was a bog, toward which the pines bowed their wind-blown heads.

It was a beautiful place, yet somehow sinister. The pond seemed black and ominous, and beyond the trees, storm clouds were gathering.

"I used to play here as a kid. I'd go swimming and jump off that rock into the water. At its deepest, the pond is maybe thirty feet deep. A good spot for perch, but they're almost black."

The boy climbed up onto a rock and skirted behind the ledge. Behind it was a large boulder leaning against the cliff wall, and between the two, a gap measuring about a foot and a half wide by three feet tall. The boy bent down and squeezed sideways through the opening.

Raid followed him.

The entrance opened up into a cavern about ten feet high, and six feet wide. Near the ceiling, a swath of gloaming sky was visible through a fissure. All indications were that the cave had been used. An old oil lamp was resting on a ledge that protruded from the cave wall, and the remnants of a fire pit lay at the rear of the cave.

"When I was kid, I'd stuff sod and birch bark over the crack up there so it'd stay dry in here. I see there's still some up there... I even spent a few nights out here..."

The boy looked at Raid to gauge his reaction, but Raid merely nodded.

"...even though I was too scared to sleep. I used to imagine that some horrible slimy creature might crawl outta the pond and swallow me whole. Oh yeah, forgot to tell you the name: Murder Pond."

"Murder Pond?"

"Yeah. You know there was a murder here once."

"Tell me about it."

"Before the wars, I mean. There used to be a logging camp near here. One time this traveling salesman drifted into camp selling whiskey, and after the loggers were all drunk, he pulled out his deck of cards. The gambling went late into the night, and he fleeced those loggers for every penny they had. Then he gathered up all his things and left for town."

The boy picked up a small rock and began to fiddle with it.

"One of the loggers was really mad, so he circled to the other side of the pond to cut the man off. When the man reached the shore, the logger jumped out from behind a rock and hit him in the head with an axe. One swing was all it took. The logger took all the man's money, tied a couple of rocks to him, and threw him in the water. He hid the man's things in this cave."

Lightning struck, and soon after, the rain began to fall. Quietly at first, then at full tilt.

"The next fall, the rotten corpse floated up to the surface, and the murder was discovered. But the killer was never brought to justice. He got so obsessed with his guilt that he went nuts and hung himself from a tree behind the camp. They found a note in his pocket, begging for forgiveness."

"What a nice story."

"How wild do you think my imagination went when I slept here as a kid?"

"Pretty wild."

The rain picked up some more. The sky was so dark that the interior of the cave was almost pitch black. The boy crawled over to the entrance. Peals of thunder whooshed across the surface of the water.

"Man, that's some thunder," said the boy. "Kinda strange. When I was a kid, I was afraid of almost everything, except for thunder. What about you?"

"Nope."

The boy scrambled back into the cave.

"You must've been afraid of something. Heights? Small spaces? Santa Claus? Snakes? Spiders?"

"None of the above."

"But something, right?"

"Right."

"What."

"Cemeteries."

"How come?"

Raid didn't reply.

"I told you about Murder Pond, now it's your turn."

"It was all my aunt's fault. Her ghost stories were just too good. My elementary school was in the middle of town, near the graveyard. In the morning, I'd ski to school, and it was always dark. My aunt lived next door, and used to tell me and my cousins ghost stories about dead soldiers coming outta their graves at night to look

260

for their missing body parts—some needed heads; others, hands. She told us that if some unlucky soul was in the cemetery just then, the ghosts would take whatever body parts they'd lost in the war. She said every now and then a body was found lying in the cemetery without a head, or hands."

The boy laughed. "Pretty spooky."

"At least for that age."

"What age were you?"

"Seven, maybe eight."

"So when did you move to Sweden?"

"A long time ago."

"You don't wanna talk about it?"

"Not now."

"My childhood wasn't so great either... Dad tried really hard, but there wasn't much he could do... I had a dog, Rob, but some fucker killed him. Tied a big rock to his collar and threw him in the lake... If I ever find out who it was, I'll strap a dumbbell to his neck and dump him in the water...and wave bye-bye..."

A few more rolls of thunder came before the clouds began to clear. Then the rain slowed, and eventually stopped altogether.

"So where's the cocaine?"

"Take a guess."

Raid looked at the boy. "Here in the cave."

"Good guess."

The boy got up, went to the rear wall of the cave, and using a stone outcropping as a foothold, he shinnied up the wall. Once near the top, he thrust his hand into a large chink in the rock and dragged out a duffel bag. He heaved it in front of Raid.

Raid opened it to find a number of bundles wrapped in plastic.

"Each one's two pounds. Two could buy you a nice flat in Helsinki. Sure you don't wanna a piece of it?"

"Yup."

"Come on. Help me out here. All I need is a good contact."

"Nope."

The boy's face darkened.

Raid threw the bag back to him. "Put it back."

The boy did as Raid told him.

"What now?"

Raid handed him the cell phone he'd taken from the Bolivians.

"You're gonna call Simon, the Bolivian who spoke Finnish. His name's in that phone's directory. Tell him you wanna return the dope, but nothing can happen to you. In addition, you want twenty grand as a reward. You gotta act shrewd, like your giving in to greed. You wanna meet them in town ASAP. Got it?"

"Do I have to...? Right now?"

"Right now."

The boy found the number, but hesitated. He looked at Raid, then pressed the call button and lifted the phone to his ear.

Once he'd said what Raid had told him to, he covered the receiver with his hand and whispered to Raid. "He wants my cell number."

"Give it to him."

"You sure?"

"Yes."

He put the phone back to his ear and recited his phone number.

"It'll take you less than an hour... Okay, don't forget the money..."

He hung up the phone.

"They were somewhere near Juva, on their way over. They'll call as soon as they get here."

"Good."

"What now?"

"Go home and make sure your dad hasn't returned. Then wait for their call and bring them here."

"But they'll kill me the second I tell 'em where it is…"

"They'll wanna see it first."

"But then they'll kill me. There's four of them, and one of you."

"Three at the most, probably only two. The boss'll send the brothers tramping through the bog. He'll just wait in the car."

"Three against one is still too much."

"Three against two. We're on the same side."

"Fuck that. I'll just get in the way."

"All you gotta do is remember what I told you."

"I'll remember. Hard to forget when your life's on the line."

"Then we'll be alright."

* * *

After waiting for almost an hour and a half, Raid heard muffled shouts coming from the bog. Shortly after, he heard the sucking sound of boots in the mud, and cursing in Spanish. The Lopez brothers' outerwear was obviously not up to par.

Raid took his position behind a boulder atop the ridge. Beside the boulder was a pine sapling that provided some cover. The distance to the cavern was about sixty yards.

He set the rifle barrel onto a bed of moss he'd scraped together on top of the boulder. Then he sighted the men through the scope.

The boy came first, then the brothers. The third Bolivian never came. The brothers were wearing suit coats, ties, and low-cut dress shoes. Their pant legs were soaked all the way up to the knees. One of the brothers had a pair of binoculars dangling round his neck.

The boy pointed toward the cave. One of the brothers stopped him and raised the binoculars. By the time they swung in his direction, Raid had already ducked behind the sapling. Once he heard the group continue on, he took up his position again. The boy led them to the bluff, and then onward toward the cave. Once they reached the entrance, they stopped. One of the brothers grabbed the boy by the hair and shook him, clearly asking a question. Just as clearly, the boy explained as he pointed to the cave. One of the brothers knelt down on all fours, and the other took out a gun and pressed it against the boy's spine. Raid saw the boy shoot a panicked glance in his direction, but it wasn't time yet.

The man was standing with his side toward Raid, and Raid aimed the crosshairs at the man's ear. He stroked his finger lightly against the trigger and found the sweet spot. The man on all fours peered warily into the cave, then squeezed through the opening. Once he had disappeared from sight, Raid breathed evenly and pulled the trigger.

The subsonic bullet went quietly to work, hit the Bolivian directly in the side of the head, and punched out the other side. Before the man fell, the boy was off and running, but he slipped on the damp rocks and fell to the ground. Raid sprang to his feet and hurried off toward the boy with the rifle at the ready. He saw a pistol emerge from the entrance of the cave, and he fired off a shot. The bullet landed close enough to the entrance that the hand quickly pulled back inside. Raid could hear the boy thrashing through the pines as he made his way up.

Raid approached the cave from the side, and was within thirty feet when he saw a flicker of motion at the entrance and a shot rang off. The haphazard shot ricocheted off the rocks and disappeared in the distance. Raid fired diagonally into the cave, so the bullet would bounce off the inside walls, then he heard a loud curse in Spanish. If the bullet hadn't hit him, the shards of rock had.

Raid set the rifle on the ground and pulled out his pistol. He cocked it, disengaged the safety and passed it to his left hand. Then he reached into his coat pocket and pulled out a drab green hand grenade.

With his pistol trained on the entrance of the cave, Raid pulled out the pin with his teeth. Once within ten feet of the entrance, he released the lever, counted to five, and lobbed it into the cave.

A brief silence, then a panicked cry: "Santa María, Jesús Cristo!"

But these devotions were cut short by the explosion, which sounded like distant thunder from within the thick walls of the cavern.

"Matti!" Raid shouted.

The boy came clambering down the rocks, his face blanched white.

"Are they..."

"Dead," said Raid.

The boy gazed at the corpse lying in front of the cave, and he began to tremble.

"And what about...?"

"In the cave."

"Who's gonna get the duffel?"

"You. But first make the phone call."

The boy remembered his orders, and searched for the number Raid had given him. His hands were trembling.

"Is this Lieutenant Jansson...? Yes, this is Matti Porola... You were looking for the four foreigners that killed my friend Sepi... I know where they are..."

He gave precise directions, and promised to meet them as soon as the remaining gangsters in the car were captured.

"So what now?" said the boy.

"The duffel bag."

The boy shifted about uneasily.

"Couldn't you just... I just feel a little dizzy... I'm kinda squeamish about blood."

"And you say you wanna be a criminal?"

The boy didn't respond.

"Either you get the bag, or it stays there."

He stalled some more, but finally knelt down, and peered into the cave. He went in up to his waist, then crawled back out.

"He's all fucked up...blood everywhere."

Raid's voice was a few degrees louder. "Go get it."

The boy crawled in once more, and this time he emerged with the bag in his hand. There was blood on his shirt, and all over his hands.

"What now?" he said.

"Get a few boulders for weights. One of them goes for a swim, the other stays in the cave. We'll close up the entrance."

Raid climbed to the top of the cave and kicked aside the moss. Some smaller boulders lay between the cave roof and the massive slab leaning against the entrance. Raid wedged a grenade into the gap, pulled the pin, and hurried to safety. The explosion hurled shards of stone high into the air, and then came a thunderous crash.

He came out to assess his work. The entrance to the cave was now five inches wide. Raid plugged the gap with boulders, took the bag, and climbed up onto the cliff, where the drop to the water was about fifteen feet. The boy followed.

"How deep is it here?"

"About twenty feet... No! Goddamnit!" he screamed as Raid tossed the duffel into the water.

Raid pulled his pistol out from beneath his coat and sent half a dozen bullets through the floating duffel. The bag began to slowly sink, leaving a trail of white powder behind it.

The boy took a swing at Raid, but Raid grabbed his fist out of mid-air and forced it down.

"The other alternative would've been worse for you. Much worse."

The boy stared at the white powder slick. He was fuming.

"Dude, look what you fucking did. You just cost me two million. What kinda patron saint do you think you are, anyway?" he bleated. "You *kill* people...is that really a better way to earn a living?"

Raid turned and walked off toward the bog. Once he'd made about a hundred yards, he heard the boy, hurrying to catch up.

* * *

"Do you know where the other two are?" Jansson asked Raid.

Diego and Simon were sitting in the back seat of the squad car.

"No."

Jansson looked at the boy. "What about you?"

"No idea," he said covering the bloodstain on his shirt.

"They probably got lost in the woods. You think we'll find them?"

"I doubt it."

Kempas emerged from the trees.

"We found a car and a body," he said. "You'll have to ID your friend, just to be sure," he said to the boy.

The body had been buried in some sandy soil about a hundred fifty feet from the road. The police had dug it out and laid it on a plastic sheet. There was still sand on his ashen face, and his hair jutted stiffly out. In the middle of his forehead was a black-and-blue bullet hole.

"That's Sepi alright."

The boy looked at his friend's sand-speckled face and shriveled appearance. His eyes began to well up with tears.

Jansson set his heavy hand on the boy's shoulder.

"Why don't you go sit in the car. We'll talk with you later. The NBI will be handling your friend's murder," he said with a glance toward Kempas, who knew to follow the boy.

Raid stayed back with Jansson.

"Our paths seem to cross in the strangest places," Jansson began.

"Sure do."

"Is it just pure chance?"

"Is there any such thing?"

"Where's the cocaine?"

"The kid destroyed it...threw it in the lake. I saw him do it."

"How'd you end up getting involved?"

"Pure chance," said Raid.

"Hopefully you haven't done anything that would conflict with my values."

268

"I haven't."

"Thanks for the help, though. We've been looking for these guys for many days."

"You're welcome."

"Were you planning on staying?"

"I think it's about time for me to leave again."

"What should we do with the boy? You think he learned his lesson?"

"Maybe, maybe not."

"What would you do?"

"I'd give him one last chance."

Jansson nodded thoughtfully. "I'll see what I can do."

22.

Erika Liljeblad took a hasty step back when Huusko and Susisaari appeared behind her office door.

"You two again? This is kind of a bad time. I have a meeting with a student in five minutes."

"Cancel it," Huusko said.

"Is it really that important?"

"Yes," said Susisaari.

Erika stepped aside and let the two officers into the room.

"I really haven't thought of anything else. What's this all about?"

"The investigation into the murders of your sister and her boyfriend, José, has made some progress. We know that a private investigator by the name of Aho was in your sister's apartment at the time of the murders," said Huusko.

"Is that who killed my sister?"

"No, but he witnessed the murders," said Susisaari.

"Last time we met, I showed you Aho's photo," said Huusko.

"You mean the guy who was with Nina at the restaurant?"

"One and the same. Why did you lie about Aho?"

"I don't quite understand."

"Aho walked in with your sister when they caught you in bed with José."

"As I told you, she never saw me."

"Yes, she did. And after the murder, you took off with Aho. In your car. Aho told his girlfriend about it.

270

We know exactly what happened. The car is being inspected right now. I'm sure we'll find Aho's fingerprints or some fibers from his clothes. And if you cleaned the car, we'll know that, too."

Erika Liljeblad was silent for a moment. "If you already know what happened, then you know I didn't kill anybody. Nina killed José, and then she died of an overdose."

"Why did you go to your sister's apartment?" said Susisaari.

Erika covered her face, but this time, Huusko wasn't fooled.

"I wanted to get back at her. José and I were dating before Nina ever met him. I wanted her to get a taste of her own medicine."

"So what happened at the apartment?"

"She came in with that private investigator and found me in bed with José. She totally lost it, grabbed a knife, and stabbed him. After that, she fell on the floor and passed out."

"And you left them both there to die?" said Susisaari.

"No. José was already dead. I checked myself, and I thought Nina was only passed out. She was still breathing. It never occurred to me that…"

She cried for a long time.

"Why didn't you notify the police?"

"Put yourself in my shoes. I'm a researcher at the university. We have a very low tolerance for scandals here. I didn't do anything to anybody, so why should I let Nina ruin my life on top of everything else she's done?"

"Last time you claimed that someone rang the doorbell."

"That's true. We went out the back door. My car was parked on the side street, and we drove away together."

"And then what?"

"I dropped him off in Hakaniemi and drove straight home."

"It's possible you could've saved your sister's life," said Susisaari.

Erika Liljeblad broke down crying again. Soon, tears were rolling down her cheeks, and gradually, her cries turned to sobs.

After calming down, she looked up.

"We'll have to arrest you," said Huusko. "Gather up your personal things. You'll be spending the night in a cell in Pasila."

"But I thought… Don't you believe me?"

"We believe that you didn't kill your sister. But we also believe that you did kill Aho."

* * *

"Well, it was a shitty job, but we got it done," said Kempas to Jansson.

"I thought it went very well."

"There's still two Bolivian gangsters on the loose."

"We'll catch 'em. In due time."

"We'll see about that."

"Have a good night," said Jansson.

He walked the dog around in front of the police station for a while before going up to Huusko's office.

Jansson told about the events in the countryside, and Huusko and Susisaari told him about Eila Tuuri and Erika Liljeblad.

"The little sister went mute on the way over," said Huusko.

"Did you ask about Aho's phone call yet?"

"Not yet."

"You think she's the one?"

272

Both Huusko and Susisaari nodded.

"So do I. We interrogated the Bolivians who went to Liljeblad's apartment. There'd been three altogether, but one was waiting in the car, and their boss was at the hotel. One of them speaks decent Finnish and he told us they saw a man and a woman exiting the back door of the building and getting into a nearby white compact. They chased it, but the car got away. He said it was an Audi."

"We'll have to search Erika's apartment," said Susisaari. "If she killed Aho, those documents might be there."

"Right. I'll deal with the search warrant."

"And one for her mom's place, too," said Susisaari.

"Her mom's place?"

"Erika's selling her mom's condo, which means she has the keys. The papers might be there, too."

"Then we'll search that, too. Sanna, tell Leimu to keep watch at one of the apartments, and Kallio at the other. Pronto."

"Got it. Shall we go have a talk with lil sis?"

* * *

Erika Liljeblad was escorted into the interrogation room, and directed to sit just opposite Jansson. Huusko and Susisaari remained standing.

"We already know what happened, but we'd like to know why," said Jansson.

Liljeblad slowly raised her eyes, but she didn't reply.

"We're conducting searches of both your and your mother's apartments, as well as your car. It's in your best interests to tell us everything."

"Do you really wanna know?"

"Yes."

"Even though he's a former police officer?"

"He was a sleaze when he was a cop, too," said Huusko.

Liljeblad made her decision. One careful word at a time, she began to come clean.

"Everything at the apartment happened just as I told you, but the next day, Aho called me at the university. He said that Nina had told him about us inheriting our mother's condo. I'm guessing Nina told him about the money we'd be getting because she couldn't pay him right away. He said Nina had owed him money, and he demanded twenty grand, otherwise he'd tell the police about me."

"He wouldn't have dared," said Susisaari. "He was at the apartment himself."

"That's what *I* said. But he just laughed and told me he hadn't done anything wrong, and didn't have anything to be ashamed of. I, on the other hand, had caused the death of my sister's boyfriend by having sex with him, and made my sister a murderer. Then he told me he'd make sure my employer found out about it, too."

"What happened then?" said Jansson.

"He told me I had two days to get the money. He said he'd call on Wednesday to tell me where to meet."

"Did you get the money?"

"Just twelve thousand of it... He called me on Wednesday and told me to come to the parking lot of the Tikkurila Shell. I met him there and got in his car. We stopped at a gas station in Keimola. We didn't say but a few words the whole trip. Then he turned onto the forest road."

"Why?" said Susisaari.

"At that time, I didn't know. He asked for the money, and I told him I only had twelve grand. Then he got very upset and started screaming at me. He said he was going abroad for a few days on business, so he needed all of it. Finally, he calmed down and told me I could pay the remainder with an installment plan of 'favors'. Once a week for a whole year. He took a pack of condoms out of his pocket and grabbed me, trying to pull up my shirt, and…"

She was silent for a while.

"I had my dad's old pistol in my bag. I'd found it in mom's apartment when I was cleaning it for a showing. So I took out the gun and shot him in the head…"

"And then what?" said Huusko.

"I had gloves on, so I didn't think there would be any fingerprints. I took the pack of condoms with me so nobody would know it was a woman. Then I grabbed a brown leather briefcase from the backseat and scattered the stuff on the ground. I thought maybe the police would think it was a robbery."

"How'd you get away?"

"I walked to the highway and got on the first bus that came by. Fetched my car, went home, dumped my clothes and went to throw the gun in the sea. I brought the briefcase to my mother's place and hid it in the attic. I'd meant to get rid of it later."

"Anything else?" said Susisaari.

"No… But that man was scum. He got what he deserved," Erika said as she stared at the floor.

"Maybe so," said Huusko. "Not that that's our official position. But about that briefcase…is it still at your mother's place?"

"Yes."

"Did you look through it?"

"I took a glance. There were some contracts and wire instructions to a bank in the Cayman Islands."

Huusko looked at Jansson, unable to contain his happiness. "Hietama and his buddies are gonna be in a pickle. We'll hand the briefcase over to the NBI... They'll have a field day with it."

Jansson nodded. "The guards will bring you back to your cell. Do you need anything? Food, books, anything else?"

"Do you have green tea?"

"Is herbal tea okay?" said Jansson.

"Sure."

"We have that."

Liljeblad was led away. In the hallway, Jansson heard the phone ringing in his office, and he hurried off to answer it.

"Is this Lieutenant Eero Jansson?"

"Yes, it is."

"This is Doctor Vehvilä from the University Hospital. I believe you know Captain Toivo Tuomela?"

"Yes, I do."

"He fell ill this afternoon, and was admitted to the hospital. He asked that if anything happened to him, we should contact both his wife and you."

"Has something happened?"

"Unfortunately, yes... He passed away. Just over an hour ago."

Jansson heard the doctor say something else, but he couldn't make sense of the words. He thanked him and hung up the phone. Then he walked into Huusko's office.

"What happened?" said Huusko, when he saw Jansson's face.

"Tuomela died. That was the hospital."

"Tuomela died," repeated Susisaari.

The dog paced restlessly at Jansson's feet.

"A heart attack, or…?" said Huusko.

"Probably. Something… this afternoon."

"Sit down," said Huusko, and he pulled up a chair for Jansson.

Jansson sat down, closed his eyes for a moment, and thought about Tuomela. They had known each other for more than twenty years, and Tuomela had always been his boss and close friend. In Jansson's mind, Tuomela had been the department's best supervisor. Always above the groping, jealousy, and backbiting, and always supporting his team, yet firm. Jansson was sure that Tuomela had died like a gentleman, with dignity, and without making a big show of it. Jansson knew that he wasn't made of the same stuff. When his time came, he would alienate all of his friends with his whining and complaining. He would feel that he'd been treated unfairly, and would beg, and plead, and pray for an extension.

"Tuomela was a good man," said Jansson.

"That he was," said Huusko and Susisaari in unison.

"I wonder what'll happen to his boat," said Jansson in a worried voice, without really knowing why. "He always kept it up so well."

Jansson noticed with surprise that tears were streaming down his cheeks, and his voice was pinched and wavering. The dog pressed itself against his leg.

"The dog's sad, too," said Jansson solemnly. "And he doesn't even have a name."

"I'll give him a name," said Huusko. "Topi, Tuomela's nickname…in his honor."

"Isn't that a little macabre?" said Susisaari.

"Topi's a good name. It's perfect," said Jansson.

"I suppose it's best if I drive you home," said Huusko, and he took Jansson lightly by the crook of his elbow. Jansson rose with some difficulty.

"Alright, then," he said quietly.

"I'm coming with," said Susisaari.

They went side by side to the elevator, three cops and a police dog called Topi.

23.

The first frost of fall had arrived the previous night, and the grass crunched beneath Raid's feet. Yet the frost-bitten apples in the trees endeavored to hang on. Raid walked to the lakeshore and gazed out at the placid waters. The yellow-gray sky reflected off the surface, and the bite in the air was a harbinger of the first snow.

In the reeds, a pike scuttled after its prey, its fin skimming the surface. Ripples, like circles of life and death, expanded on the smooth surface of the water, and then vanished. Raid took hold of the stiffened rope, and pulled the boat up onto the bank. The water at the bottom had frozen, and the ice shattered into tiny pieces when Raid flipped the boat onto its belly. He tossed the oars and oarlocks underneath it.

The Mercedes was already loaded and ready to go. Raid sat down on the cold leather seat and turned on the ignition. The engine started slowly, and ran a little rough, but Raid knew its ways. Soon it would warm up and be running smoothly. He set the levers on the heater to funnel the warm air onto the frosty windshield.

Raid left the car running while he went inside to close the dampers and lock the doors. The key he left in the same spot Nygren had always left it: in a crack in the foundation wall.

He drove out to the road and got out to close the gate. The barking of the neighbor's dog mingled with the chirping of a few birds, but no other life was in sight.

In town, it was just as quiet. The only person Raid came across was an old woman hanging out her clothes in the yard of a yellow wooden house.

Raid stopped in front of the general store just as a semi-truck was coming up the road. It swept past toward the north. After a while, a bus rolled up from the opposite direction, and pulled up in front of the store. Only three passengers were on it, and one stepped out in his shirtsleeves to walk around. Another was sleeping with her head pressed against the window, and the third was reading a newspaper.

The man in his shirtsleeves stood with his hands in his pockets and looked curiously at the Mercedes. Then he went into the store.

The bus driver opened up the luggage compartment and began unloading a few crates and packages. The door to the store swung open and the boy, dressed in a white butcher's frock, came out to help the driver. He spotted the Mercedes, stopped momentarily, and then continued on to the bus. The driver slammed the compartment shut, waved goodbye to the boy, and climbed back behind the wheel. The man who had gone into the store hurried out with a bottle of soda, and climbed into the bus.

The bus made a sharp U-turn in the lot. The boy picked up a banana crate off the ground, carried it haltingly for a few feet, and then breezed into the store without a backward glance.

Raid circled round the gas pump and caught a glimpse of the boy's dejected face through the ads in the window.

Then he pulled the Mercedes onto the road and zeroed out the odometer.

It was almost two hundred miles to Helsinki, a couple thousand to the wider world, and to where he was going, many, many more.

Also from Ice Cold Crime

Raid and the Blackest Sheep
Harri Nykanen (2010, 242 pages)

Hard-nosed hit man Raid is driving toward the Arctic Circle with Nygren, a career criminal in the twilight of his life. During the journey, Nygren puts his affairs in order, wreaking vengeance on those who have wronged him and paying penance to those he has wronged. Soon, both cops and crooks are on their trail. Detective Lieutenant Jansson and his colleagues are interested in any potential jobs the notorious criminals might be planning. In the end, the pilgrimage leaves a trail of wounded and dead in its wake.

Helsinki Homicide: Against the Wall
Jarkko Sipila (2009, 291 pages)

An abandoned house in Northern Helsinki, a dead body in the garage. Detective Lieutenant Kari Takamäki gets a case that looks like a professional hit, but the crime scene is perplexing. Takamäki's trusted man Suhonen goes undercover as Suikkanen, a gangster full of action. In pursuit of the murderer, he must operate within the grey area of the law. But, will the end justify the means?

Helsinki Homicide: Vengeance
Jarkko Sipila (2010, 335 pages)

Tapani Larsson, a Finnish crime boss, walks out of prison with one thought on his mind: vengeance. Wanting to reclaim his gang's honor and avenge those who have wronged him, Larsson targets Suhonen, the undercover detective who put him in prison. Suhonen hunts for the loose thread that could unravel the entire gang, but with every string he pulls, he flirts with death itself.

Helsinki Homicide: Nothing but the Truth
Jarkko Sipila (2011, 321 pages)

A woman sees the getaway driver in a young cocaine dealer's murder. After testifying in the trial, she finds herself the target of an escalating spiral of threats. Not wishing to uproot her life, she and her twelve-year-old daughter risk death by spurning Lieutenant Takamäki's offer of a safe house. The witness is torn between her principles and desire to keep her family safe. How much should an ordinary citizen sacrifice for the benefit of society as a whole?